WHERE THE
SHADOWS
BEGAN
& OTHER STORIES

WHERE THE SHADOWS BEGAN

& OTHER STORIES

BY BRADLEY H. SINOR

The Merry Blacksmith Press

2011

Where the Shadows Began

© 2011 Bradley H. Sinor

"Where the Shadows Began" first appeared in *Tales of the Shadowmen: Grand Guignol* (Black Coat Press, 2009)
"Late Night Double Feature" first appeared in *Double Feature* (Ghostwriter Publications)
"Lines In the Sand" first appeared in *Shelter of Daylight* (samsdotpublishing, 2009)
"Serpent's Tooth" first appeared in *Rotten Relations* (DAW Books, 2004)
"The Adventures of the Other Detective" first appeared in *Dark and Story Nights* (Yard Dog Press, 2001)
"Location Shoot" first appeared in *Playing With Secrets* (Yard Dog Press, 2004)
"Wind and Shadow" is original to this volume, ©2010
"And the Wind Sang" first appeared in *Knight Fantastic* (DAW Books, 2002)
"Oaths" first appeared in *Time of the Vam pires* (DAW Books, 1996)
"Central Park" first appeared in *Merlin* (DAW Books, 199 9)
"Final Score" first appeared in *Warrior Fantastic* (DAW books, 2000)
"John Does # 12" first appeared in *Fencon Program Book* (2005)
"Skimming Stones" first appeared in *Men Writing SF As Women* (DAW books, 2003)
"Money's Worth" first appeared in *Places To Be, People To Kill* (DAW BOOKS, 2007)
"When To Step Away" first appeared in *Double Feature* (Ghostwriter Publications)

For information, address:

The Merry Blacksmith Press
70 Lenox Ave.
West Warwick, RI 02893

merryblacksmith.com

Published in the USA by The Merry Blacksmith Press

ISBN— 978-0-61545-973-8
0-61545-973-0

TABLE OF CONTENTS

DEDICATION

To my mother, Wanda Sinor, who, when I was growing up, was always there with love, support and understanding (not to mention the worlds greatest, homemade angel food cake.)

And to my father, Harold L. Sinor, who in his quiet way taught me what it was to be a man and to take care of your family. I only wish you were here to see this. I miss you, dad.

Where the Shadows Began

Paris, 1910

Inspector John Raymond Legrasse leaned back and listened to the steady thump of the train wheels as they rolled over the tracks. The sound had long since faded into the background for him. The sound was still there, just somewhere *else*, and that was exactly where he wanted it.

Legrasse had never particularly been that fond of train travel; he just accepted it as something that you had to do if you were going to get from one place to another in any reasonable amount of time. It wasn't as if there were that many stagecoaches running any more, and, while Legrasse could drive, he hadn't yet taken the plunge and purchased an automobile.

"Not that it could have gotten me here," he mused softly. Being able to drive from New Orleans, in the United States, to Paris, France, would have been a quite remarkable trick, worthy of the pen of Verne or Wells, or something that had come out of Edison's idea factory in Menlo Park.

"Excuse me, sir. Is that seat taken?"

Legrasse opened one eye and looked up. The speaker was a tall grey-haired man dressed in a dark suit. He was pointing at the high-backed chair, one of the dozen that filled the smoking compartment, across from where Legrasse was sitting, "No, no. Feel free."

"Thanks." The stranger rummaged in his inside coat pocket and produced a leather cigar case. He carefully extracted one, cut the end with a pen knife, discarding it, and struck a match to the remaining part, holding the flame close until the end was glowing red.

"Would you care for one?" the stranger asked, shaking out another long brown tube from his case. "Hand rolled, Cuban, made for me in a little shop in Havana."

Legrasse actually preferred his pipe, but had been known to indulge in a good cigar every now and then.

"There is something familiar about you," said the policeman.

"I was wondering when you would recognize me, although it has been almost five years since I was in New Orleans and our paths crossed," chuckled the gray-haired man. "Ardan, Michael Ardan, a pleasure to see you again, inspector."

"Yes, you were the fellow that the War Department brought in, from the Baltimore Gun Club, when the New Orleans armory was broken into. They were rather insistent that we drop everything and deal with it."

"Indeed. I'm semi-retired now, but still do some consulting for the War Department," said Ardan. "And yourself?"

Legrasse chuckled. "I, sir, am "on holiday," not by choice. My superiors felt that it was a good idea that I take some time off to reestablish my health after a recent investigation."

The chief of police himself had taken Legrasse aside and explained that the inspector *would* be taking some time away from New Orleans, with pay, of course, if he wanted to be able to return to his job. There had been a matter of some political toes that had been stepped on during the investigation and the chief felt it was prudent for Legrasse to absent himself until things had been smoothed over.

"My grandmother recently passed, at the age of 90, and I discovered that I was the heir to some small properties here in France. She had not been back since the time of the '48 revolution and I was her only living relative. This seemed as good a time as any to make the trip"

Legrasse had told that story several times during his trip and almost believed it himself.

"I hope you will allow yourself time to see some of the sights of Paris," said Ardan. "It is a one-of-a-kind city."

Legrasse glanced down at the issue of the *Echo de France* that he had been reading earlier, at the three inch square advertisement announcing a performance by the Hastur Company. The ad was dominated by a yellow face mask.

"I may take in a play or two. I've always had a fondness for the theatre," he said.

———

Legrasse pulled his overcoat tighter, blocking out the wind as best he could, and looked around at the buildings, most of them sealed with weather-scored planks hammered across windows and doors. There were a few ancient business signs on some of the buildings, but most were bare of even a street number. The whole place had an air of decay, even in the middle of the day.

Legrasse turned suddenly at the sound of a clattering of wheels behind him. His hand automatically reached into the pocket of his greatcoat to close around the butt of the well-oiled revolver that had accompanied him from America. His fingers relaxed their grip when he saw that it was a large brown delivery wagon, pulled by two dapple gray horses. He watched them until they turned off to the left and vanished from sight.

That was when he noticed the other building, just down the street. It had once been a theater, though the name was long since gone from what he suspected had been a marquee sticking out over the street. Not one of the big glittering palaces like the behemoth Paris Opera, even if the place was reported to be haunted, or the Follies-Bergere, and the Varieties, but a smaller, more intimate place.

Legrasse had seen too many buildings like this back home in New Orleans, places that had long since been lost to the city and now clung by only the tiniest thread to existence. Everything about the theatre said its time had long since passed.

Crossing the street, Legrasse could feel the wind die away as he got closer to the building. The air was still and felt almost like a living thing that had taken a deep breath and was holding it.

He pushed at the door, expecting nothing to happen. Instead, it moved, just enough to let him know that it was not locked. Legrasse allowed time for his eyes to adjust to the darkness before stepping across the threshold.

A heavy layer of dust on the floor showed that no one had been here in a very long time. On the wall broken gas jets hung at odd angles across the torn and heavily water stained wallpaper.

At the far end of the hallway were twin doors with the word auditorium painted over them. A glance inside showed him tiered seating on risers that, given the size of the room, would not have seated more than fifty or so. Many of them were broken and overturned. The walls looked like they had been painted black, though the color merged so much with the darkness of the room that it was difficult to tell where the shadows began and the walls ended.

As he looked back at the front door of the theater, he noticed that there was something there, something that he would have sworn was not there when he had come inside. It was a flyer, held in place by small tack nails at each corner, the kind that were spread all over the city announcing various events; plastered up by hordes of street urchins to earn a few coins to fill their stomachs with.

Pulling it off the wall, Legrasse stepped outside, letting the daylight illuminate the paper. It featured a face mask, colored an oddly sick-looking yellow, in the center of the page. The wording was in French, but it appeared to announce a one-time-only performance of a play called 'Le Roi en Jaune'—

'The King in Yellow,' billed as one of the most dangerous theatrical creations in decades, being produced under the auspices of the Hastur Company.

The performance was at the very building where he stood.

———

"I have to admit that I had another reason for coming to Paris, besides looking up my family properties," said Legrasse. The police inspector had always prided himself on being a good judge of people, often going with his gut feeling on a situation even if the facts contradicted it. So while there were things he would have liked to know about

Michael Ardan, given their joint experience five years before, Legrasse felt he could be trusted.

"So what is it that brings you to Paris?" Ardan asked as he and the police inspector sat dawn for drinks and dinner at Legrasse's hotel.

"Two years ago there was a massacre in a local theater in New Orleans, forty people dead, literally ripped to shreds, blood was everywhere and nary a clue as to who did it or what their motive was. I've been a policeman for a long time and am no stranger to murder, but there was something wrong with what we found in that theater, something that made it feel as if the very substance of those poor people had been sucked out of them," Legrasse said. "Like marrow from a bone. Two of the policemen who had investigated the scene with me died shortly thereafter, one by drowning and one by blowing his own head off with a shotgun on the front steps of City Hall."

Ardan nodded and took a drink before speaking. "How many of the dead were audience members and how many were actors?" he asked.

"As best could be determined they were all audience members. There was no sign of the actors or any member of the production company, and we could find no trace of them in New Orleans. The Hastur Company seemed to have vanished from the face of the earth until four months ago.

"I was in the middle of investigating a drug smuggling operations when we arrested the man behind it. I found a flyer among his papers. It was an announcement of a production of 'The King in Yellow' by the Hastur Company, a single performance, set for Paris, tomorrow night."

"Interesting," said Ardan. "Especially given the conditions you described of that theater. I have a feeling that there is something you haven't mentioned about why you are here."

"While I did twist a few political noses during the investigation, I considered it a stroke of luck that the chief suggested I take an extended holiday. It's true that I don't take kindly to people being killed like that in New Orleans."

Legrasse produced an envelope from his pocket and handed it across the table to Ardan. Inside was a small piece of high grade white paper. Embossed on it were the words 'The King in Yellow', followed by a Bourbon Street address in New Orleans and the name Inspector John Raymond Legrasse.

"It appears you were on the invitation list," said Ardan.

"And I probably would have been there had I not injured my ankle the night before," he said.

Ardan nodded and said nothing for several minutes. "I have some contacts in the local theatrical community, not to mention a few more esoteric places. I can make a few inquiries, then I think that you and I shall go to the theatre."

"I appreciate the help. I'm a bit far from my usual sources of information and, while I can make myself understood in it, French and I are not always on the best of terms. There is no need, though, for you to put yourself in harm's way," said Legrasse.

Truth was, he wasn't all that confident in his own mind of what was going on, only that it was something that he could not let go of until there were some kinds of answers.

"Nonsense, you have piqued my curiosity." the older man said.

Legrasse remembered that phrase several hours later as he sat alone in the hotel bar. Ardan had departed sometime before, but Legrasse knew that if he had sought sleep it would not come. He had been nursing a glass of bourbon for half an hour listening to the music played by a quartet at the far end of the room.

"Are you as bored by this miserable excuse for music as I am?" The woman in front of Legrasse wore a provocative gown of green with a dash of black and a single emerald choker around her throat. She was tall and angular, her emerald eyes looking at him in a way that Legrasse could feel through and through.

"I never claimed to be a music critic," he said.

"Music should be able to take the listener and carry him to other places, places that were or could be or perhaps should never be," she said. Legrasse had the feeling that those last words were not directed at him. He wasn't all that sure he wanted to know who they were meant for.

"Perhaps," he said slowly. "Though one can never be sure until the musicians begin to play what the piece will do."

"Indeed. How do you feel about music and the theatre?"

"It can be interesting, if well done, painful if not."

Without asking permission, the woman took the chair that Ardan had occupied earlier. For a long moment neither spoke, listening to the music instead. When the musicians shifted into a different tune, one that sounded vaguely familiar, something changed.

"I can't help but say that piece comes close to fitting the description of painful," she said.

"You may be right," he smiled. "I don't believe we've been introduced, madam."

"We haven't. You may call me Cassilda. Should I call you John or Raymond, Inspector?"

Legrasse's eyes darted over the room, scanning the few others in the bar for any sign that they might be in league with her. She was enticing, a mystery wrapped up in an enigma, the answer to which would probably be as mundane as anything.

"Perhaps we should keep it formal and you call me Inspector. Only my late grandmother called me Raymond and I don't know you well enough to suggest my first name as an alternative," he said.

From her handbag the woman drew two small pieces of cardboard. She slid them across the table toward Legrasse, holding them in place in front of him with the edge of her fingernail. The red polish glowed for a moment, then faded to a darker shade close to that of blood.

"I've brought you something, sir. Something that you will find far more entertaining than this pitiful excuse for music that is currently assaulting our ears could ever hope to be."

Inspector John Raymond Legrasse drew a long breath and continued to stare at the woman. His eyes barely registering what she had placed on the table.

Very deliberately Legrasse reached across the table and laid his forefinger on the pieces of cardboard, carefully not touching Cassilda. He drew them toward him, turning them over. They were tickets, emblazoned with an eyeless yellow mask and the words 'The Hastur Company presents for one night only The King in Yellow' worked into the design that ran up and down the side. Across the end they read "Doors open at 7:30, no one will be admitted after the performance begins."

Legrasse felt a chill as he stared at the tickets, he could feel the weight of the other invitation in his coat pocket.

"So, are you interested?" Cassilda said, her voice a low sound that outweighed any other noise in the room.

"For me? How kind. Since there is more than one, I wonder if you were planning on accompanying me?" he asked.

"That would be difficult, since I must be on stage. Though afterwards, who can say."

With that, Cassilda rose and walked toward the far door, her figure cutting its way along the shadowed portico. At the last moment she turned and said something. Legrasse had the impression that she was speaking to him though he could not distinguish the words.

"No one seems to know anything about this Hastur Company, not even any rumors of the spicy and salacious variety, and for actors not to know that kind of gossip is damned unusual." said Ardan. "I even contacted the Diogenes Club in London and they professed to know nothing about the Hastur Company. The play's been around for a long time and there are rumors about it that are fairly bizarre."

"So I guess we have to go in there cold and see what happens," said Legrasse.

"So, tell me more about this young woman, Cassilda did you say her name was?"

"That's what she claimed. I tried to follow her but I lost sight of her in the street outside of the hotel. It seems like her main objective was to deliver the tickets, so I'm getting the feeling that we are *expected*," said Legrasse.

"Shall we be off? After all, we wouldn't want to miss the curtain, now would we?" Ardan replied.

Two cabs had refused their fare when told the address, forcing Legrasse and Ardan to walk. As they moved along the streets, the lights of Paris began to flicker into existence around the two men.

As they walked, Legrasse could not shake the feeling that they were being followed. Yet he could not spot who the watchers might be. He just felt in his gut that they were there, watching and making sure that the two men found their way to their final destination.

"I regret that I am the only one of us who is armed," Legrasse said as they neared the theater.

"What ever gave you that idea," said Ardan. He held up his walking stick so Legrasse could see the heavy metal ball that was at the end, and then he opened his coat to reveal a rather formidable-looking pistol holstered under his shoulder. "I do work for the Gun Club, after all. I've traveled all over the United States, as-well-as the world, from Opar to Shangri-La and Maple White Land. So I long ago learned the value of having weapons to hand."

Legrasse allowed himself to smile. Things were looking up, at least for a moment. He did wonder how long that feeling would last.

———

Things can change in a short time, that much Legrasse knew, but as he and his companion turned the corner onto the same street he had stood on less than a day before, he found himself amazed at what confronted him.

Most of the buildings were still as dark and abandoned-looking. Only the theatre had changed. What had been a wreck now looked as new as the first day it had opened for business; the doors were illuminated with gold filigree and the façade had a feel of opulent decadence about it. A small group, dressed in tuxedos and gowns, stood in front of the theater waiting for their chance to enter this dream palace.

"This hardly matches your description of this place," said Ardan. "I must say, these people seem to be on their toes when it comes to remodeling."

"Tell me something I don't know," said Legrasse.

"I'm pleased to see that you decided to come, Inspector," said Cassilda. The woman had come out through a smaller door just to one side of the main entrance. She wore a yellow gown draped in the classic Greek style, a thin silver headband holding her hair in place.

"How could I refuse a suggestion from so lovely a lady," said Legrasse.

"Then let me not keep you from '*The King*'." She gestured for them to follow her.

Once inside, Cassilda pointed toward a curtain that led out into the main hallway. Like the outside, the inside of the theater had been reborn, in lush colors and gilded accoutrements. A feeling of ultimate hedonism seemed to permeate everything, even the air itself.

"Bruno will show you to your seats," Cassilda smiled at Legrasse before she disappeared down a hallway that he guessed gave the performers access to the backstage area.

Bruno proved to be a medium-sized man with the palest face that Legrasse had seen this side of a corpse who had been floating in the swamp for a week. Yet there was a spark of yellow in his eyes that reminded him of a sputtering candle fighting to stay lit. He wore a tuxedo that looked as if it had been made for someone several inches taller and many pounds heavier than he.

"You are Cassilda's guests," Bruno said after Legrasse handed him the tickets.

Most of the seats in the theatre were posh red leather creations, inlaid with designs similar to what bracketed the building's front door. Here and there among the fifty or so seats were four or five, mixed in among the rest, that were also red, but a darker, harsher red.

"The performance will begin shortly," said Bruno.

The people that they had seen outside began to make their way into the auditorium; most were talking in the way of theatre patrons through the ages about dinner, about their lives and their thoughts on the coming play. From the few words here and there, broken sentences and half heard statements it was obvious that no one had much of an idea just what 'The King in Yellow' might be about, only that it was infamous and attending the exclusive performance was a social coup.

Gradually the gas lamps on the wall flickered to life, growing slowly brighter. When the stage was illuminated, Bruno stepped through the curtain. He had discarded his ill-fitting tuxedo for an imperial Roman toga that seemed to have been designed especially for him.

"Ladies and Gentlemen, I bid you welcome to this performance of 'The King in Yellow,'" he said, his voice booming out into the small room. "This play is one of the most banned in the world. I cannot count the number of cities and countries which have proclaimed that its words cannot be performed within their borders. There are those who say that when he had finished writing it, the playwright cut his own throat with the very quill that he used to pen it. Perhaps this is a warning, offering you a chance to depart, or perhaps it is nothing more than empty words, building up our performance this evening."

An uneven wave of laughter filled the room, slowly shifting over to applause.

Bruno spoke slowly, a grin breaking his passive face. "Very well, you have made your choice, so let me say simply, on with the show."

The light shifted, casting a mixture of lights, yellow, red and white, across the stage. A cowled and caped figure came onto the stage, head bowed, face turned from the audience, and moved across until it stood on the edge only a foot from the people who sat on the front row. Two additional figures, each nearly identical to the first emerged, taking up positions to form a curved line just a hand's breadth from the audience. Each of them wore identical full face masks, all three a pale, sickening yellow.

Legrasse exhaled; he realized that he had been holding his breath since Bruno had finished speaking. As much as he wanted to, he could not look away from the stage.

Something nagged at him as he watched, even more so than when he and Ardan had entered the theater.

Music came from somewhere in the wings on stage left, a harpsichord or a piano of some kind; in the distance other instruments echoed, a drum and a flute vibrating like a heart beat.

On some level Legrasse was aware of the play as it moved through scene after scene, but from one moment to the next he could not have recounted what had just happened on the stage. It was in the second act that Cassilda spoke to the man who had been designated the King.

"Along the shore the cloud wave breaks. …" the rest of the words merged into an indistinguishable din. Yet he could hear another voice, one growing stronger and louder with each word that it spoke.

Bruno came through the door at the side of the auditorium, followed by a figure wrapped head to toe in a bright yellow robe, its face also wearing a yellow mask identical to the ones that the first performers had worn. The two were shrouded in the light from the hallway, then merged with the shadows as the door swung shut behind them. Whoever this was had a thick leather-bound book that he carried in both his hands, holding it in front of him like a sacred chalice being brought to the alter.

"Hail! The true King in Yellow is among us," chanted Bruno.

Legrasse nudged Ardan and pointed toward the newcomers. The other man turned his head one way and then another as if he were having trouble focusing on the figures.

"Is it…" said Ardan.

"I don't know," said Legrasse. Around the tiny auditorium the other audience members had begun to sway, chanting the same words over and over. Clothes began to fly off and moans replaced words as arms and flesh merged in syncopation to the chant.

Legrasse felt a woman's hands moving over him from behind, her body plastered hard against him; Legrasse found himself staring into the eyes of Cassilda.

"Come to me, John. Now is the time, the time that I have been waiting for. I need you, I want you, I have to have you as part of me and mine. I reached for you in New Orleans, but you did not respond."

Around them a cornucopia of sounds, flesh against flesh, voices moaning at an animal level, filled Legrasse's ears. He found himself struggling to not lose himself in them, to not surrender to what they promised.

"What are you?" he demanded.

"More than you could conceive, not even in your wildest yearnings or nightmares," she said.

Legrasse twisted to one side, pulling back from her. The elegant gown that enwrapped Cassilda earlier was now torn and marked with splotches. He thought he could smell…something, an odor that turned his stomach. Just then his hand brushed against the butt of his gun, it was like touching the ends of an electric wire, the pain something that he could grab onto and hold, something real something that he could understand.

It took him two tries before he could close his fingers around the gun. Once it was free he slammed the gun hard against the side of Cassilda's face. The impact was a satisfying sound.

Cassilda flew to the side, slamming into Ardan and knocking the other man backwards across the theatre seat to his side. That seemed enough to drag him out of the trance that had enwrapped the audience for 'The King in Yellow.'

All around Legrasse and Ardan the sounds of moans and body against body had changed. Now there were screams; pain and terror mixed into a new unholy sound that echoed off the walls. People were ripping each other apart, the gaslights on the wall flaring like a heartbeat to illuminate the scene.

Over the whole thing The King in Yellow presided, chanting, Bruno holding the huge leather-bound volume open in front of him. With each passing second the book seemed to grow bigger, as one after another the audience members were ripped apart.

"I would say the time has come to make an ungraceful exit, my friend," Ardan said as he kicked at Cassilda who was crawling along the floor toward him, laughing maniacally.

"I couldn't agree more," Legrasse said as he fired twice toward The King. If the bullets struck the figure, Legrasse couldn't tell' the figure seemed absorbed by the book and the chant that came from beneath his mask.

Then it came to Legrasse. "The book," he shouted to Ardan. The other man seemed puzzled at first, then understanding washed over his face. Both men began to fire. One of their shots struck Bruno, whose grin did not fade as he collapsed in a heap on the floor. But a few shots struck home, and the effect was almost immediate; everything around them, people, colors, chairs, walls, the very light itself seemed to merge into one, spinning around and around. Legrasse felt his stomach go out from underneath him. It was only by some miracle that he managed to stay on his feet.

And then they were on the street. Legrasse had no memory of leaving the theater, he was simply one place and a heartbeat later he was somewhere else.

The theater was gone, or, rather, abandoned again, the boards once again blocked the doors and layer upon layer of Paris grime blackened the windows.

Legrasse looked at his companion.

"Don't ask me, I don't know," said Ardan.

Neither did Legrasse, and he had the feeling in the pit of his stomach that he probably would never know, and that was a good thing.

A ripped flyer rolled past on the wind. Legrasse couldn't be sure, but he thought he saw the image of a yellow mask and the words 'The Hastur Company presents' on it.

NEW YORK CITY, 1925

"Belknapius, would you be so good as to have a look at this."

Howard Lovecraft gestured at the wooden fence where layer after layer of advertising posters had been pasted. The particular poster that had caught his attention was half covered by another in the endless chain of advertising that adorned virtually any fence or empty wall in any of the five boroughs of New York."

"What is it, Howard?"

Howard was a walking example of the word eccentric, from referring to himself as Grandpa or the Old Gentleman, to concocted nicknames for friends and correspondents like calling Frank by a Latinized version of his middle name Belknap.

The two of them made quite a pair. Howard's long frame, that seemed to have grown leaner in the past several months, contrasted with Frank's shorter stature, neatly trimmed mustache and thick glasses. Since Lovecraft's relocation to New York from his beloved Providence, the two of them had spent many hours roaming the streets of Brooklyn.

"It's this poster," said Lovecraft. "It presents a bit of a surprise for this Babylonian berg. An acting company is presenting a bit of theatre with an unusual name. That does not suggest the sort of material that you would see on the so-called Great White Way, or that might be scored by those hacks on Tin Pan Alley."

The shorter man scratched his chin; it amazed him that his friend knew anything about live theatre, let alone musical theatre. The poster showed a full face mask, vaguely resembling one of the traditional drama masks, only this was the oddest shade of yellow.

"And what is it? Some lost Shakespeare play perhaps, or a revival of 'Our American Cousin?'"

"'The King in Yellow,'" said the tall man.

"Never heard of it," his companion replied. "I can't read all of the poster; too much of the thing is covered over, but it looks like there is only going to be one performance, which, if I understand theatre, is most unusual. Besides, I didn't think you were interested in theatre."

"Sonia has been trying to bring it to my attention. My dear wife wants to widen my horizons. Unfortunately, the date is Saturday next and I am otherwise obligated. Perhaps you could go and report back."

"Saturday, no," said Frank. "My parents and I are going to Maryland to visit some distant cousins of ours."

The long lean man let out a sigh. "I must say the few moments of culture that this town manages to bring forth are just as quickly gone."

"I shouldn't worry about it, Howard. Plays come and go, and then come back again and again. Sometimes it seems like there is no way to stop one if it is popular. Look, let me stand you to an ice cream soda."

"A capitol idea, Belknapius, a capitol idea" said Howard.

As the two men walked away, the wind whipped up and ripped another piece of the poster from the wall, leaving only the image of the yellow mask behind it.

✦

LATE NIGHT DOUBLE FEATURE

John Wayne was punching out the bad guys for the third time that day when I noticed the musketeer on the balcony stairway.

L ooking back on it, I'm fairly sure I could have handled seeing The Duke standing there. After all, what ghost would have a better right to be hanging around a movie theater showing a John Wayne triple feature than Marion Michael Morrison his own self?

Only it wasn't him standing on that stairway. Over the years I've seen a fair number of John Wayne movies, featuring him in everything from army khaki, to Genghis Khan high fashion. To the best of my knowledge he never played a French Musketeer, and that was who I saw as I came out of my office.

Now and again customers show up in costumes inspired by the movies we happened to be showing, usually the Trekkie crowd or the Rocky Horror bunch and even some from the local medieval reenactment group.

Right then I figured one of two things was going to happen: either someone would jump out of the shadows and yell 'Gotcha!,,' or maybe a couple of pink elephants were going to walk by and ask which way to the concession stand.

Neither of those happened.

Before he noticed me watching him, the Musketeer was just kind of looking around, admiring the scenery. When he saw me, he unsheathed his blade, raised it in salute toward me, then turned and headed up the stairway to the balcony.

What did I do? I did what any normal person would do; I just stood there. I wasn't really certain I wanted to admit to myself that I had seen what I had seen.

Thirty seconds or so later, I took off after him.

I may not be the world's fastest runner, but I fancy I can hold my own in a short race. Yet, by the time I hit the balcony, it was empty. There were eighteen rows of seats on a slight incline that led up to the projection booth. None of them was big enough for anyone older than a ten year old to hide behind.

I glared out toward the screen. Somehow, I didn't expect John Wayne to turn around and say "Pilgrim, the man you're looking for is sitting in the third seat from the left." After all, he had his hands full with Maureen O'Hara, and she was more than enough for anyone to tangle with.

There was a handwritten sign on the projection booth door: ENTER AT YOUR OWN RISK, followed by a drawing of a happy face with vampire fangs. The door resembled a cross between one on a bank vault and something you would find on a submarine. Back in the 20's and 30's, movie film stock was such a volatile material that fire was a distinct possibility, so projection booths had been made as fireproof and airtight as possible to protect the theater. If the projectionist got roasted, well too bad. Hey, it was just part of being in the movie business.

A pair of red lights illuminated the room just enough to get around and, hopefully, keep from tripping over the piles of empty film reels and shipping cans that were strewn all around the place.

Karl, the projectionist, had been working at the Orphium since before I hired on as assistant manager three years ago. With his shaggy, shoulder length hair, faded jeans and Grateful Dead tee-shirt, he looked more like someone who should be panhandling on a street corner or hanging out in a biker bar.

"Hey there, Mr. B. Looks like we're not really packing them in this afternoon."

"These days, who knows what will get people here. I'd be surprised if there were more than fifty people in the auditorium," I said.

"I stopped trying to figure out what gets people to go to the movies a long time ago," he said.

"You're a wise man, m'friend. Oh, by the way, you haven't noticed anyone sticking their noses up in the balcony, have you, in the last few minutes."

Karl pulled his wire-frame glasses off and began cleaning them with a shard of Kleenex he picked up from the repair bench. "No. Of course I haven't been looking that closely. But then it's a bit too early in the afternoon for couples to be trying to sneak up here for a bit of privacy. Of course, I did notice one young lady in the ticket line that I certainly wouldn't mind bringing up...just for a tour, of course," he said with a grin.

"Yeah, I know all about your 'tours'. As I recall, one of them ended with the woman's boyfriend trying to break you into small pieces. And yes, I did notice the girl you're talking about. That is, if the one in purple was her."

Karl angled his head at me for a moment. "Exactly, Bwana. I'm glad to see that you're paying attention. I'm more than willing to go downstairs, introduce myself to her and soften her up for you."

I didn't say anything, just felt my gut tighten up in knots.

"I can get my own dates."

"Then do it. Maybe it's none of my business, and you've got every right to tell me to shut up, but I'm going to say this anyway. It's been six months since the car wreck. She's gone; it's time to get on with your life."

"Karl, shut up."

"Yes, Bwana. Your wish is my command, Bwana."

———

It was 4:10 a.m. when the phone started ringing. George, my answering machine, clicked in on the fourth ring. I didn't even consider trying to take the call. I figured if something was important enough to call this late, it could bloody well wait until morning. If it were someone I really wanted to talk to…well, right then I really couldn't think of anyone that might be.

After the whirring tape stopped, was when the machine's obnoxious beeping started. It was loud enough to be heard a mile away. Why couldn't I have gotten one of those machines that just blinked its little red light on and off silently? I just lay there a few minutes, hoping the sound would stop. Finally I reached over with the intention of pulling the plug on the machine. That seemed a more practical alternative than just yanking the thing out of the wall and throwing it out the window. Groggy as I was, instead of getting the cord, my fingers banged against the play button.

The voice that emerged from the tiny speaker sent a chill through me.

"Hi, it's me. I know you probably just got in and are worn out. Well don't feel bad, so am I. I'm sick to death of this conference and can't wait till its over and I can be back home.

"Now look, when I get back we need to talk. Something has been bothering you for the last few weeks and I want to know what. I refuse to accept your standard, "Oh, nothing." I haven't been married to you for seven years without being able to tell when something is bothering the man that I love. Okay? I'll see you in a day or two. Just remember, I love yo…."

There hadn't been quite enough tape for all of her message. That was just like Betty, always just a little bit more to say than there was time for on the machine. How many times had I heard her cut off in the middle of a sentence or a word?

I stared at the machine for a long time before I found the courage to hit the play button again. Only this time it was a reminder from Ryan, my boss, that we had a breakfast meeting with a film distributor.

I didn't go back to sleep.

Who could sleep, especially after he had just heard the voice of someone who was six months dead?

Instead, I sat in front of the chess board, the one Betty had given me just after we met, the week before her nineteenth birthday. I had a chess problem laid out, but I couldn't concentrate on it. I just sat and stared until sunrise.

———•———

The forecast had been for rain, and for once in his life the local TV weatherman had gotten things right. I pulled the lapels of my trench coat a little tighter and my hat down a little lower. Not that it helped against the rain; it just made me feel like I had actually tried to do something.

After I slid my car into its assigned parking spot, I flipped open the cover of my watch with the MGM lion on the cover and checked the time. I still had a half an hour to go before the first showing started. I didn't need to get right into the theater. Mondays are always slow and I knew my head usher would have everything in order.

I had hardly walked in the front door before I noticed her at one end of the lobby. Small, maybe five two or three, auburn hair hanging nearly to her waist. She was dressed in a work-out suit over tights. I guessed her at anywhere from early to mid-twenties, but I am notorious for guessing women's ages wrong.

She was standing near a couple of movie posters, staring out the smoked glass window, and just seemed confused, like she wasn't sure just where she was.

I waited till the feature had started before going over to her. "Excuse me, Miss, but the movie's already started. Are you waiting for someone?"

She turned with a start, her deep green eyes locking onto mine. "M-m-m-m-movie?"

"Yes, but don't worry, all you've missed are a couple of ads and maybe one of the coming attractions."

"Ads and a movie?" Her eyes appeared empty and far away.

"Yeah. I don't care for them that much either, but these days what can you do about them?"

"I don't know," her voice faded to a whisper as she turned back to look out the smoked window at the street. Then she seemed almost normal as she said "Thank you for your help, Mr...Blaine isn't it?"

I watched her as she headed back toward the auditorium door. It was only after she had disappeared inside the shadowed doorway that I realized the name she had called me. Frankly I had no idea who this "Mr. Blaine" she had mistaken me for might be.

I stayed in the lobby most of the evening. It always helps to let the employees know that you're around. Of course, I was also making sure I was there when the feature let out. Trouble was, I saw no sign of the girl, either in the crowds leaving or when I walked through the auditorium between showings.

———•———

I collapsed into bed that night, dropping my shoes and shirt on the floor, not really caring where they landed. A long time later a sound in the hallway was enough to wake me. Rising up on one elbow I saw *her*, standing in the doorway; long red hair glistening in the moonlight.

She had on a midnight blue negligee, the same one she had worn the first night of our honeymoon in Hawaii.

"Betty?" A whisper was all I could manage, afraid that if I spoke any louder I would awaken from what had to be a dream. If this was a dream, then I didn't want it to end, ever.

"Hey, big man," she said, with that sultry voice I had missed hearing, as she slid into bed next to me.

"I..." Betty's finger reached out and touched my lips before I could say anything else.

"You've got a lot better things to do right now then talk." She was definitely right. The next thing I knew I was kissing her. At some point I realized that the thin silk wrapping of her negligee was gone. I had the vague memory of seeing it disappearing over the edge of the bed.

"What if I get cold?" Betty asked.

"Trust me, there's little possibility of that," I told her.

My hands began to move up and down, tracing the line of her spine, lingering in the small of her back.

"You've only got three days to stop that," she said. Her fingers worked their way around my shoulders and began to massage my neck and shoulder muscles, artfully probing and teasing at the same time. Lord, I had forgotten how good she could make me feel.

As we twisted toward the center of the bed our legs became tangled up in the sheets. Not wanting to take my hands away from her for even a minute, desperately afraid that if I did she would vanish, I tried, unsuccessfully, a couple of times to push the covers away from us with my feet. On the third or fourth attempt I managed to free one foot and use it to send the coverings flying.

"Talented, aren't you," she said.

When I awoke the next morning I lay for a long time without opening my eyes, savoring the memory of our lovemaking, knowing that when I opened my eyes she wouldn't be there. The only thing I did find was a single strand of long red hair, draped across the imprint in the pillow of someone's head.

I cried for the first time since her funeral.

———•———

I found Ryan on the roof of the theater. He's a big fat man who I've always thought would have looked more at home running a black market operation in some middle-eastern club than running a movie theater.

"Something wrong?" I asked.

"I suppose you could say that." He said, pointing at the large air conditioning unit that filled much of the roof. It was a big water cooler, standing twenty-five-feet tall with water pouring through its vents. The machine was at least forty years out of date, if that new.

"Interesting?" asked Ryan.

That was an understatement if there ever was one, considering I had personally supervised the installation of a twelve ton refrigerated air conditioning unit on the roof less than two months before.

"So when did this happen?" I asked.

"I noticed it about an hour ago."

"Would I sound stupid if I said things are getting weirder by the minute?"

"From that I take it something else has happened. Care to fill me in?"

I told him everything, the musketeer, Betty, everything. Amazingly, he didn't say he was going to make reservations for me at the local laughing academy. In fact, he asked an occasional question that made me think that just maybe he knew more than I did about the whole thing.

"So, am I crazy or what?" I asked.

"I knew you were crazy when I hired you. It helped get you the job," he said. "As for the rest, it's not your imagination; it's real."

I was wondering which one of us was the delusional one. "Real, like that thing," I said gesturing at the antique air conditioning unit.

"Yep, and I'm fairly sure that the musketeer is a fellow who goes by the name Loki."

"Loki? Like in the Norse gods?"

"Yeah, but he's no god, just a troublemaker who knows how to manage a few very special tricks. I suspect his real name is Harold Hempelmyer III."

"Harold Hempelmyer III? There were two others who were stuck with that name before him?" I should talk, considering my own first name.

"That's right. He takes a singular pleasure in confusing people and in general causing problems. I'm sure he has some very good and solid reasons for what he does, at least good ones for him, but most of the time I've never been able to figure them out," said Ryan.

Somehow it just didn't surprise me to find out that guys who named themselves after old Norse gods were hanging around the theater.

"Old Harold and I have had a few run-ins over the years. Though, if that is him in the musketeer outfit, it would seem his taste in clothes has changed considerably. It was nearly 20 years ago when a brash young manager began to think it was rather odd when he started having more people go into the theater auditorium than came out. Plus, being beat up by characters from the movies you were running seemed to be not part of the regular job description," Ryan said.

"I imagine that sort of got your attention."

"No shit, Sherlock."

Ryan suddenly looked very old, very tired. "I wish I could explain it all, wrap it up in a nice neat little package that would make a lot of sense. But I can't. It's about dreams, nothing more and nothing less. One person's dream is another one's reality. And for years people have lost themselves in these dreams we call movies in places like the Orphium."

That was when Karl came running toward us, breathing hard, his glasses hanging at an odd angle. "We've got trouble. A nut case in the lobby with a sword and a mucking big gun that he looks like he knows how to use."

Loki!

————

Loki had a very large flintlock pistol in one hand and his arm around the neck of one of the concession girls. I think her name was Valerie or something like that.

"My, isn't this turning into a real convention," he said when he spotted Karl and then myself on the stairway. "You, sir, were amusing for awhile but have gotten rather boring."

"Harold!"

At the sound of his real name Loki turned toward Ryan, who had come down the other stairway. Just then I smelled Betty's perfume and was certain I heard her voice very clearly. "Get him!"

That was enough for me. I jumped across the stair railing and went sailing toward them. So maybe I had seen too many of those old swashbuckler movies. It seemed the thing to do at the time.

I slammed into Loki, the impact sending us crashing to the floor. After that, things kind of got a little crazy. A little? I remember landing several good punches on Loki. I have a vague memory of the flintlock going off. That's a cannon roar that you can't mistake for something else.

Around me there were a lot of fists and a lot of faces all colliding with each other. Most of the time I couldn't tell who was throwing punches at whom; it felt like one of those classic movie barroom fights. Somewhere in the process I slammed my head against the side of the candy counter.

"We've got things in hand, Pilgrim."

I watched as Marion Michael Morrison and several other figures who looked vaguely familiar dragged Harold Hempelmyer III, AKA Loki, out the front door of the theater and off into fog.

"You look like you need a drink," said Ryan.

"At this point in time, several," I said.

"Here," said Ryan. He passed me over a cold can of beer. I didn't recognize the brand, but, frankly, I didn't give a damn. Right then it seemed like my main problem was going to be to get the can open. There was funny looking hinged ring gizmo attached to the top of it.

Ryan showed no sign of producing a can opener; instead he pulled the ring upwards and then pressed it back. A familiar sound of escaping pressure followed a moment later.

He smiled at my difficulty.

After several tries I managed to get it right. That had to be some of the best tasting beer I had ever had.

"Okay, you're wanting explanations. I'm not sure if I know everything you need to know. I'm not sure that anyone does."

"Before we were so rudely interrupted, you said it had to do with dreams."

"Yeah. Dreams, the dreams that we project up there on the movie screen, the dreams we all have locked up in our heads, maybe even the dreams that we need to keep us safe.

"I read an article once, by some hotshot scientist, name of Benford or Hawking or something like that, who said that there were a lot of different versions of our world, all sitting here in the same place. It's just most people can't see or touch them, never know that they're there.

"You know how sometimes you wear a shirt so much that the elbows will wear thin, but not bust through?"

"Yeah." Betty was always bugging me about getting rid of some shirts and socks like that.

"Well, in my never to be humble opinion, I think that reality is like that. If enough people dream in a certain place for enough years, it wears reality thin. It's people wanting, needing, to be somewhere else than they are that does it. If they want it hard enough. A few people who have the right frame of mind are able to find their way to these other worlds."

"And no one has noticed?"

"Most of the time, no. When someone does manage to slip over into another world, they usually manage to fit in. The ones that don't, well, every place has its share of misfits.

Don't ask me why, it just happens. I'm a theater manager, not some fancy genetic scientist or sorcerer. Why some people are good at sports or left-handed and some people aren't. Just put it down to chance. It happens. Maybe to a lot more people than we think."

"However, there are a few people, like you and me, who see these things happening around them and find out that they can move among the different dream worlds, we call it up and down The Way, any time they want. Makes for some damn interesting times, and does give you a wider choice of places to take your vacation than most people have.

"You might even run into yourself out there along The Way. I've noticed several versions of myself, each one whose life went a little different than mine. Hell, I've even seen a couple of versions of you," Ryan said.

"Me?"

"Yeah. In one world you were a writer, another one a politician and more than a few times you were a movie star."

A movie star? That boggles the mind. "So, were my movies any good?"

"The ones I saw weren't too bad. One of them was called "Treasure of the…something or other One I really liked, you played a detective who was looking for the statue of a bird."

Now, that figured. Any other detective would get the girl; me, I get the bird. I finished my beer and tossed the can in a nearby trash canister. Outside the theater the fog had gotten thicker; for a second or two I thought I saw a carriage roll by, lit by gas headlights, and was fairly sure I spotted something with leathery-looking wings sitting on top of the pawn shop sign across the street.

Ryan rummaged around in his jacket pocket and produced one of the Orphium's business cards, only this one had me listed as manager.

"This your way of telling me you're retiring and I'm being promoted."

"I suppose so, if you want the job. But I'm not retiring. I've got my eye on a little one-screen theater down along The Way, down in this alternate Caribbean, where I can sell sodas for a dime and popcorn for fifteen cents, the way it should be. My lady is already there and getting pretty annoyed that I haven't been able to join her.

"I just needed to find someone who would understand what was going on at the old Orphium before I left someone who would know how to appreciate what we have here and take care of this place. So you want the job?"

Before I could answer I heard the sounds of heals clicking across the floor. A moment later a hand settled on my shoulder and a very familiar perfume was in the air.

"He'll take the job."

A moment later my arms were around Betty; very real, very solid. Our lips were tight together for an eternity. When we came up for air I just stood holding her, staring into her emerald green eyes.

"It is you."

"You were expecting maybe the Marx Brothers?"

"Are you here to stay?"

Her answer was another kiss. Shorter this time, because Ryan started to chuckle. "Oh did I forget to tell you? In a slightly different version of reality it was you who were killed in that car wreck and Betty who survived. Sometimes it doesn't take the Traveler's Blood to walk the worlds, just a need. Though why she needed *you* of all people I will never know. You're too short and homely for my tastes."

We ignored him.

An eternity later I asked Betty. "So do *we* want this job?"

"Sure, sounds like fun."

Ryan smiled. "This looks like the beginning of a…"

Whatever else he said, neither Betty nor I heard or particularly cared. It didn't matter one bit, we had each other, again, and it looked like we'd always have the Orpheum.

✦

LINES IN THE SAND

The surf had been building up for nearly an hour. Uneven bits of white mixed in with blue reached further and further up the sand.

I had left Jack somewhere back up the beach. There had been this really intense political discussion going on between a bunch of graduate students from UCLA. It was the sort of thing he could never walk away from.

For a long time I just sat there in the cleft of two rocks and watched the ocean. It reminded me of a July afternoon, oh, so long ago, when George Barris and I had done a beach photo shoot. The wind, the sand; it had all just fitted together perfectly. I only wish we'd had time to do it again, the way George wanted.

A couple of seagulls were working their way along the shore, diving and lifting again on the wind, skimming down to the very edge of the water. I'd always felt a sort of kinship with them, so free, able to reach out so far, yet so tied to a specific set of circumstances.

"So, you're really going to try."

Leaning against the rocks was an all too familiar face. Bobby! He shook his head, absently pushing his hair back in a familiar gesture. I hadn't heard him come up, but that didn't surprise me in the least. I knew *why* he was here and I honestly don't know if I was happy or not by his making the effort to show up.

"No, I just like the beach. Are you here for another fight?" I asked. "I hope you at least made yourself useful and brought champagne with you?"

"We didn't always fight," Bobby said. "There were some good times, some very good times. Besides, you know champagne makes you giggle."

"So what's wrong with an occasional giggle?"

"You're really going to try?" He repeated.

"Of course I am. You knew that when you came." Just to the left of my foot I noticed a sand crab scrambling toward the rocks. "Wouldn't you, if you were me?"

"I hoped I was wrong. You know all it's going to do is end up hurting, hurting very badly." His accent had come back, deeper and more distinctly New England than ever.

"Why not? It wouldn't be the first time I've been hurt," I said. "You've tried. We all do. It's allowed." There were other things that I wanted to say to him right then, but I didn't.

"You're wrong there. I haven't tried, not that I haven't thought about it, but I still haven't," Bobby said. Maybe it was just his attitude. He always did have an ego bigger than his native Massachusetts. I knew that this was his way of admitting that he actually cared enough to try to stop me, without really admitting that he was doing it.

I turned and looked at the ocean again, listening to the waves, feeling them move more than actually seeing them. When I did eventually look back, Bobby was gone like he'd never even been there.

I don't know just how long I sat there, but the next thing I noticed was the last rays of the sun shrinking behind the horizon. The wind had grown colder, even though it was early summer. I hugged myself for warmth.

Finally I got up and began to walk south along the beach, taking my shoes off as I went, letting the water and sand squish between my toes.

When I could hear the cars up on the highway, I knew that I wasn't all that far from the restaurant. It had been opened by some Major fresh out of the Army Air Corp who used his retirement pay to open it, hoping to cash in on the money that was supposed to abound in sunny California.

I spotted her sitting on a rock not too far from the water's edge. The tide was moving up close enough to occasionally touch her toes. The giggle told me a lot about her mood. She had a long stick and was drawing idly in the wet sand.

Dressed in a canary yellow blouse and tan slacks, her brown hair hanging loose around her shoulders, she seemed to have a sort of innocent optimism about her. No, that sounded too much like the sort of crap the studio publicity offices put out. The problem was, it was true, in spite of the pain, frustration and desperation that I knew lurked beneath the surface.

I stopped a few feet away from her. She looked up and smiled, as she continued to draw. Finally she stopped and stared at her creation.

"It needs...something," she said.

I looked down at it. "May I?" I asked, reaching for the stick.

I began to make a series of lines in the sand next to her drawing. I had no particular design in mind; I just drew what struck me at that moment. Gradually it came closer and closer to the first one, never quite touching hers, but seeming to merge, none-the-less.

"That's very good," she said. "Are you an artist?"

I hadn't been all that sure I could get her to talk to a complete stranger. But sometimes people will open up to a stranger, precisely because they are just that, a stranger.

"I wish. I just doodle here and there."

"Well, you're good. What's your name?" she asked.

I hesitated for only a moment, my throat dry. "Mar…Just call me Mary; everybody does."

"Nice to meet you, Mary. I'm Norma. Though I've been thinking of changing my name." It seemed funny hearing that name come from her, in a voice I knew so well.

"Then you must be an actress," I said.

"And what makes you think that?" she asked, cocking her head as she spoke.

"The only people who change their names here in California are either bank robbers or actors. Since I didn't see anyone who looked the least bit like you on Mr. Hoover's Top Ten Most Wanted List, that can only mean that you must be an actress."

Norma giggled, her face flushed slightly from the wind. "You're right," she said. "Or at least I'd like to be. I haven't had a whole lot of luck with auditions, yet, but I'm going to make it."

"You sound pretty confident in yourself."

"If I'm not, who will be?" said Norma.

"Good. You're what, twenty? That would be just a wee bit early to start declaring yourself a failure and throwing in the towel." I told her.

Norma rose and walked a few steps. There weren't any tears, but that didn't mean that there shouldn't have been or that they weren't far away.

"The problem is, I am only twenty, and I do have my whole life in front of me. A whole life of failure if I don't fight things every step of the way. I've failed a lot of people, let them down, in those twenty years," Norma said, without looking up. "My mom. My foster parents. My…husband. I'm scared I'm going to fail again if I don't work very, very hard at it. Sometimes I'm even too scared to try because I might fail, and that hurts…"

I picked up the words for her. "…so much that it cuts right through you until you feel like there's nothing else. Yeah, I've been there more than once myself, kiddo."

"What do you know about show business?"

I wrapped my fingers through each other and looked toward her. "I've been in more than my share of movies."

"Extra work is easy to get. I've never heard of you."

"It happens. I've been where you want to be, and sometimes the price just doesn't equal to what you end up getting for it," I said, trying to inject as much "truth" into my words as possible. "If I were you and I could, I would take a long, hard look at things. Maybe it's not really worth it."

"Right! The only thing is, you've given up. I can see it in your eyes," Norma said. "What are you, thirty-five? By the time I'm your age I'm going to be on top of the world or dead. You may have given up, but not me. My big break is out there and I am going to find it."

"Did you ever think about what it might cost?" I asked, already knowing the answer to that one all too well..

Norma turned her head just slightly toward me. "What do you mean?"

"It's a lot of long, long hours, far too little sleep, no social life except, maybe, what the studio orchestrates for you. As for the directors and producers, forget them; they don't see you as a talented actress, just a walking talking pair of tits that needs to be told where to stand, when to speak and to stay out of trouble.

"And as for marriage, that's a joke. Tell the truth; how many Hollywood marriages do you know of that have lasted all that long and are still happy? Most of them are staying together because of pressure by the studio. And then there's kids; you and they would be virtual strangers if you're working a lot, no matter what kind of garbage the publicity department dreams up," I said.

Norma drew a long breath, pursing her lips in and out for several minutes. "I know it won't be easy," she said. "You may not know it, but I've been modeling for the last couple of years. That was long and hard and it cost me my marriage and even more." As I recalled, technically she was still married; it would be another month before the divorce was final.

"I understand."

"Besides, if I made a go of it, I don't believe those things you talk about will happen to me. I'll make it work and work right," Norma's voice had just the slightest tremor in it.

"So what does your date tonight think of your chances? "I asked. "There are an awful lot of other beautiful girls kicking at the studio gates."

"You know, it's funny. That's exactly the same thing that Jim, my ex-husband, used to say. As for Bob, well, he thinks that I've got the makings of a star." She flipped her hair back, smiling to emphasize the last word.

"So, is this Bob an actor, as well? You know, it's not a good idea to date other actors. Though the publicity department really eats that sort of stuff up."

"No," she shook her head. "He's a writer, I practically tripped over him today at the studio," she said, smiling at the memory.

"From that tone I'd say that you like him." I said, taking the wise older woman's position. "I get the feeling you like him a lot."

"I do. He's fun. He makes me feel special."

"That's important," I said. "Maybe the two of you would be better off just packing it up and going back to Ohio."

Norma picked up the stick and began to add lines to her sand design, each one cutting deeper and deeper into the sand. "You know him, don't you?" she said at last.

"Who?"

"Bob. Bob Slatzer. You know him and you want him for yourself. You must have followed us tonight." Her voice was full of venom. "If you don't know him, how did you know that he was from Ohio?"

Whoops. "I didn't follow you tonight. I'm not trying to break up your date. Norma, listen to me. Think about what you're doing. It's not going to be worth it. No matter what it seems like now."

For maybe a minute she just stared at me.

"Oh, yes, it will be! Whatever the price I pay. I think you're just a sad old has-been who wasn't willing to do what it takes," Norma turned toward me, fire flaring in her eyes. "Lady, someday I am going to be a star and nobody will remember you. You're nothing, that's all you ever have been or will be. Get out of my way or I will crush you."

That was when another voice intruded on the two of us. "Norma!"

A couple of hundred yards up the beach I spotted a young man in slacks and short sleeve shirt. My heart was in my throat; it was Bob. Bob Slatzer. Oh Bob, it was special with you, but it could have been even more special than it was.

"Norma!" he called again. Norma jammed the stick into the sand, directly into the heart of the drawing, turned and headed toward Bob at a run.

I got out of sight before Bob got much closer. He had never mentioned seeing anyone else that night. Of course, given the circumstances, the memory of making love in the sand with surf echoing around us, I could understand why.

Once they were gone I walked back around to the rock. The tide had already begun to cover the lines in the sand. I watched for a long time as the waves moved further and further up, wiping a bit more each time.

Well, that was that. The thing is, it didn't surprise me in the least. I could have talked until I was blue in the face and it wouldn't have done any good. Norma Jean was as thick-headed and stubborn as I remembered her, as I still am.

Just around the point I found Jack waiting for me. He smiled, kind of sadly, and we walked for a long time, his hand slipping into mine.

"I guess that Bobby was right," I said.

"My little brother can be a pain in the ass at times, but he's usually right" Jack said. "I didn't change a thing."

"Did you really expect to?" he asked softly.

"I don't know. I just felt like she deserved the chance to find some happiness and maybe find a way out of the hole that I dug myself into." I said.

"Are you saying you weren't happy?

"No, I was happy, at times very happy." I wasn't even sure if I was telling the truth or just what I wanted to hear myself saying.

"You want to try again? There are some other places, further on in your life. After she's got a movie or two under her belt. Maybe before Joe's gone or Arthur leaves. Then you can give her just the right push, keep things from…" He didn't have to finish the sentence.

"I doubt it. Who knows, maybe I'm saving the world from my career as an interior decorator who finally dies at the age of 65 in 1995. How many times have you tried to change things?"

He rolled his eyes up, shaking his head. "More times than I can count. Or even want to think about. Everything from trying to convince myself to stay married to my first wife to not trying to run until '64. Hell, I even tried to talk myself into staying in the Navy."

"Aye, aye, Admiral Jack. Hey, that does have a pretty good ring to it." I told him.

"Watch it, woman. I demand more respect than that from you; after all, I am the President."

"Were." I reminded him. "Besides, you were just a common politician. I, on the other hand, am a movie star."

"Don't get impudent, Norma Jean."

I think that was the first time he had ever called me anything but Marilyn. I squeezed his hand tighter and we walked for a long time; the waves lapping on the sand were so very easy to listen to.

"I think it's time to go," Jack said softly.

Up ahead I could see the light. It felt warm and inviting. I pulled my fingers away from Jack's, shaking my head. He looked at me for a very long time before turning and walking off. I watched him until the light seemed to swallow him up.

The water moved around my feet, the sand squishing between my toes as I walked in the other direction.

✦

Serpent's Tooth

(written with Susan P. Sinor)

DEAR MOTHER,

Why didn't you warn me about the problems stepchildren cause? Not that I would have listened, of course. I know, I know, I was in love; at least I thought I was. After all, he had blue eyes to die for.

Okay, maybe I wasn't really in love, but I liked the man well enough. Look, good marriages have been made from worse beginnings. So he didn't have "that" much money, but then you don't expect a second son to have much money. Not to mention he wasn't a drunkard, like my late lamented spouse. I do hope you hear the irony in those words.

Besides, I'd been a widow long enough. My girls and I needed someone to support us, and he had a daughter who needed a mother, too.

I thought it would be just perfect. You know, two broken families united to make one whole. It's just the sort of thing they talk about in all those books.

Now, there is no doubt in my mind that I did my dead level best to make this whole thing work. It was all her fault, that little brat of a daughter of his, Ella.

From the beginning I tried to treat her like she was one of my own; the girls tried to treat her like a sister. I think the idea of having a younger sister thrilled Drusilla. This way she wouldn't be the youngest.

But what did I get in return? Resentment! Nothing but pure unadulterated resentment! I just don't understand.

I'll give you an example. After the wedding I put all three girls in the same bedroom. I figured that if they were sharing a room, that would help them share each other's lives. You know, Mother, the way my sisters and I did. I wanted them to be closer, like a real family. It could have been so perfect.

So much for my dreams of perfection. It only took two or three days before Drusilla came to me and said that it just wasn't working out. Ella just wasn't cooperative, would just sit and sulk and wouldn't get involved with anything the other two wanted to do. It was like she resented breathing the same air as Anastasia and Drusilla.

All they were doing was playing with their hair. You know how young girls like to play with their hair and clothes. Well, when I tried to talk to her about it, she complained that my daughters were being cruel to her.

My daughters are not cruel people! Okay, sometimes they may tease a little, but it's always just in fun.

I sat her down and tried to have a heart to heart, mother-to-daughter talk with Ella, to make her understand that if she'd just try to get along with them, things would be just so much better for us all.

Maybe I am just an optimist, but when she walked out of my bedroom that night I was sure things were going to work out. Yeah, right. I won't bore you with the details; lets just say that by Friday night I knew things were not going to work with the three of them in the same room.

The problem was, the only room I could put her in was that little room in the attic. It certainly wasn't big enough for Ana and Dru! I hoped that she would be much happier up there, in her own private room. After all, it wasn't as if I could put her in the guest room and make any guests we might have sleep up there!

Then the complaints started. She was lonely; she was cold and she was becoming very annoying with all this whining. It was winter, after all; what did that ungrateful girl expect me to do, wave a magic wand and speed up the seasons! It was only a couple of weeks until spring, so I told her to wear something warmer to bed and gave her an extra blanket. As for being lonely, she had had her chance to make friends with Dru and Ana, but I was certain that they would give her another chance if she learned to behave. The tears and screaming didn't phase me a bit; she just wanted her own way and was not getting it.

Now you know I try to run my household efficiently. A place for everything, and so forth. Dru and Ana know that and always get their chores done quickly. I expected the same from Ella, too. I explained her responsibilities to her when I took over the household. I said I knew she wasn't accustomed to cooking and cleaning, but that we all had our own jobs and that was hers, so she would just have to get used to it.

Well, she argued with me, said there were servants to do that. But I told her that I'd had to let some of the servants go. We couldn't afford them any longer, and besides, I'd caught them slacking.

She didn't like that at all, said that I was picking on her and her OWN mother would never have treated her that way. So I had to remind her that her OWN mother was dead. I was her mother now, and she'd better get used to it and hold up her end.

Lord knows I tried to accommodate her and not sully the memory of her mother, who, looking at that house, seemed the most disorganized person I have ever seen. I have no idea what John saw in her. I tried to make friends with the people who had been friends with her. But some of them! Mother, you will not believe what bizarre people they were.

One afternoon this very common looking woman showed up at our back door and said that she was a friend of the family; at least I think that is what she said. She had such a thick accent and seemed to mumble every other word.

Truth be told, she could have been saying she was anything from being a good mother to maybe being a godmother. I suggested that if she were a friend of the family she should come calling some time when John was at home. That way he could set the Watch on her, in case she was a lunatic or something.

Add into this the half a hundred things that it takes to keep a household running. So did I have any spare time? No, but I took some and tried to work with Ella. Yet all I got from her were snide remarks and looks that would have ripped my heart out if it were possible.

One afternoon I was inspecting a new batch of vegetables that had had been sent over from the market. I asked Ella to help me. While I was deciding on the menu for the coming week, Ella was supposed to be bringing in the baskets of vegetables from the cart and putting them away. Now, this was an easy task; it wasn't as if I were asking her to master some complicated recipe for dinner. Did she do it; did she pitch in and try to do her part in this project? No!

She came into the pantry, sulking about having to do "servants' work," carrying only one basket when they were light enough to carry two or three at a time, Then she had the nerve to throw that basket down, scattering the small pumpkins in it all over the floor, and run out of the room. When I confronted her later she tried to claim that she had seen a mouse and it had frightened her. I mean, really, as if I would allow vermin in my house. You know I can't stand them. If I thought there was even the slightest chance of mice having invaded our property I would definitely get a cat, even though I find cats almost as disgusting as mice.

I tried not to be mean about it, but I had heard all I wanted to from her. It wasn't easy for me, either, taking someone else's home and husband; having to retrain and rearrange, and get things into the way that they need to be to run right.

John kept saying that this wasn't the way that he was used to doing things. Why are husbands so difficult to train? You'd think they'd want things to run smoothly and easily, but every time I made the tiniest suggestion for a slight modification in behavior, he went off the deep end and sulked for days.

I am not that hard to get along with. I just have a firm sense of responsibility, and I expect everyone else to feel the same. But I was going to tell you what happened last week

John had announced several weeks before that he was going to be away for a business trip to the provinces, so the girls and I were up early to watch him ride off.

The trip was supposed to take no more than a month, but he had told me there was a chance it might take longer if several business deals that could be worth a lot of money to us worked out.

I don't mind these long trips; I know he is working for the betterment of our family. Besides, it gives me a chance to get things done around the house without interference and without having to hear "but this is the way we've always done it."

The big problem developed three weeks into that trip in the form of an invitation to the Governor's Ball. In this province that is the key social event of the season. So there was no way in the world I was going to miss it. All right, I know it was a social no-no for a married woman to attend without her husband, people looking down their noses at you and all that, but what kind of choice did I have?

Besides, there would be plenty of eligible young men at the ball and this would be the chance to get the girls properly introduced into Society. I would attend as their chaperone, a fitting role for a married lady.

But by all that was Holy, the girls would not let their chores go by the wayside while we were getting ready. After inspecting our wardrobe I came to the conclusion that we had nothing suitable for the occasion. Therefore each of us would have to make a new dress for the ball. Drusilla, Anastasia and I got busy right away on our outfits, but apparently Ella hadn't learned the basics of needlework and was having trouble. I don't want to horrify you by describing that "thing" that she created. It would not do, not do at all.

We each offered to help her when we had the time, but she acted as if our offers were insults to what little ability she had as a seamstress. So, with so much to do, her dress was barely half-finished when the day of the ball came. There was no way that it could be completed in time for our departure, and we told her so. She would have to stay at home.

After all, it wasn't our fault she didn't have anything to wear. We had time to finish our dresses, she should have had enough time for hers, especially with our help. I did feel sorry for her as we dressed. For once, she didn't throw a tantrum. She actually helped us fix our hair. We were grateful for the effort and told her we would try to bring her something from the party. Our coach came and we waved goodbye as we rode off.

Well, the ballroom was breathtaking. There were flowers everywhere, and fountains of champagne. Uniformed servants discreetly appeared with hors d'oeuvres and disappeared with empty glasses and plates. We were treated like royalty. We were presented to our hosts and their son, Richard, who had been away at school for several years. The young man was very handsome, I would say in his early twenties, just a few years older than my daughters.

Richard seemed rather taken with Anastasia. I was hoping they might spend some time together, getting to know one another, you know. I could definitely see possibilities in those two as a couple.

Then a new guest showed up, an unescorted young lady. Needless to say there were tongues wagging before she managed to walk ten feet into the ballroom.

She seemed somewhat overcome by all the pomp and didn't quite know what to do, when Richard spotted her and practically ran over Ana to get to her. I never got a good look at her, but there was something familiar about the new girl.

The two of them spent the rest of the evening dancing in the garden. Richard seemed to have totally forgotten not only my Ana but also every other guest in the place. I have to say, that school he attended obviously did not teach him all that he needed to know about manners and how someone in a political family is supposed to behave.

I happened to have stepped out on one of the balconies and was listening to the big clock tower tolling midnight, when I noticed the girl who had been with Richard running out into the garden and toward the street gate. I stepped back inside and heard a lot of people chattering about how the girl had just abruptly turned and run away from Richard without an explanation. The thing was, no one seemed to know exactly who she was. This sort of thing would never have happened in the social circles you raised me in, Mother. I mean, really, a party crasher like that and no one had the nerve to throw her out.

We got home just after two; Ella had obviously gone to bed, since she had certainly not stayed up to greet us, which I thought was very rude.

The next day we heard all over town that the unidentified girl at the ball had lost a shoe while running down the steps, and young Richard had found it. He swore that he would search all over town until he found the girl the shoe fit.

When he came to our house I told Ella to stay in her room since she hadn't even attended the ball and there was no need to just come in to gape at the young man. But did she listen to me? No!

She sneaked down the back stairs, the ones that she seemed to prefer most of the time, and into the parlor; wearing the oldest dress she had. At least the girls and I had dressed up for the governor's son. Look, he may have been behaving a little nutty, but I figured there was always the chance he would get interested in Ana or Dru. Okay, it was a long shot, but it never hurts to try.

Mother, you'll never in your life guess what happened next! The world turned totally upside down! Richard took one look at Ella, and before I could turn around or get a word in, he had put the shoe on her foot and whisked her into his carriage and away to the mansion. He was chattering something about marriage.

I wasn't sure if I was going to faint or have a heart attack right then. There were obviously some mistakes that needed correcting. I went straight after them and demanded to see the governor about his son's behavior. This was just impossible. I told him that Ella couldn't possibly be the girl his son was looking for because she hadn't even been at the ball.

About that time Richard and Ella appeared. I wanted to take Ella off in private; she had embarrassed herself enough as it was. But neither Richard nor the governor would hear of it, so right in front of them I asked Ella what had possessed her to try to pass herself off as the girl being searched for. She was obviously trying to take advantage of this poor deluded boy.

That was when Ella told me that she WAS the girl. She spun a really strange story. Apparently, after we left, her 'fairy godmother' had appeared. I mean really, a 'fairy godmother'! This figment of her imagination apparently magically dressed Ella for the ball, turned vegetables and mice into a coach, horses, driver and footman, as well, with the warning that the enchantment would last only until midnight.

The girl was obviously lying. How was I, or anybody, supposed to really believe as ridiculous a story as that? Richard seemed to believe her, though, or not really care; he was still determined to marry her. So what was I to do? This could have some very bad repercussions for our family, socially, as well as for John and his business. Trust me, you don't want to get on the bad side of the governor.

I had one trump card left: Ella's father. I insisted that no marriage could take place until he returned. After all, Richard still had to formally ask John for his consent before they could be married. Well, I was sure that my husband would never consent to his daughter marrying at such a young age and that would be that. If necessary, I was sure I could persuade him.

Actually, I hoped that they would get tired of each other and that Richard would take an interest in Anastasia again. I really think that my daughters should marry before Ella does. After all, they are the eldest, and one should have respect for tradition.

John finally returned, ten days later than he had planned, with news that he had made a fortune off this trip. But that was a moot issue. When I told him everything that had happened while he was gone, he got mad at me! According to my dear husband I should have made sure that Ella was able to go to the ball with the rest of us, as if he thought we were supposed to wait on her hand and foot. I gave him a piece of my mind about that idea.

You know, Mother, in the long run, this marriage might turn out to be a good thing. It's not what I wanted, but you always taught me to make the best of whatever happens.

Of course, there are some advantages to having Richard in the family. He and Ella aren't even married yet and we've already started having gentleman callers at the house for Anastasia and Drusilla. Even my future stepson-in-law's younger brother has come calling, not to mention more than one highly placed government official who has started making noises about steering some very lucrative business possibilities John's way.

One odd thing happened recently. The other night I happened to look out in the alley and saw Ana talking to someone. It was that plain-looking woman I mentioned earlier, you remember, the one who said she was an old family friend. But I couldn't understand a word she said. They seemed to be talking so intensely that Ana didn't even notice those mice that were running around her feet.

As soon as the wedding date is set I will send you all the details. We have so much to do before the wedding that the girls and I just won't have enough time to make dresses for the wedding, so I had to find a dressmaker. I'm sure the dresses won't be nearly as nice as they would be if we made our own, but I guess we'll have to get used to it. After all, the wives and daughters of wealthy businessmen, not to mention the parents of the governor's son's wife, do not make their own clothes.

Your loving daughter,

Harriet

✦

THE ADVENTURE OF THE
OTHER DETECTIVE

The weeks following the return of Sherlock Holmes, three years after his supposed death at the hands of Professor James Moriarty, the so-called Napoleon of Crime, were busy ones for my old friend.

There was, as might be expected, a steady stream of visitors who found their way to Baker Street, everyone from the dirtiest pickpocket to a messenger who took Holmes to a private meeting at Buckingham palace.

I had also returned to Baker Street.

Not twenty four hours after Colonel Sebastian Moran had been led away in chains by Inspector Lestrade, Holmes asked if I would agree to return to Baker Street. "It would be the best medicine in the world for you, Watson," he said over one of Mrs. Hudson's excellent dinners.

As I look back on that night, I must admit that I was not all that difficult to convince. My darling Mary had been gone for nearly a year. Her weak heart had taken her only three days after our fifth wedding anniversary.

The end had come so swiftly that there had been nothing that all of my medical skill could have done to save her.

Even after so many months, there were moments when I caught myself turning to ask her something, or would look up at a sound, expecting to see her stepping around a corner.

So Holmes' invitation was a most welcome one for me.

Of cases there were many: *The Adventure of the Black Katana*, *The Quest for Pendragon's Sun*, and *The Theft of Alharazad's Manuscript*, to name just a few.

By the middle of October things had returned to as much of a semblance of normality as was anything around Sherlock Holmes.

The evening of the 13th I was alone in Baker Street. Holmes was dining with his brother, Mycroft, and I did not expect his return for many hours.

I declined the invitation to join them. I had no doubt that I would hear the details from Holmes, especially of the 'favor" that he would no doubt be asked to perform by the man whom he had once described as, at times, "being the British Government."

Beside my favorite chair that evening stood a stack of medical journals. A stack that I had to admit was far too high. This past year I had sadly neglected to keep up on the literature of my profession and it was something that I meant to correct.

The mantle clock had just tolled ten when I heard a furious pounding on the downstairs door. Moments later the familiar footsteps of Mrs. Hudson could be heard rushing to answer the summons.

The young man behind Mrs. Hudson looked vaguely familiar, in that way that so many people resemble others. He was bundled tightly against the night's chill.

"Sir, I am sorry to disturb you, but the young man says that it's an emergency," Mrs. Hudson said.

"I am afraid that Holmes has not returned, but if there is anything that I can do..." Before I could say more, the young man cut me off with a wave.

"Sir, it wasn't Mr. Holmes that I come to fetch, but yourself. There's been an accident."

"Accident? Where?" I said sitting bolt up.

"Three streets over," he said. "Mr. Delvechio's warehouse. It was himself Mr. Hobbs who came falling off that old balcony. I couldn't tell if he was breathing or not." Mrs. Hudson already had my bag ready. The fog that had rolled in at sunset was heavier than I had seen it in years, enshrouding the streets like a thick blanket. A half-dozen steps from the door and Baker Street was gone from sight.

"Colder than I thought it would be," I said, pausing to pull the collar on my coat up.

"Aye, sir."

"What's your name, son?"

"Arthur, sir. Arthur Pym. I'm the new accounting clerk for Mr. Delvechio. Only been there about a half year."

It was scarcely five minutes before Pym was leading me to a side door marked DELVECHICO AND SONS, IMPORTERS.

He had to pound for several minutes before anyone came to admit us.

"We got no time for..." The door was opened by a massive man with small square-shaped glasses hanging on the end of his nose. "Oh, it's you."

"Aye, Mr. Harris. I done brought the doctor. Watson's his name."

"Don't matter what his name is. Could've saved yourself a trip. If that fall did'na kill him he'll be dead soon, after doing a header into that pile of Italian mirrors."

Not since the battlefields of Afghanistan had I seen a body covered with that much blood. Around me were hundreds, if not thousands, of shards of glass. In each one there seemed to be another me, angled and bent and torn into a million different shapes. The unfortunate Mr. Hobbs lay in the center of this display, any hope that he might still be alive ended when I found the shard of glass embedded in his jugular.

Once the police had arrived and taken statements, confirming the story of Hobbs fall, I volunteered to remain until the body was removed. The constable said it would not be necessary, but that I should come to the local station house tomorrow to make a statement.

"Are you certain you don't want me to come with you, Doctor Watson?"

"Thank you, Arthur, but it is only a few blocks. Even in this mist I can find my way to 221B with no problem."

"You have a good night then, sir," said the constable as he opened the door.

I picked my way through the fog carefully. The occasional glow of a streetlamp gave a safe haven of scant few feet in the mist. I had to stop several times, unsure of my direction.

Standing there in the mist a feeling of nausea came crashing over me and I had to fight for each breath. My head seemed about to burst with wave after wave of pain. I had to struggle to keep from losing myself in the pain. For that instant I could have been anywhere: Delvechio's Warehouse, darkest Africa, or the cold wastes of the South Pole. Then, just as quickly as it came, the feeling passed, leaving only a dull ache in the pit of my stomach in its wake. I pulled myself together and began to pick my way once again toward Baker Street.

When I finally reached that familiar door I felt as if I had just run ten miles with full military field pack, uphill. A good stiff shot of whiskey and my own bed were the best prescriptions I could think of right then.

I had some difficulty making my key work. It fit, but did not seem to want to turn at first. Finally, by twisting it hard and pushing, the door came open. I reminded myself to mention something to Mrs. Hudson in the morning concerning it.

Under the door to our rooms I could see a light. Obviously Holmes had returned in my absence. Just inside I spied the familiar silhouette of Sherlock Holmes sitting scrunched in his chair in front of the fireplace. I was just about to say something when I heard a voice behind me.

"Say now, who might you be?"

Standing in the door to my bedroom was a figure with a revolver in his hand. When he stepped into the light I saw a face that I had not seen since I had left Afghanistan.

"Murray?" I said.

"I said, who are you? And why are you bursting into our quarters without so much as a..." his face went ashen as I stepped into the light. "God help me. It can't be! Colonel? Colonel Watson, sir? But you're dead!"

At that, my former Army aide fainted dead away. Holmes was out of his chair and across the room in an instant, kneeling beside Murray.

"If I am not mistaken, I believe that you, sir, are a doctor," he proclaimed.

"I am."

"Then I believe you have a patient." It was then that I realized the man was not Sherlock Holmes but none other than Professor James Moriarty.

One of the best restoratives available in a physician's pharmacopoeia is nothing less than good old-fashioned brandy. I've kept a small metal flask of the stuff in my case since I first took medical degree. As I expected, it brought Murray around almost immediately, gasping for breath, but awake.

I felt every bit as confused as Alice, having stumbled through the Looking Glass. If this were a dream, it was the most realistic one I had ever experienced. I felt entitled to a long swallow of brandy myself.

For that moment I had a chance to look around the room. Things were familiar, but subtly different. I recognized the familiar chemical apparatus in the corner, the violin in its case by the fireplace and the old battered coat tree near the door. Only the Persian slipper and its tobacco was missing from its accustomed place. Where there should have been several rows of carefully indexed scrapbooks, I found neat matching journals, many dealing with mathematics and astronomy, bearing dates that went back some eight years.. And in the far corner of the room stood a small telescope.

"Excellent work, doctor, excellent," said Moriarty.

"Thank you," I said looking at the man who up until a few minutes before I had been convinced lay dead at the bottom of the Reichenbach Falls in Switzerland. Only this was not exactly the man that Holmes had described. He was younger by at least ten years, if not more so, than I had expected. There was an ease and confidence about him that reminded me of Holmes.

"Would somebody mind telling me just what in the hell has happened to me?" I said finally.

"A very good question, doctor. Watson, isn't it?" he asked as he helped Murray to his feet. My former army aide stared at me for a moment without saying a word, and then allowed me to lead him over to the couch.

"Now, Doctor, tell me how long you have lived at 221B Baker Street?" asked Moriarty, sitting down in the chair facing the yellow leather one I had taken.

"How...?"

Moriarty grinned and gestured with one finger toward my medical bag, still sitting open on the floor. "Rather revealing, I must admit," he said. There, in neat gold letters, was my name and the address, 221B Baker Street, London.

The day I had moved back into Baker Street I had retrieved my old bag from the back of the closet.

In spite of all that Holmes had told me regarding this man, I found myself warming to the fellow. I began to describe the events of the evening. Moriarty stopped me only occasionally to ask for further details, sometimes on the oddest things, the type of doorway that had fronted Delvechio's, the uniform the constable had worn, and the location of the local police station. I wanted to know why, but for the moment thought it best to keep my own counsel. Moriarity was especially interested in my impression of the fog itself.

"A most fantastic tale that you have entertained us with this evening," said Moriarty. "You have to admit it is a bit hard to accept, especially considering that Murray and I have been sharing these quarters since the spring of 1885."

His eyes were unblinking as he stared at me, waiting for my reaction.

"Professor, I am a doctor, a man of science. If I were hearing this tale from anyone but myself I would be convinced that the speaker had far too much good Scotch whiskey and had been reading one of the scientific romances of Mr. H.G. Wells. Yet as sure as I sit here, every word that I have told you is the God's own truth."

Moriarty steepled his fingers in front of his face, deep in thought. "Doctor, I believe you."

"Professor, how can you believe him?" objected Murray. "The last time I saw Colonel Watson he was dead, an Afghan spear through his chest. I supervised the burial party myself, and that was nearly ten years ago."

Dead? Me? A cold chill ran down my spine. This had to be a nightmare, but there seemed no way to escape it. I defy anyone to hear the news that he was not only dead, but a number of years buried, and not have at least some reaction.

"What would it take to convince you that this man is John H. Watson?" asked Moriarty.

Murray thought for a moment before he answered. "Look on his left forearm." I hesitated for a moment before taking off my jacket. I rolled up my sleeve and held out my arm for Moriarty to inspect.

"There should be scar there, three to four inches in length," said Murray.

"It is there," confirmed Moriarty.

"How did you get it?"

I smiled, remembering well the hunting trip with my father and brother that had been the last time all three of us had been together as a family. I had brought down a boar, but not without the beast nearly ripping my arm to shreds.

Murray just shook his head.

"Colonel, I don't know how you managed it, but I'm bloody glad that you did," he said finely.

"Just a minute there, Murray. That's the second time you've called me Colonel."

"Aye, sir. After all, that is your rank."

Colonel Doctor John H. Watson. That did have a nice sound to it. The only trouble was that I had never risen above the rank of Captain when I had served with the Fifth Northumberland Fusiliers and had been discharged after being wounded at the Second battle of Mawand.

"But, Colonel, at Mawand you weren't injured. I was."

This difference in history seemed to please Moriarty when I mentioned it.

"Unless you are one of the most convincing madmen to come along in a long time, you, sir, are telling the complete and utter truth. The facts concerning your rank only serve to help prove my theory.

"Ever since the incident of a man who walked around his carriage, out of the view of a dozen people, and utterly vanished, I have developed a theory regarding the existence of other worlds," he said.

"Like Mars and Venus?" I asked.

"I said other worlds, not other planets," he corrected. "More precisely, worlds exactly like our own, only with differences. The result of other decisions. For instance, where the American Confederate States lost their war for independence. Mathematically, it makes perfect sense.

"These worlds would on occasion touch and allow people to pass from one world to another, usually by accident, but under the right circumstances, deliberately. Tonight it seems that the fabric of space and time was stretched so thin that it allowed Dr. Watson to walk from his London to ours."

"All in the space of a few blocks," I said. Looking out the window into the fog, I knew in the pit of my stomach his theory was right. I took a long swallow out of my brandy flask and laid it on the nearby table. It was hard to fathom that everything I had known was gone, especially when I could see much of it around me.

As it had so many times before, the conversation in Baker Street was interrupted by the arrival of none other than Inspector Herbert Lestrade. The little rat-faced Scotland Yard man had been one of the first of Holmes' professional associates who had made his way to Baker Street. Naturally, he did not know me from Adam.

"Lestrade, it is always good to see you." said Moriarty, extending his hand.

"Thank you, Professor. I'm sorry if I've interrupted anything. However, my news could not wait." He paused for a moment, looking in my direction. "May I speak freely?"

"Forgive me, Inspector, I'm forgetting my manners. This is an old army friend of Murray's, Dr. John H. Watson. They served together in Afghanistan. Dr. Watson is privy to anything said here."

"Very well then," he said, sitting down in a red leather chair opposite Moriarty. "Less than an hour ago I received a telegram notifying us that Colonel Sebastian Moran has escaped from Dartmore Prison."

"Do they know just when it happened?" asked Moriarty.

"Sometime in the last three to four days. He got into a fight with some of the other prisoners. They all ended up in solitary confinement," said Lestrade.

"And current penal theory calls for prisoners so incarcerated to see and be seen by no one, except a single guard," said Moriarty.

"Even at meal times?" I asked.

"A small metal grate on the bottom of each door allows the trays to be injected and later extracted. Moran has pulled more than one hunger strike in the past. They could see a figure wrapped up in his blanket, so even though he wasn't eating, they didn't much bother with him," said Lestrade.

"How did they penetrate the ruse?"

Lestrade laughed, leaning back in the red leather chair. "One of the other prisoners, Volmer by name, suffered a stroke. He was dying, and his last request was to see Moran. Apparently they had become friends."

"Do you think that Moran will be making for sanctuary with his old comrades here in London?" asked Murray.

"Old friend, I know he will. I am also certain that Moran's employer had a hand in this; it's just his style." With that, Moriarty was out of his chair. From behind a bust of Caesar he extracted three perfectly round metal balls. He rolled them over in his hands several times and then deposited them in his vest pocket. "How much longer did Moran have left on his term in solitary confinement?"

"Three days."

"Then whatever is going to happen will happen within the next seventy-two hours." For a time Moriarty stared at the wall calendar.

"Good lord," he said.

"What is it, Professor?" asked Murray.

"If I am right, we have little time to lose."

"I'll come with you," volunteered Lestrade.

"Thank you, but no. For the moment there are things that must be done that you cannot be a part of."

"I don't like it, Professor. This is police business."

"I am aware of that. However, there is no place for you in our party this evening." Lestrade didn't say another word; his face reflected the irritation that he was feeling. Instead, he turned and walked out the door without a word.

Murray disappeared into the bedroom that had once belonged to me, emerging moments later, overcoat draped across his arm, a twin pair of Army service revolvers in his hand. "Colonel, if you would take charge of one of these," he said.

The familiar weight in my hand was another reassurance of the reality around me. It fit perfectly into my jacket pocket. "I am to accompany you then, Professor?"

"Of course, old chap. Murray and I wouldn't have it any other way."

"Professor, I am at your disposal."

———

In spite of the fog we were able to flag down a cab in only moments. I didn't hear the address that Moriarty gave the driver, but moments later we were shooting down the street. After a few turns I lost my way completely.

"Professor, may I ask who Colonel Moran's employer is?"

"Do you know of Moran in your London?"

"Somewhat. Ex-Indian Army, number two man in a criminal organization that stretched its tentacles into every bit of bad business through the length of London, and even England itself. Prefers to kill with a custom-made air rifle," I said.

"Air rifles, nice to know old Moran is predictable," said Murray.

"And who was the head of this criminal cabal?" asked Moriarty.

I hesitated for a moment before answering. "You, Professor."

Moriarty laughed. It was the eeriest sound that I had ever heard.

"Well, why not," he said at last. "It sort of balances things out."

"Then who is the leader of the organization here?" I asked.

"Why, none other than Mr. Sherlock Holmes."

That announcement put a damper on conversation, at least on my part, so we rode in silence. The concept of Holmes as a criminal did not seem as shocking now as it might have a few hours before. In the back of my mind I suppose I still harbored the faint hope that this was all some strange dream that I would at any moment be roused from.

Our cab pulled to a stop in front of Number Ten Cudugin Square. A three-story private home; its windows were dark and a single gas light burned at its front door.

"On your toes, gentlemen," said Moriarty. "Our luck is with us. They are meeting tonight."

A liveried butler answered the door. The professor spoke a single word to the man. "Valhalla."

"Down the hall, sir, second door to the right."

As we walked along the hallway, I had the distinct feeling that we were being watched, which I told Moriarty.

"I would be worried if we weren't," replied the professor. "The security of those we are about to meet is of paramount importance."

Any interest I might have had in who we were going to meet vanished the moment I saw who had opened the door. The dark brunette hair fell loose around her shoulders, with hazel green eyes in a familiar oval face.

It couldn't be, but it was! Mary, my own dear wife, dead these many months, but there she stood. It took all the strength I could muster to keep from grabbing her up.

"This way, gentlemen," she said.

"Easy, Colonel," said Murray, his hand on my shoulder. My former aide had always been aware of my moods, many times almost before I was.

Three men sat at the heavy oaken table that dominated the room. Two of them I knew by sight. One was none other than Edward, Prince of Wales, and Heir Apparent to the throne. Next to him was a much older man. It took me a moment or two to recognize him, considering Albert of Saxe-Coburg-Gotta, Prince Consort to Her Royal Highness Victoria, Queen of England, had died thirty-three years earlier in the world I knew.   The third man was unknown to me, though he did look vaguely familiar. His thin cadaverous face suggested someone who might be found on the streets of the East End, rather than in this company. Seeing this, and most of all, Mary alive, made me pray that it was not all some nightmare.

"Professor, this is a most unexpected surprise. We haven't had the honor of your company for far too long." said Prince Albert.

"Thank you, Your Royal Highness," said Moriarty. "I believe you know Murray. This other gentleman is Dr. John H. Watson, whom I have asked to lend his aid to tonight's enterprise. I will vouch for him completely."

"That he travels in your company is proof enough of his trustworthiness," said Prince Edward, as he extracted a large cigar from his silver case. "Watson? Watson. Would you be related to the late Colonel Watson? I met him some years ago on a tour of India."

"A cousin, sir." I could hear every bit of uncertainty in my voice as I spoke. "Our parents always claimed that he and I could have passed as twins."

"Indeed. If memory serves me, you readily could have." He laughed as he lit the big cigar. "He was a good man, of whom your family can be justly proud; he was a true hero of the empire."

"Thank you."

"Now, professor," said the Prince Consort. "What is this errand that has brought you here tonight?"

"It is a matter of gravest importance. By your own statement, even the Queen does not know just how involved you and your son are in these meetings. If it had not been for your sure hand behind the scenes, I would not care to speculate what state our country would be in now.

"However, tonight matters have reached a point where I can no longer act alone. For some years you three have known of my ongoing feud with Sherlock Holmes. More times than I care to remember, this Napoleon of Crime has managed to elude the net that I have cast for him. Tonight he made a move in a plan that will involve the escape of Jack the Ripper."

The silence that fell over the room with his words was a familiar one to me. I had known it on those occasions when it had been necessary to break the news to a patient's family that they had lost a loved one.

"You are certain of this?" said Prince Albert. At that moment he seemed twenty years older than when I had come into the room.

"Yes, and moreover, I believe that events will come to a head with the next several days. In three days time it will be the anniversary of the first of the Ripper murders. It would suit Holmes' sense of humor to see the man walking free again on that day."

The silent man picked up his pen and began to write. A moment later the sheet was passed to Prince Edward. The younger man's cigar sat untouched in the ashtray in front of him, a gray pile of ash below it.

"You have guaranteed the silence of your companions, Professor. Very well, let both men understand that what they are about to hear may be the most dangerous secret in the entirety of the British Empire. What do you gentlemen know concerning the Ripper murders?" asked the Heir Apparent.

"Only what was in the newspapers," Murray said.

Holmes had, in fact, been called into the case, but had never confided any of the details, saying that it was a tale better left untold. I recalled the multitude of rumors that had echoed from every pub and street corner regarding The Ripper during those dark days.

"Six years ago Murray was in America handling the matter of the May Surveillance for me.. Dr. Watson was also out of the country."

"Very well. As you gentlemen know, for some six months in 1888, London was frightened to its core by the series of murders committed in the Whitechapel district by the person who came to be known as Jack the Ripper.

"So far as the public knows, the Ripper was never brought to book for the crime. Some of the far more speculative journals have hinted that he may still be prowling the streets of London to this day. That has not been true for more than six years.

"Thanks to the untiring efforts of Professor Moriarty, Scotland Yard and the late Inspector Allard, in early July of that year the Ripper was captured," said Prince Edward.

"Then why was the public never told of this?" asked Murray.

"Because of the identity of the Ripper. I still remember the night I was summoned to Scotland Yard. When I learned who the Ripper actually was I knew that it would be impossible for that knowledge to be made public." said Prince Albert, his voice shaky.

"Impossible," said his son picking up the narrative. "Because Jack the Ripper was none other than the Duke of Clarence, third in line to the throne of England; Albert Victor, my own flesh and blood, my son."

There had been rumors, of course, regarding the Queen's grandson. Like many others, I had heard them and just credited them to a frightened, over-active public's imagination.

"He was insane, of course, a mental disorder combined with syphilis. You both will understand the dilemma that we faced," said Moriarty.

"My grandson had to be cut out of the line of succession. The very idea that the heir to the throne was a murderer would have shaken the very foundations of this monarchy and our empire. So, like a mad dog, he was, in a manner of speaking, put down. With the cooperation of certain highly placed officials, we faked his death.

"For the last few years, Albert Victor, under the name Victor Wednesday, has been a patient at Druid's Hill Asylum. Not even my beloved Victoria knows the truth in this matter," said Prince Albert.

"You may rest assured, Your Royal Highness, that no one shall hear of this from either Murray or myself." I said.

"Thank you, doctor." This was no monarch who spoke now, but a grieving grandfather.

The third man again took pen in hand. This time the paper went directly to Prince Albert.

The old man read it and nodded. "I cannot agree with you more."

"Professor, I am going to place the entire matter into your hands. You will have at your disposal all the resources of the government if you need them.

The Prince Consort scribbled a few lines on a sheet of paper, added hot wax to the bottom, and his signet ring into it. His son looked at the result, signed it and added his own signet's impression to the wax.

"This will not only gain you admittance to the asylum, but gives you full authority to act as you see fit concerning the inmate known as Victor Wednesday," said Prince Edward.

"Full authority?"

I arched an eyebrow at those words. To me that meant the power of life and death. I suspected it meant the same to Moriarty

"Full authority," The Heir Apparent repeated.

"I understand. I will attempt to exercise it with extreme discretion

"I didn't doubt that for one minute," said the older man, quietly.

———

Moriarty had decided that it would be best for Murray to remain in London while the Professor and I would pay a visit to Druid's Hill. We, however, did not travel alone.

At the insistence of Prince Edward, we were accompanied by Mary Morstan.

"I think that she would be of very great help to you in this enterprise," Prince Edward had said.

I was the first to raise objection, fearing for her safety. I also found myself wondering if in this world Mary were one of the many 'close friends' that Bertie was known to have in mine.

"Before you object, doctor," she said. "Let me enlighten you to a few things. I am also a physician, fully board-certified and a graduate of Queens College. I have been a practicing doctor for some time. My specialty these last several years has been the study of criminal insanity."

Mary had always exhibited a healthy interest in my work, but I had never considered that it had gone that far. To say I was astonished was to put the situation mildly. I had heard of women doctors, but had never encountered one before.

"What is the Prince's condition?" I asked.

"Slowly deteriorating. He has periods of lucidity, but they don't last long anymore. Like many patients suffering from syphilis, his thoughts are confused and at times make little or no sense. There are moments when he can fly into a total murderous rage at the mention of certain subjects. In the case of the Prince, it is mention of the Queen, his grandmother. Only three weeks ago he nearly killed one of the other doctors who made an offhand remark," she said.

"You understand the danger that you are placing yourself in tonight?" I asked, realizing as I did that I was speaking to the woman who had spent considerable time in the company of Jack The Ripper these past few years and lived to tell about it.

"Yes, Dr. Watson," she said. "But thank you for taking time to worry."

"If I may ask a question, Professor?" I said.

"Certainly. Given the current set of circumstances, I would imagine that you have quite a few of them."

"That rather thin gentleman back there at Cudugin Square, the one who never spoke. Who was he? He certainly seemed to have the Prince's ear."

"Indeed he does. His name is Holmes."

"Holmes? Mycroft Holmes?"

"That is exactly who he is, Watson. I take it you know him?"

"Yes. What does he do for the Prince?"

"I'm not sure, but I think that he is the head of the secret service."

"You think?"

"That's how secret it is." At least some things were the same in this world as the one I had come from.

I shook my head and turned toward Mary. We departed Victoria Station the next morning. During the trip I found it remarkably easy to speak with Mary, she was so like the woman I had fallen in love with, and yet as different as night and day.

———

Druid's Hill Asylum. The name suggested a far more sinister-appearing place than the rather palatial-looking country estate we found ourselves approaching that evening. The house itself was more than three hundred years old; its basements had been built deep into solid bedrock. A fence, hidden in places by carefully placed hedges and trees, surrounded the grounds. The ornamental grating on the windows was actually reinforced iron.

"Definitely a fortress," I said.

"It will be difficult for Holmes to penetrate these grounds," Mary observed.

"Dr. Marstan, I appreciate the fact that you did not claim it impossible. Nothing is impossible," Moriarty said. "In just the journey here I have conceived of some five methods that would work. It is the sort of challenge that Holmes has always accepted in the past."

The director of Druid's Hill was a burly man with mutton-chop side whiskers named Throckmorton, Dr. R.A. Throckmorton. He seemed a self-important fellow who had found his niche and intended to protect it.

"See here, I will not have you interrupting the routine of this establishment. Barging in here in the middle of the night is the sort of thing that could destroy months and months of work with these patients. We walk a delicate balance with some of them. Dr. Marstan, I'm totally astonished that you would associate yourself with these….common adventurers."

Moriarty rose in his chair at those words, but settled back. His face was washed of emotion, his eyes two cutting grey lights starring at Dr. Throckmorton. I heard a tiny click, click, click sound, of metal hitting metal, and noticed Moriarty had the three metal balls in his hand and was rolling them back and forth.

"You have seen our authorization."

"Indeed I have. That piece of paper leads me to suspect that the dementia that afflicts Victor Wednesday may be only partially caused by the disease that he suffers from, and more from his ancestry," Throckmorton said.

"That statement borders on treason, Doctor," I said.

"It borders on the rights of a free-born Englishman to speak his mind, sir," replied Throckmorton. "A right that we all posses, republican and royalist alike."

"Dr. Throckmorton, this is not Hyde Park. You know my authority, where it comes from and the range of it. You know my personal credentials. My companions are physicians who will certainly see to the health of the patient. Will you permit me access to him?" said Moriarty.

"Yes," he said finally.

Albert Victor, Duke of Clarence, third in line for the throne of Great Britain, AKA Victor Wednesday, was awake. He was sitting on his bed staring at a small painting of a landscape hanging on the opposite wall.

The cell that they kept him in was on the lowest level of Druid's Hill, nearly thirty feet under ground. According to Mary, he was allowed out only under the most strictly controlled conditions. This section of the asylum was reserved for the most dangerous and psychotic cases. As we had made our way through the halls, I heard screams of pain and anger that cut into the very stones of the building.

"I've seen him sit for days just like that, not sleeping, just staring at it, absorbing every little nuance of it. Perhaps for him it is an escape," Mary said. "Other times he raves on every subject imaginable, making little or no sense. On rarer and rarer occasions he is coherent and seemingly aware of what he has done and what is happening to him."

We had been there an hour, and never once in that time had the Prince responded to any questions, or even so much as acknowledged our presence. He just sat on the edge of his bed and stared at the painting.

I could see enough of his face to recognize the family features, echoes of those two faces that I had seen only a few hours before. He had lost weight, but no matter what name he officially bore at Druid's Hill, there was no mistaking that face.

"I wonder if he knows of the plan to free him." I asked.

"I would not put it past Holmes to have contacted him. Whether he did, it is questionable whether Victor would even remember it," said Moriarty. "At his stage of the disease, a syphilitics memory is not reliable."

In the meantime, The Prince had risen and walked across his cell to make a slight adjustment to the picture. Then he began to pace back and forth, in slow measured steps along the length of the cell, holding himself with the dignified carriage and air that one would expect of a member of the royal family.

He stopped for a moment, looked toward us, gave a slight nod in Mary's direction and continued pacing.

"I do not expect the attack to be direct," I told Moriarty.

"Perhaps," he said.

"Sometimes a frontal assault is exactly the sort of strategy that works the best." Someone said from behind us.

We turned to find Director Throckmorton standing in the door that led to the upper levels of the asylum. The voice belonged to a big bear of a man standing directly behind him, his arm around Throckmorton's neck, a pistol pressed to the doctor's temple.

"If you gentlemen and the lady would be so good as to step back against the far wall it would make things a great deal easier for the lot of us."

"Please do as he says! He's already shot two of my orderlies and who knows how many other people," pleaded the director in a whiney high pitched voice.

"Colonel Moran, I presume?" I said.

"Indeed I am, and who might you be, sir. I know Moriarty and this girl, but you are a stranger to me."

"I am Colonel Doctor John Watson, late of the Fifth Northumberland Fusiliers. You may be more than a bit familiar with my old regiment." I elected to use the unaccustomed rank, hoping that it just might give me a tiny bit of equality in Moran's mind.

"A fine outfit. Now Colonel, if you don't get yourself up against that wall I will shoot you and then Director Throckmorton, in that order." he said.

So much for the idea of impressing him.

"Oh really, Mr. Holmes," said Moriarty, shaking his head. "I do think that it would be a bit more comfortable for you if Colonel Moran would take the gun out of your ear."

For the briefest moment I wondered what kind of game he was playing. Then I saw a change come over the asylum director. Moran did indeed free him, stepping back several paces. An obviously padded jacket slipped off Throckmorton's shoulder, followed by a shirt, pillow and the shock of unruly red hair and mutton-chop sideburns.

Sherlock Holmes stood stretching himself to his full height. The face was the same as that of my friend, but the lines around his eyes were harder and crueler.

"There, that is much better. The disguise was not all that difficult a thing to do, but the man has such an insufferable attitude I wonder how anyone can stand to be around him for any length of time. Tell me, Professor, when did you know it was I?"

"Not immediately. Only when I noticed that one of your sideburns was not quite glued down completely did I suspect that I was not talking to the genuine Dr. Throckmorton. Your acting was excellent. I have no doubt you would have done well treading the boards," said Moriarty.

"My thanks, Professor. Like many, I have always harbored dreams of theater. Perhaps if my life had gone down a different path. That, however, is neither here nor there. Your sudden arrival has forced me to accelerate my plans."

Holmes` slim fingers reached into his vest pocket and produced a long gray key. He fitted it into the lock, swinging open the cell door with a flourish.

"Your Highness, if you would come with me."

Victor Wednesday continued to walk back and forth, ignoring Holmes' action. When he did stop, he didn't look at Sherlock Holmes, or even the open cell door, but stared at the painting.

"Is this real or but another of these endless nightmares given form?" he whispered.

"Oh, very real, Your Highness, very real. The only nightmare invoked this night will be for those who locked you away," said Holmes.

"Good," he said.

For the first time, Victor Wednesday seemed to pass away and Prince Albert Victor took his place. As he headed for the door he casually said "It would please us greatly if you would accompany us on our journey, Dr. Marstan."

The thought of Mary in the hands of Holmes and this man who was Jack the Ripper was more than I could stand. Without a thought as to consequences, I charged at Holmes, screaming at the top of my lungs. Unfortunately, I did not get close enough to my old friend's double, because a mountain stepped between us. Moran grabbed me by the lapels and slammed me hard against the cell bars.

The last thing that I recall before I blacked out was Mary calling my name.

—·—

It was at least several eternitys before the darkness opened up for me. I struggled to say something, but lost the words echoing through the pounding in my head, which could very easily have been the changing of the Guard at Buckingham Palace. I tried to rise up, but a wave of dizziness sent me rolling back onto the floor.

"Easy, Doctor. Besides having the wind knocked out of you, you slammed your head solidly into those bars. You don't appear to have a concussion, but I think you should just lie still for a moment, until your head clears," said Moriarty.

We were in the Prince's cell; that much was quickly obvious. I didn't have to ask to know that the door was securely locked.

"How long was I unconscious?"

"Ten minutes, no more."

Seemingly satisfied as to my condition, Moriarty turned away from me to examine the cell door.

"I really don't mean to belabor the obvious," I said. "But if we don't get out of here Mary may well become the sixth victim of Jack the Ripper."

"Eighth. There were two that the public never found out about. However, I think you may well be right," he said. Just then the door swung open. He turned to me and displayed a thin wire he reattached to his pocket watch chain.

"Shall we, Doctor?"

Before I could get to my feet, Moriarty crossed to the wall and reached into a trash container near a guard post. He rummaged around for a moment and then produced the army service revolver that Murray had given me the night before.

"Moran searched us both for weapons after knocking you out. While he found your gun, his ego wouldn't let him keep a common army issue weapon. I doubt he expected us to be putting it to use quite this quickly." Moriarty passed the gun to me.

The main entrance hall of Druid's Hill was almost empty. I could hear a grandfather clock chiming ten o'clock.

"They're probably making for the carriage house," said Moriarty.

I was already a dozen steps ahead of him toward the door. Unfortunately, we were not fast enough. I had barely cleared the doorway before an open carriage came ripping past the front of the house, horses at full gallop. Whoever had the reins, and it looked to be Moran, was struggling to keep control while defending himself from an attacker who seemed to be trying to push him out of the carriage. It looked like the Prince.

"We'll never catch them," yelled the professor. "Shoot, Watson, shoot!"

I fired three times.

Whatever control Moran had was lost when the animals began to charge headlong into the sharp curve of the drive. The carriage whipped sharply from one side to the other several times before tilting too far in one direction and sending its passengers and the frightened horses sprawling across the grass.

I found Mary some few feet from the wreckage. She tried to raise up on one arm to free herself from the bushes that had cushioned her fall. However, the moment she leaned any weight on her arm, her face contorted in pain.

"I can't be sure," she said. "But I think it may be broken."

It was a clean break, thankfully. Her only other injuries appeared to be cuts and bruises.

"A fair enough trade for my life," she smiled.

We found Moran sprawled on the ground unconscious. The Prince was dead; we found him beneath the overturned wagon, his neck broken. Death had been almost instantaneous.

I did not envy Moriarty the task ahead of him; informing a father and grandfather that the fiction they had invented many years before had now become fact.

"What happened in the carriage to make the Prince attack Moran?" Moriarty asked Mary.

"I can't be sure. Moran said something to the Prince just as we left the barn; he screamed bloody murder and went for Moran's throat. I'm just glad that Moran said whatever he said," Mary replied.

"Whatever the reason, it looks like Jack the Ripper probably saved your life," observed Moriarty.

That was when it occurred to me that I had seen no sign of Holmes since the carriage had overturned.

"His footprints lead off away from the asylum," said Moriarty. "There was some blood, but I lost the trail about a quarter of a mile to the east. I have no doubt that we will be hearing from Mr. Sherlock Holmes again."

"The train is late," I said, snapping the cover on my watch closed. Mary reached out, took my hand and smiled. Her left arm hung in a sling, a reminder of our encounter with the *other* Holmes.

All right, I admit that I was more than a bit nervous. Frankly, considering what had happened to me over the last few days, I would say that I had every right to be.

This wasn't Victoria Station by any means, but, rather, a country train depot. In fact, it could have been a waiting room in any depot from Liverpool to Glasgow. There were a few people lingering around the waiting area. Professor Moriarty sat with a notebook on his lap, eyes half closed, every so often jotting down a few words or numerical notations. Occasionally I heard the now familiar sounds of the small metal balls clicking together as he rolled them across his palm.

Mary and I had talked for some time, but in the last few minutes both of us had lapsed into a silence, broken only by an occasional reassuring smile.

"I believe that the train is arriving," Mary said.

The familiar sounds of a steam locomotive filled the station. From the west I could see its lights, hear the metal on metal sound of its brakes, and moments later watch the steam cloud cut across the platform as it slid to a stop.

Moriarty extracted his watch from a vest pocket. "Nine and a half minutes late. Mathematically insignificant, especially considering the distance that it had to travel."

A number of people emerged from the train. Most went right to the baggage compartment, while a few lingered around looking slightly confused. A familiar figure in frock coat and top hat, carrying a walking cane, cut his way through the crowd.

"Holmes, over here," I called out.

I must confess that until that moment I had harbored the slightest fear that all of my memories of the other world had been one long dream.

"Watson, old fellow. It is good to see you." Holmes said grasping my hand. "I have had the most remarkable journey and have seen things that even surprised me."

"They must have been a remarkable sight, then," I said.

"They were. I am sure the return journey will present even more astounding sights," he said.

I glanced at Mary. Her eyes had that remarkable wisdom that I had always looked to for strength and support.

"Holmes, where are my manners," I said "Let me introduce you to...."

"It is my pleasure, Dr. Marstan."

"I am honored, Mr. Holmes. You seem as remarkable as John has described you. Since John has explained how you both came to know my other self, I would be most interested in how you reasoned that I am a doctor."

Holmes flashed a familiar grin. "Simplicity in itself. A number of signs gave your profession away. I shall mention only two: the slight stain of silver nitrate on your uninjured hand, plus I noticed the ear piece of a stethoscope protruding from your sleeve. Since I see Watson is still carrying his in his hat, I reasoned that it most likely belonged to another doctor, you in this case," he said.

"Remarkable!" Mary laughed.

"Elementary," said Holmes. "Wouldn't you agree, Professor?"

"Indeed I would, Holmes. I note you did not fail to make use of the station's wall mirror to note my approach."

"A simple precaution, given our history. One I'm sure you would have taken had the positions been reversed."

"Indeed, you prove once again why your doppelganger has proved so elusive for these many years," chuckled Moriarty. "It is a pleasure to meet you, Mr. Sherlock Holmes,"

"The pleasure is mine, Professor Moriarty," Holmes said.

I then saw something I never in my life had expected to see: Sherlock Holmes shaking hands with Professor Moriarty.

"The note that you sent was fascinating in its implications," said Holmes.

"You had no trouble with the formulas that I suggested?"

"None. It was simply a matter of reorienting one's perceptions of the world around us to direct the train to this particular station and your world," said Holmes. "I doubt the other passengers ever noticed the difference."

"Then there should be no problem in allowing you and Watson to return, by the next train, to your world." Moriarty pulled a time table from his pocket. "Which should depart in just a bit over ten minutes, if this schedule is correct."

It was time. I squeezed Mary's hand once more before speaking. "Unfortunately, I will not be returning with Holmes."

"Indeed. And would I be wrong in assuming that at least part of your reason for remaining is Dr. Marstan?" asked Holmes. I noticed he had a very large grin on his face as he spoke.

"You would be exactly on the mark. In our world, the path for a female physician is especially difficult. Here, though not common, they are accepted more easily. As a general surgeon, I can practice anywhere. Save for a few distant cousins, I have no family left. Beyond yourself and a few other friends, none will miss me. The Professor has offered to help establish my credentials in this world," I said.

"There is then marriage in the offing?" asked Moriarty.

"Perhaps," I said.

They both knew there was, as did Mary and I. True, I had not formally proposed, but that was a matter I fully intended to correct very soon. "For now, we are definitely going into medical partnership."

"Well, Professor, it seems a good thing that I did not accept your wager," said Holmes.

"Wager?" I asked.

At that moment both Holmes and Moriarty had the same sort of twinkle in their eyes.

"Oh yes, did I forget to mention the wager that the Professor offered me? It seems that he appended a note to his missive containing the formulas for traveling here. He suggested that you might have decided to remain here, even offered to bet me ten pounds that you would."

"I did not accept that wager because, though you have been steady as a river throughout our friendship, you have at times surprised even me. From the things told me

I had the feeling that this might just be one of those times." A porter appeared carrying two large carpetbags. "I also took the precaution of bringing some of your things I thought you might wish to retain in your new home."

"My thanks. Will my disappearance cause you any problems?"

"None that cannot be handled. I think with the aid of your friend, Dr. Doyle, we should be able to maintain the fiction that you are still writing your chronicles of my minor adventures."

Doyle was a good man, a decent physician and an excellent writer of historical tales. He had recommended me to the editors of the Strand Magazine when I had first begun to seek publication for my work. Doyle's only problem was that he had an annoying habit of forgetting my name and calling me James.

"Then this is good-bye?"

"Let us simply say auf wiedersehn, Watson. I would not rule out the possibility that we will see each other again."

I watched as Holmes strode across the platform. He had only just stepped inside one of the first class compartments when I noticed a conductor, with a worried expression on his face, approaching him.

As the train pulled away I saw Holmes nod and follow the man deep into the train.

"Do you think that there is a problem on the train, John?" Mary asked.

"Problems always seem to find their way to Holmes. Perhaps this one will not be without points of interest for him."

"Then, for Mr. Holmes, it appears that the game is once more afoot," she said.

LOCATION SHOOT

"So, when are you going to get a 'real' job?"

For some damm reason her mother's perennial question was flashing through Maggie's mind when she stepped in the gopher hole.

All right, they didn't have gophers on this world. It was a hole, whatever had dug it, and was enough to send her off balance and crashing straight into Bambi. Of course, Bambi wasn't that easy to miss, being six-four, dressed in chain mail and leather, and weighing in at around 250 pounds.

Bambi realized what was happening and, at the last minute, twisted to one side. Even so, the impact of Maggie slamming into him was enough to send them both crashing to the ground in a tangle of metal, legs, brush and briars.

"Cut!" yelled the director.

The words coming out of Bambi's helmet were not in any language that Maggie knew. The spell that allowed the movie company and the natives to understand each other only worked with the local language. But his tone and emphasis were enough to let her know that they were the equivalent of what she was thinking.

"If that son-of-a-bitch calls for a retake," Bambi said, switching to a translatable language, "I'm going to cut his balls off!"

———

"But Mama! I have a job! I'm in show business! You know... The Movies!"

"Yeah, sure. All you ever do is leap off buildings, jump through windows, and get into fights. Is this any way for a well bred young lady to earn a living?"

"Half the time when you come to see me you've got some new set of bruises or a broken this or that! If I didn't know what you did, I'd think you were into something really kinky."

"And besides, nobody knows it's you! They think its **Miss Silicon Tit Implant!** *Your name is always buried so deep in the credits that nobody but the projectionist and I ever see it!"*

———

Maggie reached out to help Bambi to his feet. Bambi wasn't his real name. Maggie was the one who had dubbed him that, since the House badge he wore featured a stag that had reminded her of the animated Bambi. The nickname didn't bother him and was a lot easier for Maggie to pronounce than his real name, M'Gerna N'cal Hastolka. Once on his feet, Bambi moved a bit stiffly, favoring his right leg.

"The pike wound still bothering you?" she asked.

"A bit," said Bambi.

Maggie suspected that it was more likely that Bambi was developing arthritis in that leg, rather than any wound giving him trouble. He was over forty and had been a mercenary since he was fourteen. Now he commanded his own sword company, The Nightwinds. Bambi had been on leave while his men were in winter quarters when he got bit by the show business bug.

"Hey, will you two move. You're in my shot and we need to get some film exposed before we lose the light," said an assistant director.

"Do you think that means we're through for the day?" asked Maggie.

"I suspect so. I think it's my turn to buy the first round of ale," said Bambi.

"I like the way that you think, sir," she laughed.

———

At the time she had gone to the Paragon Pictures production offices, Maggie had only the vaguest idea of what the movie was to be about. The producer, a little worm named Rudolph Meriwether Carmichael IV, hadn't even been willing to send her a copy of the script.

Standing by the window was the reason for the secrecy: Ean Findley. Findley was the sort of director who was either a genius or a total raving lunatic, possibly both, depending on who you talked to in La La Land. His penchant for secrecy on projects was legend. But one thing Maggie knew for certain - movies that Findley directed made money, a lot of money.

"This is going to be a tale of high adventure, of an age undreamed of before history, a story that mixes allegory and fantasy, without losing touch with mod-

ern sensibilities" Ean said. "For it, I need the services of the best stuntwoman in the business."

"Well, she's busy, so you'll have to settle for me."

"I like her, Rudolph," Ean said. "Maggie Ferguson is the person that I want in charge of all our stunt work."

"You're the genius, I just juggle the bottom line," said Rudolph. "Okay, Ferguson, you'll have a crew of fifteen to work with. Can you be ready to leave for the location in three days? We have a tight, a very tight, transportation schedule and no leeway in it."

Three days? That was unheard of. Normally Maggie insisted on at least a month to design and prepare all the stunts. She didn't like the feeling this caused in the pit of her stomach. However, since her son was spending the summer with his father and her bank account was a lot leaner than she liked it, Maggie didn't feel like she could turn this job down.

"Three days? I think I can do that. How long will we be gone?"

"Five to eight weeks. I'll messenger you over a script tonight." said Rudolph.

The tavern was actually a huge army surplus tent, erected next to a barn that the company had leased. The company's presence was a boon to the local economy; renting buildings and hiring craftsmen, laborers and extras from the nearby village.

Maggie grabbed a Diet Pepsi for herself and a can of Coors Lite for Bambi. Bambi snapped the pull tab off his can and held up the small piece of metal. "This is truly amazing. Simple, obvious and efficient, yet no one in my world has ever conceived of such a thing."

"There're a lot of things that I imagine people around here have seen in the last few weeks that no one has ever seen before," said Maggie.

"It makes me wonder how a world that could produce such wonders as these can also produce such a…what is the word you use…jerk, like Rudolph Meriwether Carmichael." Bambi stretched out the producers name for emphasis.

"Rudolph Meriwether Carmichal the Fourth," Maggie reminded him, "Rudy to those of us who know and hate him."

Rudolph hated the nickname Rudy, so everyone took every opportunity to use it.

"Oh, yes, The Fourth. Yesterday he tried to tell me, **me**, the proper way to use a short spear," said Bambi.

"I hope you offered to demonstrate the working end of the spear, on him."

"I did. I can understand when Ean does something strange; it's usually for the sake of his art, this movie. But Rudy just gives me a sour stomach."

"Me, too."

———

A three a.m. call was not a problem for Maggie. She had done more than her share of them in the dozen years since she came to Hollywood. But instead of the convoy of trucks, R.V.'s, and buses driving off to the location, all they did was form up into a big circle and wait

"Are we, maybe, expecting an attack by Indians or something?" Maggie asked one of the drivers.

"Lady, I don't know. They just told everyone to do this and make sure no one gets out," he said.

So they waited - for a half hour. Under the light of the full moon, a limo followed by a black '64 Thunderbird pulled in and drove to the center of the circle. Maggie watched as Ean and Rudolph got out of the limo followed by two figures that she recognized immediately.

Caitlin de Vres and her husband, Joseph Alexander Ellison. In the space of less than ten years the two of them had become the reigning couple in Hollywood. It seemed like no picture either or both of them appeared in finished anywhere but number one at the box office. Joseph was reported to be one of the nicest people in the business. Caitlin, on the other hand, was supposed to be a egotistical bitch to work with.

A heavy-set man wearing a full length robe and carrying a carpetbag embroidered with astrological symbols got out of the Thunderbird. Without speaking to the others he took several instruments from the bag and began to place them at various places around the cars. After drawing a number of symbols on the ground, he pulled out a propeller beanie, placed it on his head and began to chant.

That was the moment that, for Maggie, the world changed. Awash in colors and spinning shapes, everything around her, the people, the cars, the air itself, glowed, twisted and changed.

In spite of her head feeling like she had a massive hangover, Maggie opened her eyes. It was still night, but the sky had an odd coloring and two moons hung in the air. They were no longer sitting in a parking lot in Burbank, California. Now the entire convoy was parked in a huge field with only some farm house-looking buildings anywhere to be seen.

Near the limos Ean was in deep conversation with a man dressed in chain mail and a cape. Caitlin and Joseph were leaning against the limo. Of the other car and the man in the robe and propeller beanie, there was no sign.

"I'd say that qualifies as a hell of a ride," said Maggie.

With her fiery red hair and supermodel figure, Caitlin de Vres resembled some of the Irish heroines of legend. When she came into the tavern tent she was wearing the chain main bikini, knee high boots and sword that comprised her principal costume.

Maggie had always suspected that Caitlin had a large streak of exhibitionism in her and just generally enjoyed shocking people by prancing around in next to nothing. She had seen the gown that Caitlin had worn to the Oscars last year. Maggie owned swimsuits that had more material than that dress.

In addition to being the head stuntwoman, Maggie was Caitlin's stunt double, so an identical outfit to the one Caitlin had on was hanging in Maggie's tent. She was none too fond of it. In spite of the lining, the metal rings had a tendency to pinch, usually at the most inopportune times and in the most inappropriate places.

"Maggie, I should have expected to find you around Bambi," said Caitlin, her voice was just dripping with friendliness, the kind that drove Maggie crazy. "You really should give the rest of us a chance at him. "

"Hello, Caitlin. I'm surprised that you're even here today. I figured that since you and Joseph had the day off you would be taking it easy," she said.

Caitlin laughed and got a dreamy smile on her face. "Oh, we had planned on a nice little private picnic today, at that waterfall about fifteen miles or so from here."

"Oh, I know that place," said Bambi. "Very private, perfect for …."

"Yes, that's exactly what we had in mind. Wine, cheese and some assorted things were all packed. We were supposed to have the next couple of days off. But then Ean took it in his pointy little head that there were some scenes with Joseph that had to be shot now; ones that weren't even on the schedule for a week."

"Knowing him, he'll call for forty or fifty retakes of each one of them. This means, if I'm lucky, I may see my darling Joseph around midnight. Then Rudolph, that little worm, decided that *I* should have some more publicity shots taken. So I had to put this outfit on and go shake my tush in front of some pointy eared photographer. He looked like a reject from a Star Trek convention," said Caitlin.

"I'm sure Joseph will make it up to you," said Bambi.

"Oh, you better believe he will," she said.

"Since Joseph won't be back till late, I'm having a few of the other girls over to my trailer. We can kill a couple of bottles of wine, gossip and just have a great time. Why don't you join us, Maggie?"

I wonder if they're all as thrilled at that prospect as I am, thought Maggie.

"I'll try to, Caitlin."

"Wonderful. See you about eightish!"

"Of course," Maggie sighed, sagging back in her chair.

Caitlin hadn't gone more than five feet from the table before Maggie reached over, took Bambi's beer and finished it in two swallows.

Bambi said nothing.

The few R.V.'s that were being used for living quarters had been parceled out among Joseph and Caitlin, Ean and Rudolph. As chief stuntwoman, Maggie was entitled to a private tent, but she had opted to share space with two of her friends, Jenny Carshaw, a sound mixer and Sherry Hartley, a costume designer. The three of them got along well together, and were quite tolerant of the others' moods and crazy schedules.

Thankfully, this afternoon, both of the other girls were out. Maggie was not in the mood for company, no matter how congenial and understanding. Dropping a CD of Mozart's fourth concerto into her Walkman, Maggie fitted the headphones over her ears. She slipped out of her jeans and just stretched out on her cot. The music washed over her, letting her push everything else away.

A century or so later the music was suddenly drowned out by the most horrendous sound. Maggie thought for a moment that there might be something wrong with the player, but when she punched the off button the sound continued, this time coming from outside her tent. She dropped the Walkman, pulled on her jeans and sprinted out to see what was going on.

To say that the camp was in chaos was pretty accurate. There were people running in several directions at once, screams coming from all over the camp and the sound of crashing wood and metal everywhere.

"What the hell is going on?" said Maggie.

That was when Maggie saw the dragon. The creature was hovering in the air near the center of the camp. Maybe twenty feet long and eight or nine feet high, it seemed to fill the sky. Greenish silver scales glistened in the afternoon sun as its roar echoed everywhere.

One of her stunt people ran past Maggie and yelled, "Come on! The dragon knocked one of the camera towers down. Hanson is trapped underneath."

The camera tower was actually an old windmill that Ean had ordered converted to the company's use. As they got closer, it was obvious that now the thing was only kindling.

It turned out that Hanson wasn't trapped under that pile of wood. If he had been, he would have been deader than vaudeville, someone observed. He had been able to leap free and seemed to have come away with only a badly sprained ankle.

"You'd still better have the Doc check you out," Maggie told him. "If you could do that kind of fall on a regular basis, I could use an extra hand on some of the stunts."

"No thanks, Maggie. I'm crazy sometimes, but you guys make me seem stone cold sane," he said.

"That's part of the reason you love us so much."

"Hey, it's leaving!"

The dragon twisted in the air and sailed off toward the south.

"Thank God that's over." said Hanson.

Maggie wasn't so sure it was over. She couldn't be a hundred per cent certain, but she thought she had seen a figure gripped in the dragon's claws. And it sure looked like it was Joseph Alexander Ellison, himself.

———

"Maggie!" Rudolph's voice always seemed to hit the highest notes when he was either angry or scared. There was a pool going around among the crew to see who could get him to hit that high note the most times.

"Yes, Rudy," she said.

"You've got to stop her!"

"Who?"

"Caitlin, of course," said Rudolph. "Look around you. This is a major disaster.

The camp is in ruins. Our leading man has been carried off by some flying lizard. Now my leading lady has just announced that she is going to go off to play Xena, Warrior Princess and rescue him. She's going to get herself killed, eaten at a dragon barbeque, or sold as a slave. The picture is ruined!"

"You're the one who is always saying that you're in charge. I think this falls under your job description, not mine."

"Like she would really listen to me? She walked off muttering something about ripping my lungs out through my ears," said Rudolph.

Of course, Maggie might have suggested amputating a somewhat different portion of Rudy's anatomy, and through a different aperture.

"You've got to convince her to stay. We can still salvage the picture. It can be a final tribute to Joseph. His last, greatest work!"

"You make it sound like he's dead," said Bambi. The mercenary's left arm was in a sling. Maggie cast a quizzical look at him.

"I tripped over one of the script girls during the dragon attack. But getting back to the dragon, I would say that it is very possible that Joseph is alive and healthy, for the time being. From what I've heard, they like to collect their food, keep it alive, play with it and then eat it raw," Bambi said.

"Thank you for sharing that wonderful bit of culinary information with us," said the producer.

"Seems Caitlin is determined to go and try to rescue Joseph," said Maggie.

"You two would have to move fast. Dragons can fly a long way very quickly," said Bambi..

"We? Who mentioned anything about 'we' doing this," said Maggie.

"I'd go with her, myself, but not with this arm," said Bambi. "Look, you can handle yourself and are able to think on your feet. Those are skills that Caitlin may not have in abundance," said Bambi.

"Yes, yes. If you can't talk her out of it, go with her, bring her back here alive," said Rudolph.

Maggie had worked n Hollywood long enough to know when an advantage presented itself.

"All right, Rudy, it's a deal. But only on my terms."

"Terms? What terms?" She could see his hackles rising like a frightened porcupine.

"My fee is for you to green light a script I have," she said.

"Why is it that everyone in Hollywood has a script!?" moaned Rudolph.

"Maybe it's something in the water," said Bambi.

"All right, all right. You've got me over a barrel. When we get back I'll look over your script."

"No, you'll agree, right here and now, to green light my project. It's either that or you borrow one of Bambi's chain mail shirts and go with Caitlin yourself," she said.

"He agrees," said Bambi, laying his hand on the producer's shoulder. "Don't you, Rudy?"

"Yeah, yeah I agree," he sighed.

"I knew you would see it my way," said Maggie.

"Now where the hell is it?" Caitlin was pawing through the things in a closet at one end of the RV. Maggie had knocked, but when her third attempt went unanswered, she just walked in.

After a minute or two Caitlin took a black leather whip from inside the closet, pausing to shake a couple of loose socks out of its coils. Maggie considered for a moment asking why she and Joseph had a bullwhip in their closet, but then thought better of it.

"You really think you're going to need that?"

"You never know," Caitlin said. "I suppose that sniveling little worm Rudy sent you here to try and talk me out of going. Don't even waste your breath."

"Fine. But I wasn't intending on stopping you. I just wanted to let you know that I would be going with you."

Caitlin looked at her for a moment. This was definitely not the Caitlin de Vres that Maggie had known for the past two years. The 'star' egotist was gone, replaced by a different woman looking out from the familiar green eyes.

"Like hell you will. You just want me to forget the whole thing so that Ean can get his damm picture finished. Well, you can go back and tell him that I don't give a flying fig about finishing the picture. I don't care if they blackball me back in La La Land. I'm going after Joseph," said Caitlin.

To emphasize her words, Caitlin flipped her wrist out and cracked the whip across the trailer's length. The tip tore into the cloth of a pillow just to Maggie's right. Down went flying everywhere, hovering in the air like a ticker tape parade.

"Not bad,' said Maggie. "Look, Caitlin, you can yell and scream all you want, but it's not going to do you any good. I'm going along, that's a fact. The longer we stand here arguing about it, the further away that dragon is going to carry Joseph."

"The two of us are going to have a better chance to get him out of trouble than just you. So, whether you like it or not, I'm in on this whole thing and there isn't a damn thing that you can do about it," she said.

"I want to leave in an hour. Can you be ready?"

"No problem. By the way, you are going to change clothes, aren't you?" Caitlin was still wearing the chain-mail bikini. The actress didn't say anything, just gestured over to the couch where breeches, boots, a work shirt and weapons lay.

"I was afraid of this," said Caitlin.

In the last five days the two women had ridden hard, stopping only to sleep for the briefest of periods, as they headed for a mountain range that Maggie estimated was sixty or seventy miles from the company's campsite. All along, Caitlin seemed to know exactly where they were going.

"Afraid of what?" asked Maggie.

Caitlin passed her a pair of binoculars and pointed toward a place above the tree line, maybe a hundred yards away. There sat Joseph, apparently unharmed, seemingly all by himself, only the chains around his wrists keeping him from getting up and walking away..

"When it looks too good to be true, it probably is. So this is obviously an ambush," said Maggie.

"It is, it's an ambush. Look to the left and about twenty yards up into the rocks."

It took Maggie a moment to find the place that Caitlin had indicated. The dragon was not hiding, but had wound itself among a number of rocks and boulders.

"His name is Halymer and he's waiting for me," said Caitlin.

"You?"

———

"Good morning, Joseph!"

Maggie had waited to speak until she was within a dozen steps of Joseph. His face had gone pale when she spoke. He twisted around to look up toward the rocks.

The dragon sat silently, watching them both.

"Hello, Maggie. I must say I didn't expect to see you here. I hope you know what you're doing and maybe brought some help," he said.

"No, just little old me. You don't think Ean would turn loose of enough people to make a decent size posse, do you?" she said.

"Caitlin didn't come with you?"

"Nope. No way would Ean or that spineless shit Rudy let her go. You know the show must go on and all that. Rudy said that they were going to make this picture your final movie, a tribute to you," she said.

"Oh, how nice."

The dragon rose up on its hind legs and roared.

"Would you knock it off!" said Maggie. "Has he been this noisy and obnoxious since he brought you here?"

"Occasionally," said Joseph

She looked up at the dragon. "Look, I know you can talk. So stop acting like Rudy Carmichael. One of him is enough!"

"Where is she," the dragon demanded. His voice was gravelly and echoed in the back of his throat.

"That's better. Now maybe we can talk like two civilized creatures. Let's start with names. Mine is Mary Margaret Ferguson," said Maggie.

"I am Halymer! I am your death, if you don't tell me where she is! Is she a coward to ignore my challenge!" said the dragon.

"Oh come on," said Maggie. "Here we had such a nice relationship started and you go off on this macho bullcrap roaring stuff. What's next, you and Joseph going off to beat drums together?"

That was when Caitlin appeared on the rocks above the dragon. She waited only a moment and then launched herself from her perch, crashing down onto the dragon's neck.

Halymer began to twist from side to side, trying to throw her off. However, she seemed to have gotten a good grip, straddling his neck. A few seconds later the bullwhip she had carried from camp flashed over the beast's face. It struck several times, cutting into the leathery flesh.

"Stop it now! Stop acting like a spoiled brat!"

The sound of Caitlin's voice enraged the dragon even further. He began to buck, attempting to throw her off. His tail struck the boulders around him hard enough to shower the area in a rain of pebbles.

"I said to stop it!" shouted Caitlin. 'Stop it now or I'll have to tell Mom and Dad about that stunt you pulled on Aunt G'may!"

"You wouldn't dare," the dragon said.

"Try me."

"I'm going to assume that you have one hell of a lot of questions," said Caitlin.

"You could say that," said Maggie. "It looks like you were right when you said I wouldn't need my sword."

"Well, I couldn't let you go trying to play St. George and kill him. After all, as much of a pain in the tail as he is, Halymer is still my little brother," said Caitlin.

Maggie, Caitlin and Joseph were seated at a small table near the edge of a stream. As soon as the confrontation with Halymer was over, others, both dragons and humans, appeared from the rocks.

They were brought plates of vegetables, a meat dish and mugs of a warm beer. Several dozen other people were scattered around the landscape, some eating, others talking, a few walking back and forth attending to various chores. Nearly a dozen dragons of sizes varying from ten or so feet to nearly thirty were dispersed over the side of the hill, some watching what was going on , others just sitting in the sun.

One thing that Maggie did notice was that several of the people walking near them resembled each other. Plus, more than a few bore a more than passing resemblance to Caitlin. It definitely looked like a family picnic.

Maggie reached across the table and picked up something that looked like an orange and began to methodically peal and then section it.

"Okay, let's cut to the point. Caitlin, what the hell are you?"

"I suppose you could call me a were-human. Dragons are able to take human form for a period of time. It is sort of a form of camouflage," said Caitlin. "I was born a dragon; my birth name is S'lina. About a dozen years ago, because of a head injury I sustained, I was locked into human form. Not even our most powerful magi could find a way to let me take dragon form again."

"That's where I entered the picture," said Joseph. "Before you ask, I'm completely human. Plus, I come from the world that you and I both call home. The wizard who sent us here is my brother-in-law; a third rate magician and a fourth rate klutz. What my sister sees in him I will never know. About ten years ago he accidentally kicked me into this world. By the time that he figured out how to get me back, I had met Caitlin and she came back with me."

"It turned out that I had a flair for acting. With Joseph's help I manufactured an identity and the career along with it. The egotistical bitch goddess routine was just to keep people from suspecting that I was different," said Caitlin.

"The bitch goddess routine was something to keep people from looking too far into her background," said Joseph.

"And it worked. Then about six months ago, just right after we had signed to costar in this picture, we got an invitation from my parents to attend a massive family reunion and celebration of their golden wedding flight anniversary," said Caitlin.

"Problem was, we were committed to this picture. The contract was iron clad. Luckily, I was able to convince Ean that if he filmed in a true fantasy world it would add just that special touch to the picture. He fell for it hook, line and sinker," said Joseph.

"I'm sure you made Ean think it was his idea."

"According to the original shooting schedule, we were supposed to have four days without any scenes at all. The plan was that we were going to go off on a camping trip. My cousin S'gan would pick us up and fly us to and from the reunion. Then Ean started changing the schedule and out of the blue my little brother shows up," said Caitlin.

"Yeah, why did he do it?"

"Who can know for sure? Adolescent rebellion? A need to show off in front of his friends by beating up on his big sister. He's really a good kid at heart. The family couldn't interfere in an official challenge between siblings. It was up to me to show him who's the boss," said Caitlin.

"Would he have hurt Joseph?" asked Maggie.

On that she could see Caitlin hesitate. "I'm not sure. But I'm just glad it didn't come to it."

"So what are we going to do about this? We certainly don't want Ean to know the truth about Caitlin," said. Maggie. She picked up her mug and began to swirl the contents slowly around. As the liquid lapped up to the edge a sudden smile came across her face.

"Oh, this is just too good," she said.

"We're running out time, Ean," said Rudolph Meriwether Carmichael IV.

Rudolph had found the eccentric director in the editing tent at the far end of their camp, his face only inches above the screen of a moviola. Every minute or so he would pull another frame through the viewer.

"According to the schedule, we've only got two more scenes before the Caitlin and Joseph stuff has to be filmed. After that, everybody is going to be sitting around on their duffs twiddling their collective thumbs," said Rudolph.

Shouting from outside the tent interrupted anything that Ean was about to say.

One of the assistant film editors, Gene Smith, stepped into the tent, a pair of binoculars in his hand.

"It's a dragon, heading this way," he said.

"Are we being attacked again?" asked Rudolph.

"No! Maggie, Caitlin and Joseph are all three riding it."

Ean pushed his coffee cup toward Rudolph. "Be a good fellow and get me a refill, please."

"She was trying to what?"

"I think I said it clearly enough the first time, Rudy. S'gan was trying to audition, just like any other actress," Maggie said.

Rudolph stared at the dragon. Luckily, no one had noticed the slight difference in coloring between S'gan and Halymer. Maggie was fairly sure she heard him mutter something about S'gan looking hungry and wanting to know why she kept staring at him.

"You think it would be a good idea to hire, her?" asked Rudy.

"As a matter of fact, it would. She protected Joseph, got us back here in a couple of hours, where we would have taken a week if we had ridden, and seems to have a good bit of acting talent as well," said Maggie.

"How can we negotiate a contract with something that doesn't even talk. Even if we could, she couldn't sign it, no hands," said Rudy.

"Just wait." Maggie turned toward S'gan and nodded. The dragon stretched her wings wide, raised up on her hind legs and then vanished.

In the dragon's place was a woman. The dragon hadn't faded away slowly to be replaced by the woman; the change had happened in less than the blink of an eye.

She was tall, not beautiful, but striking. Her face was sharp angles and lines. Hair the color of rust hung down below her waist. There was no doubt that this was the same being, even though the forms were utterly different. Every movement, every nuance was the same.

"Rudy, m'boy, this is. S'gan."

"What just happened?"

"Oh, did I forget to mention that dragons are perfectly capable of shape-shifting into human form?" asked Maggie.

Ean stared at the woman called S'gan for a long time. Maggie knew the expression on the director's face. She had seen it more than a few times here on the set.

"Yes, you will work perfectly. I already see ways to integrate you into the remaining scenes," he said. "In fact, your very presence changes my whole concept of the true subtext in this story. Please come along with me and we can talk about it."

"Hold it right there," said Maggie. "We had an agreement and I fulfilled my end."

"Maggie, baby," said Rudy. "You're exhausted. You need to rest. Let's put that project on the backburner until this production is done. Once we're back in our world, call my office and we'll take a meeting over your script."

"Look, you S.O.B.! You gave me your word!" she said

"I'm afraid it will just have to wait. Then we will see if we can come to an agreement on your project," said Rudolph, putting on his full executive mode.

"I don't think it will wait, Mr.…Rudy, was it? I believe that you did give your word to Maggie that you would, what is the phrase, 'green light" her project for production. Among my people keeping ones word is a matter of life and death.

"I feel that if you don't keep your word to her, then I'm not sure I can trust you to keep any agreement that we make." S'gan's voice was soft and sexy, while her expression had that same hungry look that had made the producer nervous.

"I must have her, if I am to be expected to finish this film," said Ean.

"She's just trying to save you from yourself," said Caitlin. "After all, you are a man of your word."

"Yeah, but who's going to save me from her. She looks hungry," said Rudolph.

"Trust me, Rudy, I'll save you," said Maggie.

"Besides," said S'gan. "It is doubly to my advantage for you to keep your promise to Maggie. I will know that your word is good on any agreement we make. Plus I will also be getting 15% of what Maggie receives."

The color ran out of the producer's face at S'gan's words. "Fifteen percent? That sounds an awful lot like you're…you're…her…"

"Agent," said Maggie. "Besides being an actress, and when we've finished training her, a stunt woman; in between times S'gan will also be working as an agent. I'm her first client."

"Hmmm…An agent who looks like a supermodel, acts, has brains and isn't afraid to breath fire when necessary," said Joseph. "I think she will fit right into Tinsel Town with no problem at all."

"I'm not sure if Hollywood is ready for this," said Caitlin.

"Then it better get ready," Maggie and S'gan said in unison.

Bambi was standing to one side, struggling to keep from laughing.

"Maggie, you're good, very good. Are you sure you won't stay here and join The Nightwinds?"

"What, and give up show business!"

✦

WIND AND SHADOW

It was going to rain. Michael knew that as certainly as he could see the thin line of clouds and the full moon hanging near the horizon. There hadn't been a word about rain in the television weather forecast; he just knew it would happen, probably within an hour.

The pale moonlight bathed the whole area making the sign at the cemetery gate almost luminescent. Michael smiled slightly as he read it, Floral Haven Cemetery. How many times had he driven past this place since he had gotten his drivers license or come here to watch them put family members and friends into the ground?

The moonlight was enough to help him pick a path across the gravel road and between the few thin trees that stood as narrow shadows above the ground hugging tombstones.

It had been three hours since the funeral.

He had been there, though not among the crowd gathered around the gravesite; preferring to watch from the protection of the abandoned convenience store across the street from the cemetery. Once the limos and other cars were gone, that had been when he had known it was his time to visit the grave.

Michael hadn't said anything to make the grave diggers stop. They just looked up, saw him, backed a respectful distance away and then headed off toward the maintenance building. Latecomers to a graveside funeral service were a normal sight for someone who worked at a cemetery. It was also a good excuse for a cigarette break, so they disappeared quickly.

Standing next to the coffin, he hadn't been sure just what he should be thinking or remembering just then. Finally, Michael reached over and put his hand on the cold metal next to the flower spray of white and red roses.

"Good bye, Dad. I love you."

He'd known all along that there would be one more visitor; that was the reason for the vigil. The sound of footsteps coming from behind him proved him right.

"When did they say that the marker would be put in?" asked the newcomer.

"According to the funeral home people, the permanent one won't be ready for several weeks. They're supposed to have a temporary one in place in the next day or two." said Michael.

"Good. It's nice to see you, Michael."

"I wondered when you would hit town, James. Where were you when you got word about Dad?" said his brother

"Seattle."

"Seattle? I thought you didn't like coffee."

"Times change, kiddo. You still down in the Big Easy."

"You know it," said James. "It's definitely my kind of town"

"I really need to get down there for a visit. You can show me the decadent underbelly of the place."

"Like I would know it?"

"Like you wouldn't?" said Michael.

"True," laughed James. "I notice it didn't take you long to get out of Tulsa and not look back."

"I may have been born here but that didn't mean I had to stay here," said Michael.

Michael looked at his brother. The two of them had not stood face to face in nearly ten years. Yet in that time, James seemed not to have changed, though his face was paler than his brother recalled. Michael didn't need the mirror to show him the changes in his own face; gray in the hair, more and more lines around the eyes and mouth. That was quite a difference for brothers born only a year apart.

"Were you at the funeral?" asked James.

"No," Michael sighed. "I watched from across the way. I really didn't feel like putting up with *our dear* relatives," Michael gave a dry chuckle. "I'm sure that just added grist to the mill of their gossiping about what a disgrace to the family I was and all the heartache I caused Dad."

"I figured you would have been there, if for no other reason than just to irritate them."

"I considered it. Dad would have enjoyed that. But I just couldn't. I had enough of them up at the hospital. At least I got to see him before he died."

"Yeah, that's what was what was important, seeing him," said James.

"The night I got back into town I went straight to the hospital. A half dozen of our cousins and aunts were holding court in Dad's room. You would have thought that Death itself had come walking in among them the way they looked at me. You should have heard dear Aunt May, so condescending it made my stomach turn. After all, as if dying weren't enough, her *"poor brother"* now had to put up with having his gay son waltz in and annoy him," said Michael

"There are times when I wonder why Dad ever claimed her and the rest of that sorry assed bunch as relatives of ours. The only thing they were interested in from him was his money and political contacts. How do you think they would have reacted if they had seen me?" James reached into his jacket and pulled out a cigar case, along with a box of old fashioned wooden matches.

"Considering that most of them were at *your* funeral I imagine not well at all."

James's tombstone was not a dozen steps from where the two of them stood. Michael remembered the shock when, two days after his brother's funeral, he had found James standing on the balcony of his apartment.

"Yeah, well, I'm not surprised, considering some of our relatives. At least Dad accepted me, and you. I know that it couldn't have been easy for him" He took a long draw on the cigar and then let the smoke out slowly

"Hey, first he finds out that one son is gay and then he finds out that the other one has become a vampire. Not that either of us had much choice in the matter. He was a strong man; he had to be. I'd like to think that we both inherited a share of that strength," said Michael.

"So, what did Dad say to you when you talked to him?"

"And what makes you think that I was even there? How do you know I didn't just get in from Seattle a few hours ago and drive straight here?"

"James, this is me you're talking to, so cut the crap. I don't know just how long you've actually been here in town, but I know that you were here before Dad died. I know you, and I know that nothing whatsoever could have kept you from here; unless you were dead too."

"Michael, in case you haven't noticed, I *am* dead. I've even got the paperwork to prove it," James told his brother

"Your point?"

James chuckled. "You certainly have a lot of faith in me, little brother."

"Hey, I saw how you got out of trouble when you were dating the Delvechio triplets, all at the same time. Anyone who could do that can accomplish almost anything."

Of course, what Michael hadn't mentioned to his brother was a conversation he had had with a third-shift nurse at the hospital the night before his father died. That nurse had told him about someone showing up very late to see him; the picture of James in Michael's wallet had been enough to identify him.

"You're right." James blew out several smoke rings, then dropped the cigarillo, stubbing it out on the dirt. "We did talk, for nearly an hour. He actually seemed pleased when I came into the room. We said good-bye. I think we both knew that was what was happening."

Michael took a deep breath, and held it. Shifting his weight to one side, Michael rammed his elbow hard into James's side. The blow was so unexpected that James bent forward, a gasp of air hanging in front of James's face. Then just as swiftly as the first blow, Michael struck his brother again, the force knocking him to the ground.

James laid there for a moment, confusion washed across his face stunned.

"What the hell is the matter with you, Michael? Are you insane?" he demanded.

Michael knew what he had to do, and do quickly. James was stronger than four men, and unbelievably fast, so he knew he had only a few seconds.

"Oh, I'm very, very sane, kiddo; maybe more so than I've ever been." Michael drove the flat of his hand hard against James's chin, then jammed the point of his heavy boot into James's knee, and then his groin.

James's face went paler as he struggled for breath. "Why?"

"You know as well as I do. Because of him. Because of Dad."

"Dad? "

"You could have saved him. But you let him die!"

"Save him?"

"Yes, you asshole. Save him! You could have made him like you are. He didn't have to die."

James struggled to his feet, back arched like an animal ready to spring. "What makes you think that I didn't offer?"

At that, James threw himself hard against his brother, the impact staggering the two of them. Both men struggled to remain on their feet, hands grasping at each other in a blind struggle. In an instant it was over, Michael found himself yanked away from his brother.

"Damn it, boys! Stop it, both of you!"

The voice was familiar, all too familiar, yet both brothers knew that it was impossible. Standing between Michael and James, dressed in tan slacks and a dark blue flowered Hawaiian shirt that he had bought one day to annoy his wife, was their father, Saul .

"Dad?"

Saul Gideon stared at his sons, slowly shaking his head. Looking at him, Michael realized that his father was standing on two good legs, which was astounding, since a year before his death Saul's left leg had been amputated because of diabetic infection.

"It hasn't changed since the two of you were tiny. You're either trying to beat the daylights out of each other or be each other's best friend. Are you two ever going to grow up? I'm not going to be around to pull you two apart any more," he said.

Saul reached into his pocket and pulled out a cigar. Without taking his eyes off his two sons, he unwrapped the stogie and stuck it in his mouth. Ever so slowly the end began to glow red and a thin line of smoke emerged. He looked ten, no fifteen, years younger than he had when he died.

"Dad, didn't the doctor tell you that you had to quit smoking. It's bad for you," James said.

"Somehow I doubt that it will bother me much, now," chuckled Saul. The older man took a long draw of the cigar, obviously savoring the taste. Michael realized that parts of his father were solider then others; he could see through the man's chest but not his arms or face. He also looked no older than forty, though Michael knew he was twice that age.

"Dad, don't take this wrong, but you're dead." He gestured at the coffin.

"Ya think? Is believing in your father as a ghost any more difficult that believing your brother being a vampire?" said Saul "Look, I don't have all that long here. There are places that I should be, but I had the feeling that I would need to be here one more time."

Saul walked along the edge of his grave. Behind him the moon had been covered by more and more clouds. Michael noticed that the smell of rain was heavy in the air.

"So, what were you going to do, Michael, after you had beaten the day-lights out of your brother? Maybe hold him down until you could drive a stake through him heart?" asked Saul.

"Maybe, probably not. I just wanted to make him hurt, for not saving you." said Michael.

For a moment Saul's face showed all of his eighty years, but then shifted back to the younger iteration. "Thank you, Michael; not for what you were going to do, but for caring enough to think you had to do something. I know you were hurting. But you didn't have to do something like that. That last night in the hospital, James offered to make me like him. I said no."

"Why not, Dad?"

"Because I was just tired. Ten years of pain, a slow creeping kind that never gave me a minute's peace, was the reason. When we lost your mother last year, that was the moment I knew that I didn't want to go on without her."

"I knew you felt that way, but I had to give you the chance, a way out if you wanted it," James said. "And the same offer is open to you, little brother, if you want it. This isn't an easy life, but it is a life."

Michael embraced his brother, not sure what his feelings were right then.

"Now, will you two promise me there won't be any more knockdown drag outs?"

"Can't promise that, Dad," said Michael, a half smile on his face. "But let's just say there won't be any more tonight."

"James?"

"What Michael said."

"Good. I won't be seeing either one of you for a very long time. I want you both to know that I'm proud of you. I've always loved you both." He reached into his shirt and pulled out a pocket watch. "Yipes, I'm late. Your mother is probably wondering where I am, and if I don't get a move on he will be madder than hell," said Saul.

As suddenly as he had come, Saul Carter was gone, leaving nothing but Michael and James's memories in his wake.

"I don't know about you, but I could use a drink right now," said Michael.

James pulled a metal flask out of his inside coat pocket and passed it over to Michael. He unscrewed the top and took a swallow, a moment later gasping for breath.

"Kiddo, that's something," he said handing it back, slowly. "Please tell me there wasn't any blood mixed in there."

"No, why would I waste that on you? That's nothing but good old Kentucky whiskey. So kiddo, are you any better with a pool cue than you used to be?"

"Good enough to beat the stuffing out of you."

"I don't think Dad would object to you trying that," James said.

"I don't think he would, either." Michael grinned and wrapped his arm around his brothers shoulder.

"So," James said. "Hows about we head for the Sho-Bar and find out."

"You have been gone awhile. They turned the Sho-Bar into a C&W place about a year ago."

"Yuck! That is an offense against the natural order of the universe!"

"The Gold Dragon is still around: that okay with you?"

"Yeah! Is Samantha still the head dancer?"

"Head dancer? She owns the place now! After you "left" she became quite the businesswoman—owns The Gold Dragon and a half dozen other businesses," said Michael.

"Will wonders never cease," said James.

As the two brothers walked away from the grave, wrapped now in the wind and shadow that filled the cemetery, Michael felt the first few drops of rain begin.

✦

AND THE WIND SANG

The man who now called himself Eric Karlson sat on a rock near the tree-line. From that perch he could look down the hill, toward the castle and the town that had grown up around it. As the sun began to burn off the night fog, the view became clearer.

He could see the roads leading in and out of the gates and figures moving to and fro along them. If anyone happened to look in his direction, it was hardly likely that they would notice him, save as an unmoving shadow, just another part of the forest.

This was a place that Eric had not seen for over five years. A place that he hadn't expected to see for many, many more years, if ever again. The place he had called home for more than two decades. The place where he had lost his heart, had fallen in love, and had died.

"Camelot," he said, softly to the wind and memories that surrounded him.

Tethered a few feet away from his perch, Eric's mount stirred, drawing his attention, but the horse settled back after a moment; whatever had bothered it was now gone. The pack animal next to it hardly moved, lulled into sleep by the concert of the night insects and the song of the wind as it moved among the trees.

"Camelot," he sighed.

No, he corrected himself. It was Camelot no longer. With Arthur's passing, the entire area was now held by Earl Seamus MacLeod, who had renamed the castle and town Camlin. Not nearly as striking a name, Eric observed, but good in its own way.

The name Camelot was now the property of bards and storytellers, some of whom said it was easier to make rhymes with than Camlin. Not that Eric could have told; he was tone deaf, and on the rare occasions he had attempted to sing, it was not a sound that listeners had rejoiced in hearing.

81

Eric reached inside his tunic and pulled out the letter; a single, carefully folded sheet of parchment; unchanged since the first time he had laid eyes on it. Had that really been only eight weeks ago when he had found it the first time, buried deep inside his saddlebag, in a place that no one else knew about. The firelight had been enough to see the wax seal; a crow and an owl holding a single chess piece in their claws. The hand that had penned the words was all too familiar, the words still the same ones he had read that night.

> IT HAS COME BACK TO CAMELOT. PEOPLE
> ARE BEING KILLED. YOU ARE NEEDED.
>
> NIMUE.

The words sent a shiver through Eric, and brought back memories of things best buried and forgotten.

An hour after sunrise, Eric knew that there was no putting off what he had to do. As much as he had dreaded it, the time had come for Lancelot du Lac to come home. Pulling himself into the saddle, he headed his horses out of the forest and onto the road toward Camlin.

Behind him a single figure, clad in armor that seemed to glow green in the darkness of the trees, watched Eric's departure.

The Three Hearts Inn was not the most luxurious accommodation the town had to offer, but the place suited Eric's needs exactly: a private room, a well tended barn for his horses and an innkeeper who, for enough coins, asked no questions.

With the ease of a practiced campaigner, Eric opened each of his saddle bags and inspected the contents. Clothing, armor, a few mementos, all seemed to be in good shape. From under the carefully rolled bundle of chain mail he extracted three leather bags. Hefting one of them, he rolled it over in his hands. Even through the leather he could feel strength radiating from it. A thief would only find dirt inside and perhaps make some comment about a knight's peculiarities.

But for Eric, the rich and fertile dirt inside each of the bags was as valuable as gold. It was his native earth. He wondered if any of the bards who told the tales and sang the songs of Lancelot could ever in their wildest dreams imagine that their hero now bore the curse of the vampire.

The irony was not lost on Eric; he was not that far gone in cynicism. But practicality was a habit he had learned long ago. Native earth was necessary to his survival, so he kept it close to him. Let any who saw it just assume it a bit of eccentricity. Eric Karlson, Lancelot du Lac, and the other several names he had worn in the last few years, had all seen their share of eccentricities; some far stranger than carrying bags of earth.

"Some of them make me seem almost normal," he smiled.

———

"Some things never change," said Eric, turning his face into the breeze and wrinkling his nose. The wind had shifted, out of the south now, and bore with it the highly distinct smells coming from the tannery and the small lake where the town's refuse was emptied.

The streets were muddy, wagons flinging it up as they passed, while passersby sometimes sank up to their ankles in it. A pair of young boys came dashing out from behind one cart, sticks in hands like swords, dueling away, laughing with each stroke of their weapons. Moments later, their trousers stained knee high with mud, they headed off, their quest taking them in search of some goal known only to them.

This was the norm, Eric reminded himself. Kings might come and go, battles rage, people die, but always would children play, be it in the center of chaos or calm. He smiled and wished them well.

As he walked, Eric cast a wary eye along the street, studying everything. Five years did much to change memories, as-well-as people, but he still worried that someone might recognize him.

Despite the fact that he much preferred to be clean shaven, letting his beard grow had seemed a wise precaution. Not a piece of his clothing, armor or weapons was native to England, and he hoped his years among the Germans and northmen had blurred his French accent. If the circumstances were right, memories could be rearranged. Ideally, that was a problem that might not have to be dealt with.

Eric had come only a little way down the cobbler's street when he heard a scream. Just ahead of him a group of people had gathered around a rider who had come from the east.

0The man was mounted on a small dark war-horse, with a second horse tethered behind him. The rider wore chain mail and leather, a heavy cloak that had seen better days around his shoulders, lance and shield strapped to his mount's saddle.

It was what the second horse carried that seemed to hold everyone's attention. A body, wrapped in a rough-spun blanket, had been strapped in place on the animal between several saddle bags. A single bloody hand dangled free, bouncing with every step the horse took.

"It's happened again!" someone yelled.

"Who is it?" demanded a man in a blacksmith's apron. In spite of the question, no one moved forward, everyone just stood staring, at each other and at the body. Finally two men stepped up to lift the blanket clear.

It was a woman. Flies had already found the body. There were sounds of revulsion as people saw what had happened. Her throat had been ripped apart, not enough to pull her head away from her body, but nearly so. Dried blood stained her features, marking the maze of cuts and bruises. One eye had been ripped from its socket and was nowhere to be seen. Eric couldn't help but think that there were more injuries, concealed where people could not easily see.

"I think it's Marie O'Conner," said one of them.

"I've known her since my girls were small," said a woman. "What happened?"

"It's obvious, isn't it! That thing is back, back murdering people." Those words raised the hackles on the back of Eric's neck. He hoped against hope that Nimue's words had been wrong, but the scene in front of him said otherwise.

"Good people, please!" said the rider. His voice was clear and strong, with the tone of command in each word. "Someone summon a priest, so that he may see to this poor woman's soul. Then send someone to your constable and the Earl's Seneschal. Tell them what has happened and that I will come to report in a few minutes. It is unseemly to stand here with this woman newly dead, gawking."

People scrambled in several directions at one. The rider slid from his saddle, patting his horse on the forehead, and produced something from his pocket that he offered the animal.

From his position, Eric could get a better look at this stranger. He was perhaps an inch or two shorter than Eric, but he had broad heavy shoulders, and moved with the manner of an experienced soldier.

His mail and sword were worn, but looked of quality make, but they lacked either badge or device to identify the rider. In addition to the weapons on his saddle, there were daggers protruding from his boots and one strapped to his arm.

"And who might you be?" Before the man could answer, a woman came toward him, her brown hair streaked with gray, shaking her head as if she could not be certain of her own memory.

"I...I...know you," she said.

"I am Lancelot du Lac of Joyous Guard, once of the table round and King's champion to my best and truest friend, Arthur Pendragon," said the horseman.

—·—

It was true, Eric had to admit. This man who was calling himself Lancelot did bear a passing resemblance to him. At least the image of himself that Eric remembered; he hadn't actually seen his own reflection in some years. Though, to be brutally honest, he suspected that this stranger more resembled the idealized paintings that Eric had encountered from time to time.

"Your pardon, good knight," Eric said, deciding to make himself known. "Everyone assumed you dead, slain in the final battle; or returned to France and taken holy orders."

Both tales were rumors that Eric had done his best, at various times, to spread. If someone thinks you're dead or cloistered, they won't be looking for you.

"I've hard those stories myself, along with a half a hundred others," Lancelot nodded. "Some even had a kernel or two of fact in them. I was indeed sorely wounded in the final battle. It took nearly two years before I recovered at my home in Joyous Guard. Since then I have traveled much."

An interesting tale, thought Eric, as the other man said, containing a kernel or two of truth in it. Eric had indeed returned to Joyous Guard after the last battle. But he had remained there only briefly, seeing his lands into the care of cousins. As accepting as his people were, they would not have been happy to find their ruler was one of the "undead".

There had certainly been no mention of another "Lancelot" recuperating there at the time.

"Lancelot du Lac! You heathen sinner! How dare you return to Camlin! You should be spending the rest of your miserable life on your knees pleading for God to forgive you the sins that you have committed!" The voice belonged to a man in the robes of a priest who came pushing his way through the crowd. A cross of rough-hewn pieces of wood hung around his neck.

"Who speaks?" asked Lancelot.

"Aye, Lancelot du Lac, I'm surprised you don't remember me, Father Xavier! I know you," said the priest. Eric remembered him, much to his chagrin. The man was a self-righteous prig convinced that even the most minor deviation from holy scripture would damn someone to hellfire.

The priest walked over to the woman's body. He rudely pulled the head up and stared at the damaged face and neck. "Another sinner gone to face God's wrath," muttered the cleric. He growled something to several members of the crowd. They came forward and made quickly to bring the body off of the back of the horse.

"Take her to the church," said the priest. "Is this your doing, du Lac?"

"Hardly," said the man who called himself Lancelot.

"Mayhap you didn't wield the sword, but I know you were hip deep in responsibility. I have prayed and beseeched God for a sign, a sign that would awaken these people to the danger their souls are in. I've asked him to give me the way, the way to save them," the priest proclaimed. "This is the same curse that rang across this land in those last dark days before Arthur's death. Death walks among us as it did then, taking the guilty and the innocent. And with it you have come du Lac, your hands as bloody as ever."

"Believe what you will, priest. Just know that I found this woman a few miles from the town. I would say she was killed sometime last night. Now, Father, if you will excuse me, I must make a report, one I wish to God I didn't have to," said Lancelot.

———

With the advent of this other Lancelot, Eric decided it might be time to retire to the Bearded Cockerel. He had early on determined that the Cockerel was one of several places that he should avoid, except under the most dire of circumstances.

He had spent far more time than many at court thought proper at the inn. It had been the place he would seek out when he wanted not to be the King's Champion or "Sir Lancelot," but just another person. A place for thought and dream and forgetting himself for a time.

The only thing that seemed to have changed about the Cockerel was the fresh painted sign that hung over the door. When Eric walked through the door he felt as if the last few years hadn't happened. The big heavy tables, the soot-covered beams and the enormous fireplace were all there and virtually unchanged.

Taking a table back against the wall, he settled into a chair and motioned for one of the serving girls to bring him ale. The dozen or so other customers had looked up when he walked through the door, but then turned back to their own business.

Bits and pieces of conversation drifted to Eric. He could put faces to most of the voices, but that was of little import at the moment. For the most part their words dealt with everyday life: who was rebuilding a barn, the need for a new wall at someone's farmstead, how much the Earl might increase taxes next year. The words of two men sitting near the door dealt with something entirely different.

"...neck was ripped out just like Sean Farina last month. I don't care what the Seneschal says. It were no wolf! They say that a couple of the dead'ns looked like big chunks had been ripped out of them and eaten. Martha Tattershall said that she saw something, a man she thought, standing over the body, and 'e was glowing green."

Eric considered the possibility of striking up a conversation with the two men; if he stood for the drinks it might loosen their tongues even more.

"Your drink m'lord." Instead of the young girl he had given the order to, an older woman, perhaps thirty, stood next to Eric, holding a wooden mug of ale.

"Thank you," he said, holding two coppers out for her. Her fingers brushed Eric's hand and the Bearded Cockerel was gone.

Eric looked around in stunned silence. He still sat in the same chair, but now it was in a room filled with shelves and tables, covered over with apparati, books, scrolls and sputtering candles.

He knew this place. Merlin's Lair. Not the tower, the one that everyone in Camelot had known. No, this was a private place, buried deep in the catacombs beneath the castle. Here, Merlin did his real work, delving into dark secrets that few beyond Nimue understood.

"Good evening, Lance."

Sitting in a chair only a few feet from him was Nimue. Her ink black hair and dark blue eyes glistened in the dim light. When he had first met her, a few weeks after arriving at Camelot, Nimue had seemed no more than one and twenty; not a spinster, but more than a bit past prime marrying age. Yet she had moved through the court, a force to be reckoned with, as Merlin's public voice. The passing of the years not seeming to affect her only added to her mystique.

"Still good at making an entrance, I see," said Eric.

"One does what can. Of course, if you can do it with a bit of style, that does help things along." Her lips never moved, her eyes never left his. The only sounds, besides Eric's own voice, was the shifting of air and what might have been the slow dripping of water in a cave.

Nimue spoke in his mind, her voice his memory of what had been.

"Doing things with style. Yes, that suits you." Eric reached across and touched Nimue's hand. It was real, warm and soft to the touch.

"Old friend, I am here and yet not here, locked away in a place of safety if not of my choosing," she said. "But we must speak quickly as I can only hold you here a short span of minutes."

"Is this Merlin's doing? Did you two have a lovers' quarrel?"

"Nothing of the sort. Know that Merlin is elsewhere and cannot take a hand in these matters, no matter how much he would desire to do so. I cannot either; my powers are, for the moment, limited. It has fallen to you to do again what you had to do before."

"You're being as obscure as the Old Crow." Nimue inclined her head toward him as he spoke.

A broken piece of metal appeared on Eric's lap. He let out a long sigh, but didn't touch it. There was no need. The carved rune representing a name was quite familiar. Loki.

The seal, the sight of it made his stomach revolt, was a thing of evil, used to lock away a thing of worse evil. When that had been done he'd prayed it could never be undone. But it had been undone.

"Why? That armor was to be locked away forever. Even Arthur admitted that it did more damage, destroyed more dreams than a hundred armies," said Eric.

"On that there is no disagreement. Armor forged for the trickster should never have been brought into this world in the first place. It was a mistake, one of many that cost Arthur the throne. But that is the past. This is the present. The seal is broken, Loki's armor is loosed again in the world. People are dying, and without cause. It falls to you to stop it, Lancelot du Lac," her pronouncement was solemn and final.

"I am not so sure any..." before he could complete the sentence the Bearded Cockerel was once again around him. The woman's fingers had lifted the coins from his hand.

Day gave way to night and Eric again walked the streets of Camlin. The darkness brought him strength, more than human. Merlin's magic let him walk in the daylight, but only with the strength of a normal man. The night gave him more and he would need it.

The armor of Loki. Eric spit at the very thought of it; helm, breastplate, gloves, and ax. At the behest of Arthur, Kay, Gallahad and he had brought it back from a place that would have put fear into anything that drew breath. Laid before the King, he had proclaimed it the answer to dealing with Mordred and his invaders.

"Poor, poor Arthur, if you had only known." Death had followed in the footsteps of whoever wore it. Not just the death of warriors, but of the innocent, as well. Once someone wore the armor, there was no controlling them.

Only by chance and Eric's own uniqueness as a vampire, had they been able to seize it and lock it away. "So much for forever," he muttered.

Then without thinking about why, Eric drew a deep breath, closed his eyes and let his mind reach in itself. The moment of transiting from solid form to mist hurt as much as anything ever had.

He let the wind take him, drifting over houses and streets. The temperature had begun to drop before sunset so there were bits of fog lingering on the street, mixing with plumes that came trickling out of smoke holes in various roofs, so one more bit of mist was hardly noticed.

The sound of metal striking metal caught his attention. It was not that of honest work, a smith laboring long after dark, but familiar sound of combat coming from an alley just ahead. There were two men attacking a third. The victim was on one knee, but still held a sword and was giving a good account of himself to fend off his foes.

Eric came to human form without thought to the pain, and in a single move his own sword slid free, almost before he was fully materialized. He'd never liked two on one, no matter who was involved. Besides, he admitted to himself, he was in the mood for a fight.

The advantage of surprise was enough for him to put an end to one of the attackers; a blow with the hilt of his sword across the man's face, and swift kick to the knee brought the man down. Perhaps it wasn't the most knightly kind of tactic, but it worked.

The other was more of a problem. Eric dodged the man's sword thrust, but a dagger in his other hand drove into Eric's chest. Had he been wearing his chainmail shirt, it might have deflected the blow. Instead, the blade cut through leather, cloth and into flesh itself. It was more surprise than pain that made Eric's fingers go loose from his sword.

Not that it didn't hurt; it hurt a lot, enough to reach behind the walls he had fought to hold in place since *that* night that he had died and been reborn as a vampire. The Beast, the animal who considered humans his rightful pray, roared in pain and took Eric in its grip. Fangs sliding into place, the vampire that had once been Lancelot du Lac stood in his place, savoring the pain and the fear that hung in the air like solid objects.

Iron muscled fingers grabbed the attacker, grinding through cloth and into flesh, as Eric lifted the man off his feet. A look of uncomprehending surprise was the bandit's only reaction.

Eric drove for the man's neck. Flesh parted beneath fangs, fear roared through the man, radiating out like heat from a blazing fire. He could feel the liquid rolling down his throat, over his lips, staining his teeth. The bandit thrashed about, but Eric's grip was tight and unyielding.

In a single fluid movement Eric lifted the man above him. Blood from his victim's neck dripped down like a slow rain. Then he slammed him hard onto the ground, mud splattering over the body like a shroud.

Eric turned toward the victim of this attack. He arched his eyebrow in surprise, coming back to himself, the Beast sated, more easily pushed back into darkness. It was the 'other' Lancelot.

Instead, Eric didn't move. He locked eyes with this stranger who wore his name, pushing his own thoughts into the man's mind. The memories of the last several minutes were exactly what Eric expected to find; exhilaration, fear, all pulsing like a single torch in the darkness.

It took only a moment for Eric to wrap those memories in a cocoon and push them so deep into the man's memories that he would never recall them. In their wake he whispered a slightly different version of what had happened.

"I thank you, sir, for the aid. I could have handled these ruffians, had I not tripped over a thrice damned dog whose rest we seemed to have disturbed." he said. "I'm sure the dog felt as upset as you."

"Damn!" Lancelot moved several steps, shifting his weight from one leg to the other, testing them with a few steps each. The pain that shot through his features told the results. "I appear to have twisted my ankle. "

"I wouldn't try running any foot races for a day or two, at least," said Eric

"The problem is, I don't have time to wait for it to heal." he said. "My friend, I must ask for your aid again. Are you willing to fight at the side of Lancelot du Lac?"

"Lancelot du Lac? I would be honored," said Eric. The irony didn't escape him. "How came you here? Who were those two assassins?"

"I know not who they were. Earlier this evening one of the night watch reported seeing a figure in green glowing armor in this area of town. I have been searching for him most of the evening," he said.

Loki's Armor! There could be no other like that. "You think it perhaps the killer of that woman you found today?"

"Indeed." he nodded. "I hoped to find and face him. But with my ankle injured I am at somewhat of a disadvantage."

"We will try to change that," nodded Eric. "I will stand with you this night. But I do not think we will need to search far for the one you seek."

"Why?"

"Because, we are not alone." Eric gestured toward the far end of the alley. A figure stood there, dressed in chainmail and helm, gauntlets with inches long, flesh-tearing claws built into them, a tattered cloak, and holding a large ax in one hand. The green glow only emphasized the danger.

"Lancelot!" The newcomer's voice echoed from several directions at once.

"Loki," muttered Eric.

"I am Lancelot. Who calls me?" said the man at Eric's side.

"Lancelot."

Eric considered their options. With Lancelot's injured ankle, escape, while not an impossibility, would not be that easy. He also had the distinct feeling that the man was not the sort to be willing to run from a fight, even when prudence might demand it.

"What do you want?" demanded Eric.

Lancelot did not wait for an answer. Moving awkwardly, he pushed in front of Eric and waited, sword drawn. The green warrior's first blow, though stopped by the flat of his sword, had enough force to knock Lancelot off balance and almost off his feet. He had to struggle to keep from going down.

The man raised his ax and began to bring it down in a final swing. That move was interrupted when the ax went flying forward and so did its wielder, flying head first into the wall just behind Lancelot. He lay there in a heap, mud half covering him.

When Lancelot managed to turn, he found Eric with a long piece of broken marble in his hands.

"That was hardly fair," said Lancelot.

"Fair is surviving, my friend," said Eric. "Anything damaged?"

"Nothing. Did you really have to attack him from behind?"

"It struck me as the safest way." He knelt at the fallen man's side, extracting a knife and cutting the helmet's chin strap. "Now, let's see who you are."

Once neatly trimmed gray hair and beard, now scraggly and matted with blood and dirt, surrounded a face that Eric new all too well.

"Hello, old friend," the man said in a raspy voice.

"I would hardly call you a friend, Merlin," said Eric.

"Merlin?" asked Lancelot.

"Aye," muttered Eric. "Merlin."

———

Eric began stripping every piece of metal off of the old man, throwing it all as far away as he could. "Why?" demanded Eric as he worked..

The magician shook his head. "Call it the fault of my own vanity," he said. "That we weren't able to destroy the armor has always nagged at me. I should have had the power! But it eluded me! Then a few months ago I found an ancient text that suggested a way it might be done. I felt I had no choice but to try."

"Then it was you who broke the seal, breached your own spells," said Eric. "Why couldn't you leave well enough alone?"

"I only wish now I had. Help me up," the magician had to grab Eric's arm to brace himself, but managed to get to his feet. "As you can imagine, the results were not what I anticipated. Part of the spell required my wearing the armor and invoking Loki himself."

"Loki!" said Eric. "Merlin, I'm beginning to think you more of a lunatic than I ever did before."

"I deserve that remark. However, I never got to that particular part of the incantation. The power of the trickster's armor was too much for me. I lost myself to it. I don't even want to think about the results."

"Think about them! With every breath you take, think about them. Let them remind you that you cost innocent people their lives, and by your own hand, not through some political manipulation or magic spell," Eric told him."By your own hand!"

"And Nimue could do nothing?" Eric asked.

"She also, in her own way, was my victim. I tricked her into a place of safety and by my arts sealed her away. I imagine she is not particularly happy with me right now," admitted Merlin.

"I'll leave her to express her feelings on that matter to you herself. But you should know that it was by her doing that I am here at all."

"Resourceful as always, isn't she, Lancelot."

The 'other' Lancelot had not spoken since they had freed Merlin. "What did you call him?" he asked.

"I called him by his right and proper name, Sir Lancelot du Lac, Knight of the Round Table, one time Champion to Arthur Pendragon, High King of Britain," said Merlin.

"This cannot be!"

Merlin walked slowly toward him. The magician's eyes had always been his most striking feature, capable of causing terror in the heart of an enemy or bringing happiness into the smile of a small child. The man looked to either side of Merlin, refusing to look him in the face.

"Who are you?" Merlin said. He spoke so softly that Eric doubted the man's voice could be heard more than a few feet away. There was no answer

"Who are you?" he said once more. "What is your name?"

The man who had called himself Lancelot seemed to have to struggle to find his voice. His eyes had grown glassy and unfocussed. "My name is…. Collum Naismith from the village of Myra in Weston Shire."

Eric knew that place. It was fifty or so miles southwest of Camlin. An isolated place as he recalled, quite nice, quite peaceful. Far from the madness that seemed to have engulfed much of England these last few decades.

"So why have you laid claim to my name?" asked Eric.

"I was a soldier in Arthur's army. I fought in many battles. In the last battle I saw the High King fall. Try as I might I, and others, couldn't reach him before that happened. If I had been closer, and a better soldier, perhaps it would have made a difference," said Collum.

Eric reached over and patted Collum on the shoulder. There were no words, at least none that were worth the saying at that moment.

"It took time for me to recover from my own wounds, to regain my skill with a blade. By chance, someone mistook me for you and I did not disabuse him of that belief. Because of that I was able to help them. Then I was able to help others, to keep the dream that all of us had fought for alive."

"You are not a knight?" asked Merlin.

"No. As the son of a blacksmith, I was not a noble and could never aspire to the spurs of a knight. I would have liked to have been one," he said. "But I did what I did, not because people thought me knight, but because they needed me. I gave them hope."

Eric remembered the people in the plaza when Collum had arrived. Their fear was gone, they had hope. It was something that Arthur would have approved of.

Eric stared into Collum's eyes. To him it was as if looking at his own reflection. He knew what he had to do. "Know you, Collum Naismith, that I have found you as noble and worthy as any man who sat at the table. In your heart is everything that Arthur lived and fought for at Camelot. I have no children; I will have none. Will you allow me to adopt you as my son?"

Collum looked from Eric to Merlin, puzzled, uncertain of how to react to the offer. "I would be honored."

"Then, as was the custom of our Roman forebears, I formally adopt you as my son and heir. You will always be Collum Naismith, to honor the parents who reared you, but from here on you will also bear the name Lancelot du Lac, the younger. Now kneel, my son," said Eric.

Collum complied, uncertain of just what would happen next. With Merlin nodding his approval, Eric took out his sword and touched it to Collum's shoulders. "As my son and heir I pass all titles, and the obligations they carry, that are mine to you. Lancelot du Lac, I charge you now, as a knight, to carry on the traditions laid down by Arthur Pendragon and to bear my knighthood as your own. Do you so swear to do this?"

"I do so swear." Tears rolled down the new knight's face. It was not the ceremony that Eric had taken part in when he won his spurs, but for Collum it would be enough.

"Then arise, Sir Lancelot." said Merlin. "I agree with Lance, Collum. Arthur would be proud to call you a member of his band and have for you a seat at the table."

Father and son embraced.

"Oh, such a sweet scene." Standing near the end of the alley stood the priest, Father Xavier. In his hands he held the chain mail shirt worn only minutes before by Merlin. The sickly green glow had flared to life at his touch..

"What do you want, priest?" demanded Merlin. "You are playing with forces that you know nothing about."

"Oh, I know about them, you pagan devil, Merlin. I had thought you dead and sent to the fiery fate that you so richly deserve. I know exactly what this is, what has happened and what is going to happen. You have laid the groundwork, which I shall carry on. This is the answer to my prayers." The priest pulled the chainmail over his robes. "I shall bring terror to the hearts of the people, drive them from sin and back into the arms of our Lord. I shall be the hand of God among them!"

"You would use the weapons of a demon like Loki to do God's work?" demanded Eric.

"If necessary," growled the priest. His face began to shift into something not quite human. The flesh of his arms merging with the metal gauntlets.

"No! God himself would deny you!" yelled the newly christened Lancelot du Lac, the younger. He threw himself at the priest, sword drawn, but was met by the green glowing ax that moved, seemingly with a will of its own.

"Who do you think you are?" roared the priest. "How dare you interfere with God's Work!"

"I! I am a knight!" He drove his attack harder, striking so quickly at times that Eric could not see the blows being thrown. One stroke of the priest's weapon drove hard against Collum's shoulder, cutting leather and mail and flesh with a dull thud. Blood spurted, following the weapon's edge as it pulled free.

Collum made a sound, deep in his chest. Perhaps it was a word, perhaps something else. He threw himself against the priest, pushing the man's weapon aside, grabbing him up in a bear hug. Then, with all his strength, Collum crashed Xavier down across his knee. The sound of bones breaking rang in the darkness of the alley as both men collapsed in a heap.

Eric was on them in a moment, pulling his 'son' away. Then, as he had for Merlin, he stripped the armor away from the priest as swiftly as he could. Only then could he turn back to Collum.

"Alive?" asked Merlin.

"Xavier is dead, a broken back."

"What about Collum?"

Eric didn't have to answer. "I live," the voice was whispery and rough.

"Had I my full powers, perhaps I could heal you," said Merlin. "But my magic has not returned." The three of them knew it would only be a matter of minutes.

The wound on Collum's shoulder was worse than Eric had expected. Try as he might, Eric could not stop the bleeding. The ax had cut too deeply.

"I thank you, Merlin. But even if you had your powers, I'm not sure I would want you to use them. I've never trusted magic all that much," said Collum.

"You sound just like your father," said Merlin.

Both father and son smiled.

"Am I truly a Knight?" asked Collum.

"You are, my son," said Eric.

Collum said nothing as he closed his eyes for the last time. As the night insects and the wind sang around them, Lancelot wept for his son.

✦

OATHS

"**S**o you were the ones," Ryan DuLane said.
        "Not entirely, but I suppose I did my share. It was more a matter of what had to be done at that moment than anything else," said Brother Ellis.
        "Isn't that always the way, Brother?" DuLane hoped that the distaste that he had for most religious types echoed in his voice.
        Normally he would have barely even spoken to the monk, not to be deliberately uncivil, but simply out of preference. Over the years, DuLane had come to be highly selective about whom he spent time with, and church men were not high among his preferred company. There were exceptions, but this man was not one of them.
        Tonight, however, DuLane seemed to have little choice in the matter if he wanted company of any sort, which at the moment he really did not but the monk would not leave. The few other patrons of the Inn of the Crossed Scabbards had long since sought their beds, leaving DuLane and Brother Ellis alone in the large common room.
        Located at the intersection of two growing trade routes, the Crossed Scabbards did a brisk business most of the year. But spring wasn't due for another four weeks, at least, and six days of freezing rain had kept away all but the most hardy of travelers.
        An hour's ride west of the inn, DuLane had come across the remains of a bandit ambush. Three ragged bodies, bandits from the look of them, covered with blood and mud, lay where they had fallen. But they had not been the only casualties. Nearby there had been two quickly-made cairns and crude crosses, the last resting places, he learned later, for some of Brother Ellis's companions.
        In spite of the roaring fire, the cold and dismal atmosphere that had settled over the countryside seemed to have penetrated even inside the tavern. They could hear the wind howling outside and the rolling crash of thunder.

"However I may have performed with my sword, the bandits took two of our number with them," said the monk.

"But you did survive, Brother Ellis, much to your credit. From the looks of those wretches, that would have been no easy task. Besides, I learned a long time ago, it is survival that matters. I'm just surprised you didn't bury them, it would have been the Christian thing to do."

"Survival, yes, a good thing. But even so, we did not come through unscathed. Given our own wounds, myself and the others felt it best that we see to our own dead and ourselves.

"The one of our guards who lived required a dozen stitches to close up the wound in his leg. If it escapes infection he will need at least a month to recuperate." DuLane caught himself studying the monk; his tonsured hair streaked with gray only added to the lean and wolf-like appearance of his face.

"Still, you don't often associate a religious man with a sword," DuLane said lightly.

"Before God called me to the church, I found I had a small talent with the blade. It has been our Lord's will, as well as my superior's in the order, that I keep that talent sharp; in the service of God, of course, rather than temporal princes. God needs many skills in his service, Captain DuLane. Yes, your name was not unfamiliar to me," said Brother Ellis.

"Indeed? To you personally, or to the Inquisition?" DuLane didn't know what the monk was looking for, but all he would find would be a man who had lived through too many battles, lost too many comrades and could barely remember what having a home and family were like.

The monk arched an eyebrow, the barest hint of a smile touching his face. "Both. I serve the church as God would have me, protecting it against heretics and those who would work against His Holy will."

"And which am I?"

"As are all men, a little bit of both. There have been incidents regarding you that have come to the Church's attention, it is true, but nothing to make the Holy Inquisition consider you a heretic…yet."

"I'm so very glad to hear that." DuLane ran his finger around the edge of his cup, collecting a few drops of wine.

"You are traveling early in the season, Captain. It must be a matter of the gravest import for you to risk the weather," he said.

Trying to be diplomatic, but still find out things, are we? observed DuLane to himself. "Indeed. I must reach Sicily by the end of March or this whole journey, as inconvenient and painful as it has been, will have been for nothing."

"Then I wish you well." The monk wanted to know more; that much was obvious. It was a minor victory to leave him hanging, but one that pleased DuLane. If asked directly, perhaps DuLane would explain, but then again, perhaps not.

In his saddlebags was a letter from his old friend Karl Lysroni in Palermo. DuLane had served with him in a half-dozen campaigns, and, though Karl didn't know it, with his father and grandfather. Now, Karl was to be married and wanted DuLane to be his best man.

"Besides, who better deserves to stand with me?" DuLane had laughed when he had read the letter.

Brother Ellis leaned back in his chair.

Just then a young woman emerged from the kitchen. She balanced a tray with two bowls and a large pitcher on it that she set in front of the two men. DuLane had barely noticed her earlier, a glimpse or two through the kitchen door. This time, however, she was standing only a few inches from him and he found himself hard pressed to believe his own eyes.

She was no more than sixteen. Her dirty blonde hair tied in a single braid and then wrapped to hug her head. The face, the figure, the mannerisms, even the voice were all as he remembered them. It was a memory as fresh as a spring breeze and oh, so very old, at the same time.

"Ginnie?" he finally managed to say.

"Sir?"

"Ginnie?" he asked again.

"No, m'lord, my name is Emma."

A blanket of sadness fell across DuLane. It was the response that he would have expected, should have expected, if he had not let his heart speak.

"Have you been employed here long?" he asked.

"Near three years, sir. I was born in the village just down the road. Is there anything I can get for either of you?"

"No." DuLane waved her away. But his eyes followed her out of sight.

"You know her?" asked Brother Ellis.

"No. She just resembled someone that I knew a long time ago. Of course it couldn't be her; she's been dead a very long time."

"If I were a minstrel, I would imagine that I could make a great deal of what just went on," laughed the monk. "I imagine it would make a fine ballad, of lost love, heroic deeds and valor uncounted."

DuLane said nothing, knowing just how close to the truth the annoying monk was.

DuLane waited in a shadowed corner in the inn's upstairs hall, where he could see but not be seen. Not that long later the monk had gone to the room where the injured guard slept, paused long enough to look in the room, then went to a separate one further down the hall.

Not a few minutes later she came, candle in hand as she went to a doorway at the far end of the hall. It led to an attic area, where he suspected she slept.

Ginnie.

Guinevere.

No! He reminded himself that her name was Emma.

Ten minutes went by before DuLane could bring himself to follow her. He paused at the door. The sound the ancient hinges made echoed loudly in his memory. In between two breaths he shifted form, becoming mist and slipping beneath the door.

A long time before, when he had discovered the ability, it had been painful, but that had passed. Even now he did not know just how he could do what he did, only that he could. The first time he had shown Arthur, the king had stood slacked jawed as a peasant at a traveling carnival.

The wind outside of the attic room was enough to mask the sound from the wood taking his weight as he assumed solid form again. There were no windows. Emma's candle had been carefully extinguished, so it was pitch dark. That was no problem for DuLane. He had been born with good night vision; since the change, that had only grown better and better.

There were few things to mark it as anyone's home. A small curtained alcove protected her few bits of clothing, a broken piece of mirror hung carefully in a niche on the wall, and a small wooden ring held a section of cloth from which needles protruded.

The girl lay beneath a blanket, snuggled down into a pile of straw for warmth. It would have made more sense for her to sleep in the kitchen, near the fire, but this worked well for DuLane. She stirred as he came closer, murmuring in a dream.

DuLane knelt next to Emma.

He had not fed for nearly a week, since leaving Bordeaux. The Hunger was something that was never completely gone from him, just muted. It was something he accepted, an annoyance that he had long since learned to control.

He knew he should not have needed to feed again for another few days, but as he knelt there, DuLane felt it begin to grow.

And with the Hunger, the need for blood, there were also memories.

Sunlight playing over yellow hair.

Laughter. Silk sliding across satin.

Water flowing.

The subtle movement of a smile that reached into the depths of his heart.

"Guinevere," he whispered.

Outside he could hear the wind rushing around the eaves of the tavern.

Darkness.

Light being washed away in blood.

Pain.

Green eyes swept away in a flood of red.

Another voice rang in his mind as well, the voice of the man, the man who had been his best and truest friend.

"Swear by all that you hold sacred that you will stand for the right. That your sword will defend women, children and all who cannot stand for themselves."

"This I do swear."

"Then stand forth and join us at the table as our brother. Rise Sir Lancelot."

Over the years he had answered to many names, worn many faces, and now it was DuLane who opened his eyes, staring at the girl.

"Ginnie," he said. His voice a hollow echo within the storm. It might be Ginnie's face, but it wasn't her. That much the man who had been Lancelot du Lac knew in his heart.

She probably had never heard of Guinevere the Queen, except as a sad ballad at harvest time. DuLane forced himself to stand, turning away from the girl's sleeping form. He could feel her blood, still, pulsing just below the skin, a sweet wine that could bring him strength and touch places in him nothing else had ever touched.

He remembered the oath he had sworn that long ago day in Camlin, or, as it was remembered now, Camelot. On his knees before the throne, feeling the steel of Excaliber as it touched each of his shoulders in turn. The words burning into his very soul.

"Swear by all that you hold sacred that you will stand for the right. That your sword will defend women, children and all who cannot stand for themselves."

He had broken that vow many times over the years, as the centuries had rolled by; he knew he would again.

Only not this time. He would not touch her.

———

Emma came awake with a start. She had to struggle for every breath of icy air.

The feeling that she wasn't alone filled her.

For a long time she lay unmoving, waiting. But all Emma could be certain of was that a slight mist seemed to hang in the still air near her.

It faded slowly away.

———

The wind whipped through DuLane, cutting beneath his cape to his heavy fleece vest and jacket. If there was a warm spot on him, he didn't know where it was. At the moment he really didn't care.

DuLane bent forward as he slid through the barn's side door. Inside he could hear the sounds of the animals murmuring. His own horse, along with its tack, was in the stall at the far end.

He cursed a small cat that brushed against his leg. The feline hissed, then vanished into the shadows. None of the horses or cattle took even the slightest notice of him.

The sound of the wind faded to a distant drone as DuLane moved among the animals. He selected a small shaggy pony, one belonging to the innkeeper, and then touched the animal between the eyes. The strength of the animal echoed in its blood. DuLane could feel his fangs sliding into place as he drank deeply from the animal.

A few minutes later, the Hunger had once more faded into the background. DuLane wished that the memories of Ginnie, Arthur, and all the others were so easily put away.

From the other side of the barn came a voice. His hand dropped to his sword as he listened. Singing? The barn was divided into three sections. The largest was given over to the animals, as it should have been; the other two were for storage.

DuLane recognized the words as being Latin. Some sort of hymn?

That there were plenty of empty rooms in the inn made this all the more curious, not to mention the weather being a good argument for remaining indoors. He crept close to the far wall, peering through a crack in the wood.

It was a monk, but not Brother Ellis. No, this one was younger, a teenager at best, his arms wrapped tight around himself for warmth, the singing obviously an attempt to keep himself awake. Brother Ellis had mentioned a companion, Brother Francis. Obviously this had to be him. Perhaps he was serving some sort of penance and barred from the company of others.

Prudence no doubt would have dictated that DuLane not involve himself in the monks' business. But curiosity had been his downfall on more than one occasion in the past.

Shifting again to mist, he drifted into the room, coming back into human form so that he was standing just behind the monk. DuLane grabbed the man by the shoulders, his fingers grinding into hard taut muscle, as he pulled the young man to his feet in a single motion.

The two men's faces were only inches apart. DuLane reached out with his mind and seized the monk's will, freezing it before the young man was even sure what had happened to him.

"You cannot move," he commanded. The young monks face went slacked jawed, his lips hanging open as if waiting for the sounds of the next verse of the hymn to come forth. "Now then, Brother," he said, stepping away from him. "I have a few questions for you."

Before DuLane could say anything else he realized that they were not alone. Hunched up in the far corner of the room was a man, bound hand and foot, not even with a blanket covering him against the cold.

"So, now I see it. You're a guard," said DuLane. "That looks like a truly dangerous fellow."

The prisoner was gray and bent, his hair matted and covered with blood and dirt. One of the man's eyes began to open, slowly, unfocussed in the dark, turning toward DuLane. "Why have you come?" The prisoners voice was a cracked whisper. "Haven't they tormented me enough?"

"Who can say what is enough," asked DuLane. "You ask who I am. Tell me who you are."

The prisoner did not speak. DuLane repeated himself. He was reluctant to try to influence the man's mind; it seemed to be on the edge of becoming unhinged.

"If you don't know me, then it is best that I be forgotten. I only wish I had been. I don't even know me anymore."

There was something about the raspy voice that sounded like one DuLane had known, once a long time ago.

"I'm not here to hurt you," DuLane said.

"Then you are a dream, a nightmare, given to torture me. If you're not here to hurt me, then help me," he pleaded. "If nothing else, kill me."

DuLane found a water skin hanging from the guard's chair. He squeezed a palmfull of liquid into his hand. Lifting the prisoner's head, he offered a few drops to him.

"Help me," the man said.

DuLane stared at him. "Why do I let myself get into things like this?" he asked no one but himself.

Turning back to Brother Francis, DuLane shook his head as he stared at the young man.

On occasion, DuLane had wondered if people he controlled this way were aware of what went on around them. Not that it mattered. A few words, a gentle push with his. voice and the entire encounter would become at best a fleeting memory.

"All right, monk, it's time that we talked," he said. "What do you know of this man?"

The young friar seemed to have trouble finding his voice. "He is a heretic. Arrested at the order of the Bishop of Marseilles, to be handed over to the Inquisition."

"What has he done?"

"I don't know, beyond the fact that he stands accused of heresy. Brother Ellis ordered me to accompany him and the other brothers. He didn't tell me why. I didn't ask."

"I don't believe you, Brother. Even monks have their gossips and I refuse to believe that the Inquisition does not have theirs. You may not have been told it officially, but I'm sure you've overheard a thing or two." DuLane reached out and pushed with his mind, into the thoughts of the young monk.

"Y-y-y-yes...I overheard about him. He is a member of a dissolved outlaw order...monks...warrior monks. Brother Ellis thinks that he can lead us to some of their supporters here in France," he said.

An outlaw order? Now that was interesting, thought DuLane. "I've heard nothing of any recent dissolvings of any of the martial orders."

"It was a long time ago. I heard them mention the papal bull that dissolved them, the *Vox in Excedo.* I had never heard of it either. Brother Ellis told me to mind my prayers and do as I was told."

DuLane arched an eyebrow at those words. He knew that document all too well. *The Vox in Excedo* had been issued by Pope Clement V to formally dissolve the *Pauperes Commilitones Christi Templique Salomonis*, the Poor Fellow-Soldiers of Christ and the Temple of Solomon. The Knights Templar. The thing was, that had been more than eighty years ago.

"Are you saying he's a Templar?"

"Y-y-y-y-es. That's what Brother Ellis thinks." Even though they had been extinguished in France, chapters of the Templars had found homes in Portugal and Scotland, many of them prospering. Mayhap this unwary fellow was Templar after all.

"So who is he? Does he have a name?"

"I heard someone called him Penne. Oliver de Penne."

Penne! A chill went through DuLane. He looked over at the figure on the floor. It couldn't be! Oliver de Penne had been one of the prime instruments in the betrayal of the Templars during that dark October so many decades before. He had traded his own life and safety for those of hundreds of his brothers in the order.

"If that is who he really is, then he deserves everything that you and yours can do to him, and more."

The engraving on the medallion was worn, but DuLane didn't have to see it to know that it showed two figures, a pair of knights seated on a single horse. Around the edge were the words, written in Latin *"Non nobis domine non nobis sed nomini tuo da gloriam."* —Not to us, Lord, not to us, but to thy name give glory.

It had been in Jerusalem, in a place that some said had been built on the remains of Solomon's Temple, that DuLane, then called Karl Ramirez, had first heard those words.

There, on the hot sands of the Holy Land, in a place given over by Baldwin II, King of Jerusalem, he'd sworn the vows that made him a Templar. The others who stood there that night had little known that one of their number had stood once in Camelot and now walked the world as a vampire.

DuLane turned the medallion over and over in his hands, remembering faces, voices, comrades, all fallen into dust, just as the order had a hundred a and fifty years after its founding. Not because there was no longer a need, but, thanks to the cruel betrayal and greed of King Philip of France, the Pope and one of the Templars, himself a betrayer whose name, for DuLane and the surviving brothers, stood with that of Judas Iscariot--Oliver de Penne.

DuLane had barely escaped arrest himself that 13th of October in 1307. Only chance had allowed him to escape Paris. Countless others had been arrested, many tortured and many of them sent to a fiery death at the stake.

Reverently he wrapped the medallion again in what had once been a blood red piece of silk. The colors of the cloth were faded with the passing years, another memory struggling to hold. Then he carefully placed it deep inside his saddle bag.

With a practiced eye he checked the room one more time for anything, any trace of himself he might have left behind. As so many other rooms had been when he had left, the place was empty.

He thought once more of the man in the barn. Was it not such a far stretching miracle that Oliver de Penne might still be alive. Lancelot du Lac still walked the earth. Though the man was not a vampire; DuLane would know one of his own when he saw him..

If this was Oliver de Penne, the betrayer, then better to let the Inquisition have him; they would stretch out the pain far longer than DuLane might; though he was certain that none of them could enjoy it as much as he would

Swear by all that you hold sacred that you will stand for the right. That your sword will defend women, children and all who cannot stand for themselves.

This I do swear.

Then stand forth and join us as our brother. Rise, Sir Lancelot.

For a long moment DuLane heard his own voice and he also heard Oliver de Penne's plea. *"Help me."*

It would be far better to take himself away from here..now.

DuLane had no sooner stepped into the hallway than he heard the creaking of hinges just behind him. Wrapping himself in shadows, he watched a single candle pass, held by the serving girl, Emma. She moved slowly, careful to make as little noise as possible.

Once she was out of sight, DuLane found himself at a crossroads. He could leave, as had been his plan, but there was gnawing inside him. He wanted to look one more time into the face of the woman that he had loved and hated so many years ago.

Again, he reminded himself that she was not Guinivere. But that did not matter.

The girl had gone straight way to the kitchen. The small candle she had carried was shrouded behind several large boxes.

"Emma?" DuLane said.

The girl turned with a start, her face white with fear. In her hand was a piece of bread and a small sliver of cheese.

"M'lord?"

"It seems we both couldn't sleep." He stepped close enough for her to see him.

"Can I get you something, m'lord?"

"No. I couldn't sleep. I was considering leaving. I have a long road ahead of me."

"Leave? In this weather? It would be hard traveling and dangerous, even for you."

He reached over to touch her cheek. The throbbing of blood, her blood, echoed like thunder to DuLane. Only, the Hunger wasn't there. He had feasted too well. For now it was just a lonely echo. An echo of a love lost that he would never find again.

Ginnie! Ginnie! She had been the center that both he and Arthur had found themselves jointly moving around. It had been Morganna's curse that had wrapped that golden vision that was Guinivere in blood. She then, in turn, had dragged him into the darkness making him into a vampire, as was she.

Together the two men that had loved her, along with Merlin, had tracked her, who had once been the Queen of Camelot, to a lonely castle in Scotland. There they had freed her from the curse the only way they could. DuLane could still remember the silent look of peace on her face after it was over.

It had been Arthur who had denied Lancelot the same freedom, for reasons of his own, ones that DuLane had long suspected were a mixture of vengeance and pain and love. The command of his king and the arts of Merlin, imbedded in the wire-wrapped ring Lancelot wore, had allowed him to walk in the sun as a normal human, even if he were no longer one.

The girl pulled back slightly at DuLane's touch. No doubt other patrons had approached her, with fairly obvious intentions. No doubt that with the proper persuasion, she had and could be most accommodating.

"Don't worry," he told her. "I have no amorous plans for you, little Emma."

"You don't?" She sounded both puzzled and hurt, cocking her head slightly in the same way that Guinevere had the first summer he had met her.

"No," he said gently.

"You loved her? And she hurt you? Now you don't know what to do?"

This time it was DuLane who was surprised. "That's right."

"And I reminded you of her?" She smiled with the faintest bit of seduction on her face.

It occurred to DuLane that he had become something of a challenge for this village girl. "You seem much wiser than I expected," he said.

"Me?" chuckled Emma. "I'm so stupid that the local priest couldn't even properly teach me my letters. Not that he should have been trying, anyway. He had other plans for me."

DuLane laughed. The sound seemed alien here in the darkness. "Even so, Emma, let me pose you a question. If you had once, a long time ago, sworn a mighty oath that bound your very heart and soul, would you stand by it? Even if you were the only one who remembered it. Even if it involved doing something for someone that you hated with every fiber of your being?"

It was Emma's turn to laugh. "Oaths, binding your heart and soul? M'lord, you're talking words that are too much for my head. I don't know if I can tell you the things that you want to hear. Just do what is right. Perhaps we can talk about it later, upstairs where it is warmer, together."

"Perhaps, but not right now."

———

Midnight.

Brother Francis had taken to pacing about the room. He occasionally stopped and warmed his hands in front of the brazier, though his breath still hung in the air.

"Doesn't this man ever sleep?" DuLane muttered. He'd implanted the idea, not only to forget his earlier visit, but that the young monk should sleep. The latter idea seemed to be something Brother Francis was unable to do.

No time like the present, he muttered, and transformed into mist.

He was in the room in a matter of seconds, but before he could resume solid form, the outside door flew open, wind and rain rushing in with two people in its wake.

"Brother Ellis?" asked the younger monk. "What are you doing here at this hour?"

The older man had a tight grip around the arm of Emma. She followed him, struggling with every step.

"Is there a problem?" the young monk asked.

Brother Ellis looked grimly around the room, face wrinkled in disapproval, as he sniffed the air.

"We may have trouble tonight," Ellis said. "This little lost lamb was consorting with a man who was acting a bit too strange to suit me."

"You think he's a Templar, sent here to free de Penne?"

"I don't know what he is. I overheard a part of a conversation between him and this wench in the kitchen. It made me expect a visit from the man tonight, so I brought her, maybe as a bargaining point, maybe not. It never hurts to be prepared," Ellis said.

All the while de Penne hadn't stirred; he lay a huddled mass in the corner. Asleep, unconscious, or dead, observed DuLane. The last would solve a number of problems.

Leaving Emma in the hands of his young cohort, Brother Ellis walked over to de Penne. "You are in a great deal of trouble, my friend. You will speak, have no doubt about that." DuLane found himself wondering if Ellis was addressing de Penne or him. "You cannot escape God's justice. Like your grandfather, you will help us to exterminate this vile plague of the Temple."

Grandfather? Now that was interesting. It would explain a few things. It was far easier to believe than this was the same de Penne that DuLane had known. But it didn't really matter who he was; it had never really mattered. DuLane had simply forgotten that. In his mind he saw the Templar medallion that he had hung around his neck. *"Non nobis domine non nobis sed nomini tuo da gloriam."* Not to us, Lord, not to us, but to thy name give glory and heard his oath as a knight of Camelot echo in his ears. "to defend those who asked for his help."

Shifting his insubstantial self as close as possible to Brother Francis, DuLane took solid form again.

This time his hand was knotted into a fist and hurling toward the monk. It connected with the man's chin, the impact staggering the monk. That was long enough for DuLane to hit him again. The monk went down with a most satisfying thud.

Brother Ellis turned, rising as he moved; a sword that DuLane hadn't' noticed leaped from the sheath around the man's robes. Ellis was fast, far faster than DuLane might have expected, moving with a speed that he did not hesitate to use to his own advantage.

DuLane's own sword came free, he moved to one side at the same time, feeling rather than seeing his opponent's blade pass within inches of his body. There was a not a lot of area for maneuvering in this part of the barn.

Shadows mixed with what little light there was as metal clanked against metal in the darkness.

Whatever advantage DuLane gained, the monk countered quickly, as did DuLane on the monk. It seemed a contest of endurance. Then, as quickly as it had begun, something unexpected happened.

A cat, perhaps the same that had confronted DuLane earlier, leaped out of the rafters, screeching, to strike against his face and chest. Claws dug into flesh, hissing filled the air. DuLane twisted and tried to push the animal away.

That was enough of an opening for the monk. His sword slid through leather, cloth and fleece to drive itself hard into DuLane's flesh.

Pain. DuLane managed to shove the cat off as he went down to his knees, sword falling from weakened fingers. A curse in guttural French managed to escape his lips.

"I don't know who you are, Templar, bandit or hired assassin, and frankly, I don't care," the monk said.

Ellis pulled his sword free. DuLane watched his blood follow it, leaving a dark stain on his tunic vest and a trail of dots across his clothing and onto the floor. At least he had the style not to rub the thing in and clean it with my own clothes, DuLane observed.

The pain in his chest had already begun to fade. DuLane knew that deep within him torn muscles, broken veins, and ripped cartilage had begun a tedious route to mending themselves.

"Aren't you going to give me Last Rites?" whispered DuLane.

"I'm a monk, not a priest. Sometimes I think you heretics would have trouble telling your right hand from your left," said the monk.

"I have not been declared a heretic, yet. So brother, hear my confession while there is still time," he said.

"Very well," Brother Ellis knelt beside DuLane. "Are you prepared to confess your sins, renounce your heresy and free yourself of sin in the sight of God?"

"I am." DuLane's voice was a raspy whisper.

"Then I will hear your confession, my son."

DuLane managed a faint smile. "Thank you, brother. My confession is…I don't like you."

His hand shot up and grabbed the monk's robe. DuLane's leg trembled under him as he struggled to his feet. Holding the other man at arm's length, DuLane felt the battle rage filling him.

"I could prolong this," he said. "At another time I might have, but not now."

With that, he slammed the monk down hard against his knee. The sound of bones breaking filled the barn. From the cross beams above them came the satisfied sound of an owl's hoot.

Brother Ellis tried to say something, but blood filled his lips and then he went limp.

Through the whole scene Emma had stood quietly against the wall. Her face was a mask of confusion, looking from DuLane to the unconscious form of Oliver de Penne

"What are you? A demon?" she asked.

"Just a man," DuLane answered. "A man who has had to do things that you might not understand because he was a man and had pledged himself and his honor."

She stepped closer, looking at his chest. The dark patch of blood had grown bigger. "We've got to get a doctor to stitch that together or you'll die."

"I hardly think that is what I need."

Emma held her hand out to him. DuLane took it, his fingers gently wrapping around her wrist.

As his lips touched her skin, it was the sweetest wine that Lancelot had tasted in nearly eight centuries.

✦

CENTRAL PARK

The desk clerk at his hotel had given Anthony Zane a worried look after hearing that Zane was going for a walk in Central Park. It was two a.m., and that was definitely not the sort of behavior that visitors to New York were encouraged to engage in.

"This might not be a particularly safe thing for you to do. Perhaps you might want to wait until the morning," said the desk clerk.

"No. But thank you for your concern," Zane said. "I can take care of myself."

"Whatever you say, sir."

As he walked away from the check-in desk, Zane couldn't help but smile when he overheard a single, muttered word from the clerk.

"Tourist."

Personal safety hadn't been a worry for Anthony Zane in a very long time. Not that he felt any need for weapons, but fourteen hundred years as a soldier made him prefer to err on the side of caution. Tonight, a 9 mm Browning rode in a specially-made shoulder holster under his jacket, and a tempered steel knife lay hidden in a wrist sheath on his left arm. It didn't hurt to take precautions.

He had barely crossed the boundaries of the park when he noticed a group of shadowy figures in the distance. For perhaps five minutes they followed him, but then moved back into the darkness in search of easier prey.

Zane drew out his pipe, filled it with a new blend he had purchased from the tobacconist that afternoon, and fired it up using on old-fashioned wooden match. Once he was happy with the way the mixture was burning, he carefully stubbed out the blackened end of the match and dropped it into his pocket.

Standing in the center of a small stone bridge in the southwestern part of the park, he could look out over a small stream at a grassy knoll at the far

109

end of the bridge and up at the moon, letting the sounds of the city fade, if only for a moment, into a distant murmur.

"It certainly isn't Camelot, but it does sort of remind me of that little stream about ten miles or so into the woods, near the waterfall."

"Oh, Lance, this place is just so lovely. It makes me want to stay here forever and listen to the sound of the stream and the birds."

Lancelot looked down at the face lying against his shoulder. He reached up and gingerly touched her cheek. The resulting smile sent a feeling of calm through him.

"Ginnie, I'm afraid if we tried to do that there would be a squad of knights out scouring the forest in a matter of hours," he said.

"But how would they know where to look? We could lose ourselves here, forget politics, forget wars, just make a life for ourselves."

"Ginnie, oh, my Ginnie, if only we could. But you and I both know that is impossible. Neither of us was raised that way. I know my best friend. If we are gone too long he will have a squad of lancers out searching for us, probably convinced that we have been murdered by bandits or taken for ransom by some rival."

"I suppose so. Arthur does tend to look on the gloomy side of things at times. But, for a few hours, before we have to go back, and I admit we do have to go back, let's just live for ourselves," she said.

Very slowly, Guinevere began to loosen the cords that held her blouse in place.

Zane knew that voice.

That he hadn't heard the speaker's approach didn't surprise him in the least. He just looked to his left and the man was standing there. The stranger was short, barely coming to Zane's shoulder; his iron gray hair was neatly coiffed, a silver-headed walking stick in his hand. His clothing, though simple, had an elegant cut and an expensive air.

"Good evening, Merlin," said Zane. "As I recall, Old Crow, you were always either ensconced in your tower or the catacombs, or enroute to a meeting with Arthur during your tenure at Camelot.

"You never seemed to stop, or even have time for a little bit of fun. So it rather surprises me that you even noticed the forest, let alone a stream."

"That's what Nimue was always telling me. She said I needed to just relax a bit," said Merlin. Memories drifted across his face, giving birth to a smile that was gone in a moment. "As if I had the time. I had a kingdom to help maintain. Not only were there dark forces of magic and evil abroad, there were political necessities, balancing acts to be walked between petty rulers, deals to be struck that would buy us a year or a month or even just a few days more of peace."

"Even so, I did manage to steal a few hours when I tried to let my mind linger not on the next thing on the kingdom's agenda, but on her, instead,"

"Indeed?" said Zane.

"Oh, my dear Lancelot. There is a lot more to me than you've ever suspected."

It had been almost a century since anyone had addressed him by the name he had been born with, Lancelot du Luc.

"Otherwise, how, 1,400 years after the fall of Camelot, would I be standing here talking with you? In those days, had anyone suggested it, I would probably have accused them of being quite far gone in their cups."

"Of course. Lancelot du Luc was known to bend his elbow with the best of them," said Merlin. "As have many other men, whose shoes you have walked in, down through the years. Or perhaps I should be addressing you by the name that you go by now. What is it?"

"As if you didn't know."

"Indulge me, Lancelot."

"Zane. Anthony Zane."

"How many names have you worn, over the years? How many lives have you led?"

Zane sighed; it was his time to remember, as dozens of names, some his, some belonging to people he had known, now long dead, ran through his mind.

"Too many, I think; perhaps as many as you," he said. "After awhile one loses track. All of the names, the lives, the people become blurry, distant memories. Much the way Camelot is now, a faint distant memory of a time when things were better, for me and perhaps for the world. Maybe that's what helps me keep my sanity, if I have any left, that is."

Zane noticed a group of three teenage boys approaching the bridge. They were dressed in identical jean jackets, with matching bandannas around their heads, no doubt a local gang 'uniform'. The three of them paused for a moment at the end of the bridge, half in and half out of the shadows. Zane knew predators, or would-be predators, when he them. He shifted just slightly, so he could reach his gun with no problem.

One of the teenagers came toward Merlin and Zane.

"Evening. Don't mean to intrude on the time of two fine-looking gentlemen like your selves," he said.

"Good evening," answered Merlin.

"Gents, let's get right to the point." At that moment the sound of two switchblades opening came from the others. Zane was fairly sure he could see the handle of a gun shoved into one's belt. "We're collecting for our favorite charity this evening, ourselves. So why don't you two hand over your wallets, any jewelry, cell-phones, stock certificates, loose change, you know the drill. Then we'll just leave you two alone and you can get back to making whatever arrangements you were going to, before I so rudely interrupted you."

"I think not," said Merlin.

"I guess we get to have a little fun, cut you up and still get all the goodies," said one of the other boys.

"I'll handle this," said Zane.

"Unnecessary."

With that word Merlin came round, his walking stick raised, and hit the first teenager hard in the stomach. The young man doubled over in pain. Before the other two could do anything, Merlin sketched two quick gestures in the air. All three of the would-be muggers were frozen in place.

"So, what are you going to do now?" asked Zane. "Something creative, I hope, that will leave a lasting impression."

Merlin walked over to each one. First he touched their temples, then placed both of his thumbs on their foreheads just above the eyes. Once he had finished with the last, they dropped their weapons and walked slowly off into the darkness

"Are they going to turn themselves in to the police?"

"Please, Lance, give me credit for more originality than that. Our young friends will have a strange and eerie tale to tell, about how they barely escaped with their lives from a horrendous monster.

"If the rumor mill, not to mention the local tabloid press, works the way I expect it, two days from now people will say that there are a half dozen such beasts prowling the park.

"After that, our young friends will find themselves drawn to a profession that is more honest and worthwhile, perhaps professional wrestling," he said.

"My compliments, Merlin," said Zane.

"Thank you. Now, getting back to the question of your sanity. You are quite sane; I have no doubt about that. If you weren't, then you wouldn't have any worries about your sanity," said Merlin.

"You're as reassuring as some of the talk shows," said Zane.

The old magician laughed, pointing in a southwesterly direction. "I think the last time I saw you was not quite a hundred years ago. Just outside of Teddy Roosevelt's office at the Port Authority."

"You still haven't lost your ability to change the subject at the drop of a hat. Besides, Theodore's office was at City Hall, not the Port Authority," said Zane.

"Oh, yes. I suppose it was, wasn't it."

"So how did you know I was here?" asked Zane.

"I have my ways."

"Come now, Merlin. I've known you far too long to let you get away with a comment like that."

Merlin reached over and touched the heavy ring on Zane's right hand. In its center were two stones, one gray and one amber, wrapped in wire. The amber one began to glow, illuminating three tiny dots of red at the center.

"Let's just say I always know when my work is near," he said.

Zane stared at the ring. He needed no light to see the glow; he rarely needed light to see anything. Three tiny bits of blood: Arthur's, his own and Ginnie's; he knew they were there, where they had been for fourteen hundred years.

——

"Lancelot!"

Merlin grabbed Lancelet's sword arm. The French knight had not even realized a weapon was in his hand.

A dozen steps away stood Arthur Pendragon. In the long months since Guinevere had fled Camelot his hair had grown grayer and the lines in his face deeper. The king's iron grip held his queen by her arms, even as she struggled to escape his hands.

Only this was not the beautiful woman who had dazzled all of Camelot. This woman, her skin white and bloodless, was snarling like a beast. In the flickering torchlight Lancelot could see the long incisor fangs and the blood that ran from them, staining her lips and face.

"Lance! Lance! Help me! You've got to help me. Arthur and Merlin are mad. They want to murder me!"

Guinevere.

The Queen.

The women that both Lancelot and Arthur loved.

That voice, whispery and sensual, was the same one that had enchanted him and haunted his memory since the first day he had arrived at Camelot. He had seen her standing near a flower-covered lattice, supervising one of the many gardeners who worked around Camelot, and from that moment Lancelot du Luc had been in love.

"No," said Merlin. "She can never be yours or Arthur's, again. If you truly want to free her it must be done my way."

Merlin held a sharpened stake of hawthorn wood, three feet long, in his left hand. Lancelot looked at it, Ginnie and then at his best friend.

Arthur nodded.

Merlin moved toward Guinevere.

——

"You know I wanted to die that night, the night we killed her. And I should have, as well. One vampire died that night; killing a second one would have been no problem," he said

"Even after she had ripped your very soul to shreds and made you a creature of the night, you still loved her," said Merlin.

"Of course. One's heart knows little of the real world, of political realities, of dabbling among the shadows and the light. Yes, she made me into a vampire, nosferatu, a blood drinker, a creature of the night. But that doesn't change the way I felt about her, even to the end."

"I know, and she would have approved of what I did for her and for you. Thanks to my arts, I gave you back the day, and helped to add to the strength within yourself to fight the Beast that consumed her," he said.

"Yes, but why did it have to be with *her* blood?"

"And your own. It was that blood and the love that you had for her, she for you and Arthur for both of you that gave you back some measure of your humanity."

"Humanity? Was that what it gave me, or an eternity of punishment, full of recriminations and pain?"

"We had no choice in the matter, Lance, no choice at all. I needed you, Arthur needed you, the kingdom needed you, to help hold it together. They needed a hero, and that is what you were and are, my friend, a hero, nothing more, nothing less," said Merlin.

"So what did me being this hero get us, the table broken, Camelot fallen, Arthur dead and every bit of good we had done lost to the winds of history. What did it accomplish? To most people now Camelot is an hour and a half in a dark room with pretty pictures flashing on the screen, a book of tall tales or a bunch of people prancing about on the stage singing.

"As for me being a hero? Now, that's a laugh. I fought to stay alive, to hold the Hunger at bay. I wasn't always that successful; when the Hunger came over me it was more beast than soldier that my foes faced," said Zane.

"Lancelot, Lancelot, after all these centuries, you still tend to feel sorry for yourself at the drop of a hat," Merlin said. "I suspect that if I could change one thing about you it would be that."

"Lancelot."

The chill that went through Zane was as cold as the grave. It was not the low familiar voice of Merlin.

He turned toward the figure standing next to him. It wasn't the small, neatly dressed one of Merlin; the magician was nowhere to be seen. He had been replaced by a tall lean figure dressed in chain mail, a rough woolen cape around his shoulders, a familiar long sword hanging at his side.

Arturius Rex. Arthur Pendragon.

"Remember, as long as you live, no matter where you go, everything that we have believed in, fought for, died for, will continue. As long as you live, Camelot lives."

"My liege, I am not worthy of the trust that you placed in me."

"You are worthy, my brother. You have proved it many times over the years, and will continue to do it."

Then Merlin stood at Zane's side once again. "He knew this road would not be easy for you. That's what made him such a good commander and king for so long."

"But not for long enough," said Zane.

"Lance. Look, we've had this conversation before, why are you bringing it up again?"

"Maybe because you're the only one around who can understand me, even a little bit, Merlin. After all, how many other people are there walking the streets of New York who have stood on the same piece of land as Richard the Lionhearted and The Beatles?

"I've been struggling with the idea that all I've done has been for nothing, that no matter how much trust Arthur had in me it was for naught. I struggle and it seems to do no good.

"Plus, there is the date. I think the reason I'm so despondent is the date. Fourteen hundred years ago, this very night, I watched you drive a stake through the heart of the woman that I loved."

"You think you're the only one who loved her, Lance? Arthur loved her; it may have been an arranged marriage but he still cared for her. All of the kingdom loved her. I loved her, in my own way, like a daughter," said Merlin.

Before he could say anything else, Merlin looked down at the ground.

"Well, it seems we are not alone," he chuckled.

Standing next to the magician's leg was a gray tiger-striped cat. The animal didn't appear to be afraid; it just stood looking at Zane and Merlin as if it expected to be the center of their universe. Carefully, Merlin reached down and picked the cat up. The animal studied the two men, then began to wriggle itself around until it could shove its head up under Merlin's chin and began to rub.

"I think you've made a new friend," said Zane. "I'm sure you could use one."

Merlin ignored the comment, but did begin to run his hand along the cat's back.

"Lancelot! You have a problem."

"I know that, so be serious, please."

"I'm very serious, young man, and you are a young man compared to me; and don't go asking how much older than you I am; you won't get an answer. Look, given everything that has happened to you since you left Joyous Guard, I can understand that you are feeling depressed. Hell, you would be insane if you weren't, and I think we have established your sanity.

"There have been times when I felt the same way. Like you, I have buried friend after friend, watched those I love die, the work of decades crumble away to nothing, wondered why I even bothered.

"I think what you need to bestir you from this blue mood, friend Lancelot, is a quest," said Merlin.

"A quest?"

"Yes! A quest!"

"For what? The Holy Grail? Been there, done that."

"I know; I was the one that suggested to Arthur that you and the rest of the Knights be dispatched to search for it. Besides, you wouldn't need to look far for The Grail. It's in my New Orleans condo, next to one of the bird statue props from **The Maltese Falcon**."

"Then what?"

Merlin didn't say a word. Instead, he shoved the cat into Zane's arms. The animal was as startled as Zane. After a second or so it attempted to scramble out of his hands, first by leaping down to the ground, then by sinking its claws into his jacket and scrambling over his shoulder. However, Zane's hands went tight around the cat's body and held it firmly in place.

"There is your quest, Sir Lancelot du Luc!"

"Have you lost all grip on reality, man? What in the hell are you talking about?"

"Your quest is to find this cat's owner and return it to him."

"Yeah, right, some '*quest*'."

"Whoever in hell told you that all quests had to be grand things with lives and the fates of nations balanced on the edge of your blade? Did you not swear an oath to do whatever you could to help not just the greatest but the least of people who were in distress?"

"You know I did," said Zane.

"Well, this cat is too friendly to be a feral animal, so it obviously belongs to some family who is no doubt in distress at its disappearance. So there you have your quest; find that family and help them," he said.

"Why don't you just turn yourself into a cat and escort the animal home? I think that would be much simpler," said Zane.

"Lance, you've read too much T. H. White and seen too many Disney movies. You know that shapechanging was never in my repertoire. So get on with it," he said.

Zane realized that he had begun to gently rub the cat behind its ears. He was about to say something to Merlin when he realized that he and the cat were alone.

"So, why don't you tell me where you live?" Zane said to the cat.

———

A little after ten o'clock the next morning, Zane had a cab drop him on West 35th street. He knew the area. A few blocks further on was the office-home of a private detective he had occasionally had dealings with.

From his pocket he produced a small piece of paper, an address written on it. The cat, who rode quietly in the crook of his left arm, watched the whole thing with an air of indifference.

It had not been all that difficult a task to find the cat's owner. Covered by the animals long hair was a rather expensive collar, complete with the name of the pet shop where the collar had been custom made. Two phone calls and a ride across town had brought Zane and his companion here.

A moment or two after ringing the doorbell, the light on the intercom came on.

"Yes, can I help you?"

"I believe that you folks are missing a cat."

"Lancelot?"

Zane froze at the sound of the name. The door came flying open, a small form barely four feet tall appeared and the cat leaped toward it.

"You're back! Mommy, Lancelot is back!"

Zane found himself looking at a young girl; he guessed her at about ten years old, with long blonde hair hanging down to her waist. She clutched the cat to her chest like the long lost member of the family that it was.

"I'd say you are home," he said to the cat.

"She's been worried sick about that fool cat for three days," said a woman standing just behind the girl. She was the image of the child, 20 years later, lithe figure, long blonde hair, a knowing smile. "Hi, I'm Elaine Appleton."

"Anthony Zane. I'm just glad I was able to bring....what was his name? Lancelot back," he said.

"Camelot just hasn't been the same without you." The girl ignored the two adults and spoke directly to the cat, who acted as if it were his due. Which, in the cat's opinion, it was.

"Camelot?" asked Zane.

"That's what she calls her playroom, where the cat sleeps. She is totally enamored of this Knights of the Round Table thing. She has a very vivid imagination," said the girl's mother. "But then, considering her name, I suspect it would be a little hard not to."

"Her name?"

"Guinevere, Ginnie for short."

Zane felt a hard lump in his throat. Yet it was good feeling. The quest had come to a very good conclusion.

"Mommy, may I show this nice man Camelot?"

"Ginnie, I think, he probably doesn't have time."

"On the contrary, I have plenty of time," Zane said. "Lady Guinevere, if your Lady mother will give permission, and would join us, I would love to see Camelot."

"Good! Then it's on to Camelot!"

———

A crow with gray streaks cutting across its black feathers sat on a tree branch just outside of the brownstone door. Teaching lessons to hard-headed warriors was not a new experience for him.

The bird lingered for a few minutes after Zane had gone inside, then leaped into the air. Maybe it was time to take that vacation that Nimue was always nagging him about.

✦

FINAL SCORE

"Can I get you something, m'lord?"

For a moment, Ashe was sitting once again at his favorite table, just to the right of the door at the Bearded Cockerel Tavern. The place was a dump; the thatched roof needed patching, the rafters were cracked and burned and the ale was heavily watered, but the memory of it was as precious to Ashe as anything. That was a moment he would have given anything to make last.

"M'lord?"

As they all do, memories fade. Only this time Ashe found himself facing something *almost* as pleasant. A young woman, dressed in a dark green blouse and brown skirt of a style that would have been at home on any of the tavern wenches at the Bearded Cockerel.

He caught himself about to address her as Cassie, the name of a woman near fourteen hundred years dead. But Cassie would never have been wearing a pager on her belt and a button with the inscription "Goes From Zero to Bitch in 4.5 Seconds."

"I'm sorry. I let my mind wander a bit," he said.

"It's early," she smiled.

"So, what can I get for you, m'lord?" The girl was at least not trying to affect a British accent. Most of them came off sounding like something you hear on reruns of *Fawlty Towers.*

She was one of several employees in what had been dubbed The Cross-eyed Tavern; one of over two dozen refreshment tents and booths that were part of the three-day-long Medieval Fair staged by the University of Oklahoma.

In the twenty years since its beginnings, the Fair had outgrown its original campus site. Now it was staged at a nearby park, in the shadow of the towering gothic spires of the university's library and Owen Stadium, home of the O.U. Sooners football team.

119

"I don't feel like coffee this morning, and it seems far too early for anything stronger," said Ashe. "With those restrictions, what would you suggest, m'lady?"

"I take it caffeine is your drug of choice?"

"Exactly."

"Well then, we do have several very good breakfast teas." She pointed toward a large chalkboard just to the right of the bar.

Ashe scanned the list. Most of them had names like King Charles Best and Queen Anne's Delight.

"Try the Prince Alfred special. It's really a variation of Earl Gray, heavy with caffeine."

"Kind of the Jolt Cola of teas?"

"Exactly!"

Ashe accepted a styrofoam cup from her. The smell was strong. He had tasted better, much better, but for the circumstance this was far better than he had expected.

The girl watched him for a moment. "Is this your first time?"

"Drinking tea?"

"No, at Med. Fair, silly?" she laughed. Ashe smiled at the sound of her laughter. It was a momentary light in the darkness.

"Yes. I've been to some in other places, but that was a long time ago."

"If you want a guide, stop by just after noon. I'll be off work then."

"Maybe," said Ashe.

"No maybe about it."

———•———

Ashe sipped his tea as he watched the sea serpent. It wallowed from side to side in an ungainly dance, slowly cris-crossing the small man-made pond. The water was just dirty enough to hide the guide wires that were pulling it, unless someone stood on the stone bridge and watched for more than a few minutes. An odd-looking section of rock next to the bridge seemed to be where the motor had been hidden.

It had been the serpent that had brought Ashe to Norman, Oklahoma, and to the Medieval Fair.

He didn't need to pull the much folded sheet of yellow paper out of his wallet.

It featured an elaborate pen and ink rendering of a sea serpent rearing its head out of the water, the turrets of a castle in the background. Duplicates of it, blown up to poster size, had been spread out all across Norman and surrounding towns announcing the three days of the annual celebration.

He had found the flyer crumpled up in the corner of a certain cheap house in a Baltimore suburb. But, knowing the occupant's obsession, it had been enough.

The serpent, at least, was an attempt at something special. Not a too successful one, especially since the rivets in its metal hide were clearly visible, but an attempt none- the-less. Ashe took another drink. The caffeine left a warm, welcome feeling in his throat.

Below him a half dozen ducks and a lone goose paddled across the pond, carefully steering clear of the serpent. It would be quite the unexpected surprise if the beast were to accidentally run down one of the birds. Ashe wouldn't have been surprised if that happened.

"You've got to be less cynical, stop expecting the worst, let yourself enjoy life a little bit more. Don't be so afraid to just live."

He could still hear her voice. Hannah Cortez. Half Spanish, half Irish and bloody proud of both sides of her heritage. When he closed his eyes he could *almost* feel her standing next to him, a gentle touch on his hand, whispered breath along the back of his neck.

"Hannah," he whispered, crushing the Styrofoam cup into pieces, the remaining tepid liquid dripping between his fingers.

Ashe had met her only sixteen months before. It had been a glorious time, a time he had been happy. That any who he loved would die eventually was something he had reluctantly grown used to in the fourteen centuries since he had watched Camelot fall around him. But Hannah had not been taken as a casualty of war or as part of the natural order of things. She had been murdered; cruelly, painfully, slowly.

Now, as he had when he had been a knight of Camelot, when he had been a brother of the Knight's Templar and so many other things, it fell to him to find her killer and exact justice.

Ashe let the styrofoam pieces of his cup fall into the dirt near the bridge.

———

The Medieval Fair actually covered nearly ten acres. Parking fanned out along the edges of the grounds and then snaked down through the neighborhood, forming an intricate kind of spider-web along the streets.

The radio had said that there was a better than fifty percent chance of rain, so he had his choice of whole rows in the parking lot. Until the weather cleared, only the hardiest would venture forth. He hoped the man he was looking for would fit that description.

Ashe walked with no destination in mind. The food booths and the artisan's tents had been laid out in no obvious order or logical pattern that he could discern. Right now he just wanted to look and listen and wait.

Later in the morning, Ashe stood watching a small man dressed in a vaguely medieval costume made up of the most outlandish combination of colors: purple scarf, orange shirt, a black feathered cape. The little man was deep in conversation with a fellow wearing what looked like a dark brown tuxedo jacket, jeans and no shirt.

Ashe smiled.

No doubt the two of them thought they were being outlandish, original, standing out from the crowd. He had seen it all before, more times than he could count, and each time watched the would-be rebels blending into an ocean of sameness.

"You are looking far too philosophical for your own good."

Standing almost at Ashe's elbow was the young woman who had waited on him that morning. She was smiling and had exchanged her apron for a beaded vest and matching gypsy-style head scarf.

"Really?" he said.

"Really."

"Well then, if not philosophical, how should I look?" asked Ashe

"I'm not sure," she said. "Maybe like you were having fun?"

Ashe chuckled. There was something infectious in the girl's attitude. "Hmm…fun? Now what is that?"

"Fun. F…U…N. Fun. It is definitely something that I think you should have," she said. "And I'm going to make sure you have it. Yes, and you can't say you weren't warned. I did tell you this morning that I would see you again."

"Well, seems you were right. If you're that good at predicting things, how are you on the lottery, or maybe the daily double at Fair Meadows Race Track," he said.

"I might be afraid if I were right and just as afraid if I were wrong," she laughed.

"A wise attitude. One that I think a lot of so-called seers would have been better for, had they adopted it," he said.

"You *are* quite the philosopher, m'lord, *quite* the philosopher. I've not heard many of the fellows around here saying things like that. They mainly speak longingly of the glories of war and the prowess they would bring to battle," she said.

Memories of battles without end danced among Ashe's memories; the pain, the stink of blood, the screams of the dying, the utter exhaustion that permeates a soldier, both in the body and soul after a battle.

"The only honor in battle is in having survived. The only glory comes in those tales told by fools and the songs sung by minstrels. A great adventure is what you have when you're telling the tale over a pint and a good meal afterwards; when it's happening you're scared out of your wits and certain that you will die in the next second, if you're thinking at all. Anyone who isn't is a fool, a fanatic or a fake," he said.

"You certainly don't sound like the medieval reenactment guys I've been hanging around with," she said.

"Each to their own. It occurs to me, m'lady, that I have not had the honor of knowing your name."

She grinned and curtsied, almost colliding with a boy in a jester's hat. "M'lord, I. am Serina de Lyman. I am most pleased to meet you."

Ashe bowed at the waist in the courtly fashion that he had been taught in Italy.

"A beautiful name for a beautiful lady. I am Landon Ashe."

"Actually," she smiled. "It's actually Serina Smith. I added the last part for the Fair and for medieval reenactment events."

"None-the-less, it is lovely. So when do you have to be back at work?"

"By pure chance, I'm off for the rest of the afternoon."

"Pure chance, indeed? Since I'm a stranger in town myself, I'm still in need of someone to show me around the fair."

Serina grinned. "I think we can find you a guide."

"That is a most unusual stone in your ring, sir. I don't think I've ever seen one like it before."

Ashe and Serina were standing in front of the large tent of a vendor who dealt in jewelry which ranged from lost wax designs to wire wraps to what appeared to be hand made specialty designs. Serina had spotted a small necklace done in a Celtic design around the profile of a bird in flight.

Ashe nodded. The ring was unusual, the stone a piece from the Giant's Dance, and crafted by no less than Merlin.

"The man who made it was an old friend. He gave it to me for luck."

Ashe couldn't help but smile at that. Over the years he had called Merlin many things; in those first days, when Ashe had been known as Lancelot, that had actually included friend.

"And has it brought you luck, sir?" the jeweler asked.

"I suppose you could say that."

"Well, if you were inclined to part with it, I have an idea it would fetch a pretty penny. The workmanship is so detailed. I'm not sure what kind of stone that is, but it is one that holds the eye." The thing was, if Ashe did part with it, the effects, especially if he were caught out in the direct sunlight, would be most unpleasant and very painful. He did not like to recall the few times that had happened.

"So, what do you think? Is it me?" Serina held the necklace around her neck. It hung to the edge of her low cut blouse, the silver surface shining against her skin.

"It looks as if he made it with you, and only you, in mind," said Ashe.

"Oh, get off with you now," she laughed.

Serina had turned to the jeweler when Ashe felt someone grabbing his shoulder pulling him sharply around. He found himself facing a man in his early twenties, dressed in a black and white musketeer's style costume. The man's buzz cut seemed as out of place as a Grateful Dead tee-shirt on a samurai.

"What the hell is going on here?" said the stranger.

"Michael! What do you want now?" yelled Serina. She obviously knew him, and just as obviously did not like him. The young man called Michael ignored her, moving at Ashe until he was only inches from the other man's face.

"What kind of man are you, trying to put the make on my woman?"

The crowd, sensing a fight about to begin, moved back clearing a rough circle in front of the booth.

"Michael! I told you last week that we were through. You're only making a fool out of yourself! What does it take to get through that thick skull of yours, a two by four?" she said.

"Shut up! I'll deal with you later!"

"If I were you, Michael," Ashe said softly. "*I* would take what the lady says to heart. And I would be wary of how I spoke with her, if *I* were you."

"Are you threatening me? You're not me and I don't need your advice!" hissed Michael. As he spoke, a dagger dropped out of his sleeve into his hand.

"I'm tired of this macho bullcrap!" said Serina. Instead of turning away, she jammed herself in between Ashe and Michael.

"Get out of the way, Serina," said Michael. "This is between him and me."

"Wrong answer!" Serina slammed her knee hard into Michael's crotch. His face contorted with the sudden pain, a loud groan rolling out of his mouth. The knife dropped, hitting the side of the counter before it clattered to the ground.

He looked at her, pain, surprise and confusion rolling across his face. He tried to speak, but before he could, Serina punched him hard in the stomach. The impact was enough to send him to his knees. Around them the crowd, who had been yelling encouragement, broke into applause.

"M'lady Serina, it's obvious you don't utter threats," Ashe said. "Remind me never to get you mad at me."

———•———

"I don't know why he can't understand that we're through and I never want to see him again," said Serina.

She and Ashe sat on a small boulder near the pond. Around them the voices that were the Medieval Fair and its participants rose and fell. Serina hadn't spoken for some time, hadn't even looked at Ashe, just watched the ducks and the sea serpent.

It had taken less than a half hour to explain things to the off-duty police officers who were working security for the Fair. Thanks to more than a dozen witnesses, not to mention Michael's fairly long police record, Ashe and Serina had been allowed to go with no problem.

"Just because he said he was sorry after I caught him in the sack with two different women, at the same time, he thinks I should forgive him."

"Two?"

"Yeah, two," she sighed. "When I walked in on them, the asshole had the gall to suggest that I join them in their little games."

"That just proves what I already knew; Michael is an idiot."

"On that we agree." Serina grabbed Ashe and pulled him tightly to her. Their lips met in a hard passionate kiss, her hands moving up and down his back. Ashe's hands responded gripping her shoulders tightly.

"My apartment is only a couple of blocks away. Think you can show a girl a good time, mister?"

"I think I can."

"You better."

———•———

Ashe gently touched Serina's shoulders. Then he began massaging her shoulders and neck. Serina let out a long sigh as his fingers worked her muscles back and forth.

"You only have about a week to stop that," she murmured.

Ashe smiled and continued to work. Every now and again a sound would give him proof of her approval. Slowly, he let his hands begin to work their way from her shoulders, first to her arms then around her breasts. He cupped one, then the other, moving in low regular motion. He began to kiss her neck and then moved gently along her shoulder.

"Oh yes," Serina murmured. She turned, facing him, pushing her breasts hard against his chest.

Ashe felt his fangs sliding into place. He touched them to her wrist, her breasts and then her neck.

"Ah, m'lady," he said softly.

As he drank deeply from Serina, Ashe's hands worked swiftly, slipping her blouse off her shoulders, and then her skirt flowed to pool around her ankles. Her own hands had begun to pull Ashe's clothing off of him.

"I want you," she murmured hard into his ear.

———•———

The party, hosted by the local chapter of the medieval reenactment organization that Serina belonged too, was being held in a loft that covered a half a city block in downtown Norman.

Serina had outfitted Ashe in a knee length tunic, soft suede boots, cape, hood and sword. The style was 10th century Welsh with a dash or two of Scottish.

"You look fantastic. It's like you were born to wear this type of clothing."

"Perhaps I was," he said. "In another lifetime, of course."

"Maybe so, m'lord," she said.

Serina had opted not for her tavern wench outfit but for a more elegant fourteenth century Spanish style gown in green and black. Ashe had noticed her slipping a few things into her belt bag that he definitely didn't remember from that time period, her cellular phone, a roll of breath mints and a canister of pepper spray.

As Ashe and Serina made their way along the street, they spotted a man in Roman armor standing in deep conversation with a woman in a Russian style gown. Nearby, a Japanese samurai was puffing on a corn cob pipe.

"I think this must be the place," Ashe said to Serina.

"I wonder what could have ever given you that idea. Could it have been those two dressed so strangely?" She gestured at a couple of guys, standing in front of a theater marquee across the street; wearing football jerseys and shorts.

"Exactly. They're such an anachronism when compared to normal people like us."

"I'm beginning to wonder about you, m'lord," Serina said, smiling.

"Good," said Ashe.

Serina led them up a long outside stairway. Once inside she was recognized almost at once, even as the door herald announced their arrival. "Lady Serina de Lyman and Lord Landon Ashe."

They were no more than twenty feet beyond the door when someone motioned Serina over. Ashe recognized the woman as the other person he had seen at the tavern tent that morning.

"It's my boss," Serina said. "She's supposed to have the shift schedule for the rest of the Fair."

"Go make nice," Ashe told her. "It always helps to have the boss on your side."

"Okay. This may take a few minutes," she sighed. "Could you possibly get us some wine?"

"No problem."

The walls that had once separated the loft into a variety of rooms had been removed. Screens and curtains had been hung to create smaller areas, but not lose the spacious open feeling. At one end there was organized singing and dancing. In another corner, a demonstration of fighting techniques. Any number of groups were just standing and talking about everything from the Fair to current politics to the latest fantasy movie.

That was when he heard *the voice*. He had heard it only once before, on Hannah's answering machine, but it was something he could not forget. Standing a dozen feet from him was the tall, square, blondish figure whose face matched the Polaroid photo in Ashe's suitcase; the one he had found in the same house as the medieval fair flyer.

The man was a killer. The F.B.I. and a dozen different local police organizations had files on him, by deed but not by name. Eight killings were to his credit, with another four suspected, all in and around medieval and renaissance faires. Ashe had no doubt that there were F.B.I. agents prowling the Faire. He also had no doubt that they would not discover this man in a million years, unless he was presented to them on a silver platter.

"I tell you, m'lords and ladies, we are living in the ass end of history, in the dregs. Society today knows nothing, I say again nothing, of the concept of honor and pride. In older, better times men understood things like that. They were ready to die for honor.

"We saw that today, when one of our own was attacked by a clod who knew nothing of honor, truth or justice. All this scum wanted was a chance to get into the pants of a woman. Then he did not even have the heart to stand and fight himself, he let a woman do it for him!"

The crowds around the man laughed. Ashe had seen these people before, with a hundred different faces in a hundred different places. They courted what seemed new and daring; the minute it bored them they were gone.

"So there you are!" Serina came up behind him, smiling, with two glasses of wine in her hand. "I had the feeling that you would never find the wine. I was wondering where you had run off to. I hoped I wouldn't find you in the arms of some ravishing wench, because I would have had to cut her tits off if I had."

"I would never risk your wrath, m'lady. Besides, why should I settle for second best when I am with the best," he said. "No, I was just listening to this fellow discoursing on what a terrible age we live in."

Serina looked over toward the crowd. The look on her face told Ashe that she knew the man. "I was hoping *he* wouldn't be here tonight. Though I can't honestly say I'm surprised. He blew into town a couple of months ago and has been trying to wrap the entire barony around his little finger. He disgusts me. Michael and he have become best buddies. Sometimes I think that they're attached at the hip, or maybe in some other organ of the body."

"What's his name?"

"Chalker. Ian Chalker. He sometimes uses the medieval name of Rudolph von Tarquin."

"But we're here to have a good time. Come on, there are some people I want to show you off to."

"Your wish is my command."

———

Ashe waited in the parking lot. He had left Serina talking to several other ladies, which suited him just fine. What he needed to do now, he needed to do without her.

Holding himself in the shadows, he watched as the square-shaped figure of Chalker came closer. The sounds of the party drifted out open windows, voices and music blending together like a steady heartbeat.

Chalker had a half empty bottle of champagne in one hand, his car keys in the other. Ashe waited until the man had stopped in front of a station wagon. That was when he came out of the darkness, grabbing Chalker and slamming him hard against the car.

Keys and champagne bottle crashed to the ground. Then he pulled Chalker around, to face him. Ashe's hand, now holding a dagger, pushed the edge against Chalker's throat.

"Move and you're dead! Speak without my permission and you're dead! At this moment you may thank whatever dark gods watch over you that I'm allowing you to continue to breath, even for a little while. Do you understand?" Ashe said.

Chalker nodded.

"Now listen and listen well. I know who you are and I know what you've done. Call yourself Ian Chalker, call yourself Groucho Marx or Stephen King. Call yourself any damm thing you want. I don't care! *I know who you really are!*"

"What are you?" whispered Chalker.

Ashe drove his fist hard into Chalker's stomach. "I told you not to speak unless I said you could. I don't do second chances. You've had your one strike. Next time I will be ripping your lungs out through your ears.

"But I will answer your question. I am fear. I am death. I am everything that you've ever seen when you stared into a woman's face, every bit of pain and terror you've pulled out of all those dead girls over the years. Now, I think it's time you say something in your own defense. If you can even have the gall to try and have one," Ashe said.

"I don't know what you're talking about," Chalker said. "You're insane. If it's money you want, take it. Take the car. My watch is a Rolex, that will get you at least a grand from a fence. Just take them and be gone."

Ashe shook his head. "I don't want your money. I don't want your watch; it's as phony as you are. I've come for your life. That's all that I want. In case it interests you, I'm the one who you were talking about earlier. I'm the one you said had no honor, no sense of pride. My pride and my blood have led me to you. Your friend Michael got the beating he deserved, from the woman he had mistreated. I'm here to give you something of the same."

"Then you're street scum, nothing but the lowest form of trash, you have no idea of how a true man fights his battles, otherwise you wouldn't have ambushed me from behind." Chalker said.

Ashe laughed as he watched the man swelling up with pride. It was the same bravado he had seen earlier in the middle of the crowd.

"One does what one has to. You don't know who it is you are bandying words with about honor and heart, punk. I have forgotten more about true warriors and what it means to fight for honor than you have ever known," said Ashe.

"I'm sure that you know all about honor."

Ashe could feel his fangs sliding into place. The beast within him was struggling to get out. In his mind's eye he could see himself ripping Chalker's throat to bloody shreds. The image overlaid with one of Hannah as he had found her that night four months ago, carved into bloody pieces, her skin carefully removed and laid neatly on a white bridal bed.

"I'm going to give you more of a chance than you deserve."

With his last word, Ashe vanished. Chalker sagged back against his car, his breath coming in ragged gasps.

Then Ashe was there again, his form coalescing out of mist, standing only a few inches in front of Chalker.

"Owen Stadium in one hour. If you are a man of honor as you claim, a man better than this decadent age we live in, be there, with your sharpest sword. If you are not, I will hunt you down like the dog that you are and not give you the mercy I would a dumb animal."

Then Ashe was gone.

An almost tomb-like silence filled Owen Stadium. As Ashe walked along the sidelines, he knew that not a hundred yards away, beyond the southern wall of the stadium, cars were filling up Norman's main drag, the sounds of their engines like a distant buzz of insects. Here there was only silence, and memories.

Football stadiums had always reminded Ashe of the old Roman arenas in Britain and France. The ones close to his family's ancestral holdings had been in ruins, but those near Camelot had been almost intact. The game itself was just another version of cavalry maneuvers, all the players needed were horses and sabers.

He remembered the long debates with Arthur about refurbishing the arenas. Arthur had wanted them left abandoned, remnants of a pagan past, but Ashe, or Lancelot du Lac, as he had been known then, had proclaimed them perfect for cavalry training. In the end, he had won that argument and given Arthur the best mobile infantry of the time.

From a custom-made case in the back of his van had come a broadsword. It had been designed just for him, made of the finest Toledo steel; the blade was razor sharp, the edge honed with infinite patience and practice.

The weapon was hidden by a long overcoat that Ashe carried over his arm. The local police would not be happy if, even during Medieval Fair, someone were caught carrying a sword, especially one like this, away from the event site.

Suggesting that they return to Serina's apartment, Ashe had left her there, asleep, with the implanted idea of a night full of passion to come. He spotted Chalker standing to one side of the home team's bench.

Ashe had discarded his medieval clothing, exchanging them for a black tee shirt, jeans and a biker's leather jacket. Chalker, on the other hand, had gone to the opposite extreme. He now wore a full shirt of chain mail and a tabard emblazoned with a heraldic house badge, a helmet held under one arm and a fearsome looking sword resting on the ground.

"I wondered if you would show up," said Chalker.

"Really?" Ashe chuckled. "Since I issued the challenge, you doubted I would be here? That's muddy thinking; gets you in trouble every time."

"Honorless scum such as you have been known to lose their nerve."

"Honor?"

"I should expect someone like you to know little of honor and to disparage an honorable warrior. It is honor that will guide my blade in a fight," said Chalker.

"Speaking of fighting," said Ashe. "Did you come here to fight or to stand here chattering like a magpie all night. I noticed at the party that you seemed very adept at that latter skill."

The fury in Chalker's eyes blazed as he pulled the helmet over his head. Ashe dropped his jacket and unsheathed his sword.

"I suppose you know you won't walk out of here alive. But before we begin, tell me one thing," said Chalker. "I've never laid eyes on you before tonight. So why?"

"Why? Why do I want your life? Because you are a no good murdering piece of offal that persists in trying to act human. I make no claims to being human myself, but you, sir, are scum. Does the name Hannah Cortez mean anything to you?"

Chalker looked puzzled. "No. Should it?"

Ashe shook his head. "Cleveland. Four months ago. She was tall, with long brown hair, emerald eyes and an enjoyment of life like none I have ever seen. You should remember her. You should remember them all. You killed her, slowly, painfully."

Chalker grinned. He had sensed an advantage and meant to press it. "Oh, yes. Cleveland. Now I seem to recall her. I made her last for four days. Did you realize that she begged me to kill her? But I did it very slowly, very slowly. I made her last and savored each scream.

"You know, it's an art form. I did her a great honor taking her. She was one of the whores, you know. One of the ones that it is my holy charge to rid the world of!"

At that, Chalker pulled his sword up and went for Ashe. Turning to one side Ashe let the other man's blade pass inches away from its target. Chalker whirled and struck again. This time Ashe deflected the blow by pushing his blade hard forward.

That his opponent had experience with a sword was obvious. He knew how to land a blow and to counter more than a few moves. Ashe let himself wait, attacking a few times, mostly to learn, to see how Chalker would react. Ashe himself had not stood to blood combat with a sword in nearly five years. There had been no call. But old skills, learned first in the practice fields of France, honed as one of Arthur's commanders and then used over the centuries, had not faded. Ashe had begun to carefully drive Chalker back when the last thing in the world he expected happened.

Someone fired a shot.

The bullet came from behind Ashe, echoing like a backfiring truck among the empty seats of the stadium. Ashe swung wide and away from Chalker, turning as he moved back toward the stands. The gunman was making no attempt to hide himself. Standing just behind the metal railing at the fifty yard line was the same figure he had seen that afternoon, dressed in a black and white musketeer's outfit. Michael, Serina's ex-boyfriend, his hands wrapped around the butt of a very large gun.

The second shot struck the turf not a foot from where Ashe stood.

"Looks like if I don't get you," laughed Chalker. "He will."

"Some man of honor you turned out to be, having your lackey ambush me!" said Ashe.

"One does what one can," said Chalker.

"I told you to stay away from her. Serina is mine. She will never belong to anyone else," Michael shouted. "I told you! I saw the two of you together, there in her bed rutting like animals! I warned you! Now you're going to pay."

Michael drew the gun up, assuming a firing stance, but before he could fire he suddenly lurched forward, crashing into the railing, the gun flying free from his hand to land on the fifty-yard line below him.

Standing behind him was Serina, a long wooden pole in her hand.

"I told you I'm not your girlfriend any more!" Michael managed to stay on his feet, turning toward Serina. She produced a can of pepper spray and sprayed him directly in the eyes. That sent him screaming to the ground.

Ashe turned just as Chalker charged him. He managed to bring his sword up at the last moment, blocking the edge of the other man's blade as it sliced hard toward Ashe.

"You have no chance against me," Chalker's muffled voice said. "My skill has been honed for lifetimes, generations beyond anything that you can do."

"Indeed?" Ashe said.

Chalker struck at him three times in succession, slicing into the leather that wrapped around Ashe's arm.

"Indeed. My soul is an old one. Once I wore the name of Galahad of Camelot! I learned from the masters: Gawain, Arthur and even Lancelot himself!"

Ashe laughed. The very thought that this "man" could be carrying the soul of Galahad was a repugnant one. He struck hard against Chalker, his sword cutting into the chain mail the man wore.

"You are not Galahad. If your soul were his, he would have killed himself before allowing you to do the things that you have done. I knew Galahad. Galahad was a friend of mine. You're no Galahad!"

"What would you know? You're nothing but street scum, not even fit to clean the stables of Camelot."

"*I*? I am Lancelot!" With those words Ashe drove his sword down hard pushing aside the other man's blade, his weapon cutting deep into chain mail and then flesh of the Chalker's stomach. His foe stood there, staring, uncomprehending. Ashe pulled his blade clear and then drove it into Chalker's neck. The bone and flesh clung together for only a moment, and then cut through. The head lingered where it was for a few seconds, teetering from side to side, before rolling from his shoulders; blood washing it and the green turf.

With a single movement Ashe kicked the head straight between the goal posts.

"He scores, and the crowd goes wild," he said.

———·———

"I hope you take this in the right way," Ashe said. "Understand, I am grateful as all hell, but I would like to know just what you were doing there? I expected you to be sound asleep until morning."

Serina laughed. "You're welcome. You should learn to never take anything for granted."

They had left the stadium quickly, retrieving Serina's bicycle and then heading for an alley near the student union where Ashe had parked his van.

"My place," she said.

"Okay, but I'm still waiting for an answer," he said.

"And I'm still waiting for my stomach to stop churning. It isn't often that I see somebody decapitated," she said.

Ashe could understand her reaction. Even through the dim mists of centuries, he could recall the first time that he had ridden to battle with his father's army. His reaction after the fighting was over had been anything but heroic. The sight of Lancelot du Lac throwing up was not one that fit the legend that had come to be associated with the name. But then again, Ashe had never felt like he wanted to fit *that* image anyway.

"I heard what he said to you," she said slowly. "About killing all those women. Was it true?"

"I only wish it weren't." He wasn't sure if the police would be able to connect Chalker with the killings or if this would be listed as some bizarre gang execution.

"And what about Michael?"

"Oh, him?" grinned Ashe. "I don't think we'll have to worry about a thing with Michael."

Ashe had roused Michael and then carefully *suggested* to him that he had not seen any one of them that night. Instead, Michael had gone out after the medieval party and gotten plastered, failed miserably when he tried to pick up a couple of coeds, then headed for his own home to sleep it off. If any of the memories ever returned to him it would be in the form of nightmares that would make no sense.

"Normally, when I implant a suggestion in someone's mind, they do what I require of them." Ashe had now and again encountered those who were immune to his abilities. Thankfully, this had been one of those times.

Serina grinned. "You guys think that all you have to do is snap a finger and a girl is in your power. Hello! I've got news for you. I've never been that easy to hypnotize. When you tried to do it I decided to follow you and see if I could find out what was going on. Just consider yourself lucky that I did."

"Oh, that I do, m'lady."

"Now, just on the off chance that the police question you about Chalker's death," said Serina. "Just tell them that you spent the entire night with me. Besides, you didn't think that I was through with you? Did you?"

"I wouldn't think of being that presumptuous."

"Of course not."

✦

JOHN DOE #12

It had been a hell of a fight.

The first officer to arrive had described the scene as looking like a mini tornado had touched down in the alley behind the Wal-Mart Super Center. Gutters ripped loose from the wall, piles of kindling that had once been shipping crates, dumpsters overturned and leaking trash out onto the blacktop, not to mention the blood streaked along the road that gave mute proof that the first reports had been accurate.

Detective Sergeant Jack Logan squatted next to the loser of that fight; at least he assumed this was the loser, since the young man was dead.

"I hope you gave as good as you got," muttered Logan to the body as he took a last drink out of the styrofoam cup of coffee. The liquid was barely drinkable, at best an echo of anything like heat lingered in it. It felt like more than a century since he had bought it at the convenience store north of the university campus.

"You ready for me, Jack?" asked Neil Ketchum. Besides being a police officer,

Ketchum was one of Norman's four crime scene investigators; he was also the lowest in seniority, so he was on the graveyard shift.

"All yours," Logan said.

Ketchum pulled on a pair of latex gloves and began to examine the body. Logan pulled a pair from his own pocket and put them on. He had never cared for the gloves, but had long since accepted that they were a necessary part of the job.

"Looks like rigor hasn't set in, so we're talking a time of death within the last several hours," said Ketchum. "No wallet, no pieces of paper in the pocket, no PDA, not even a comb or a piece of lint."

135

The CSI motioned for Logan to help him turn the body onto its side. Underneath was a sword, the end of it a broken ragged edge.

"I think we may have our murder weapon, I wonder where we'll find the other one," said Ketchum.

"Other one?" asked Logan. He really hoped this wasn't going to turn out to be one of the string of murders at Medieval and Renaissance Fairs that had been going on for more than two years all over the Midwest. A serial killer stopping for a visit was all that Norman needed.

"Oh yeah, it took something big and nasty to do this kind of damage to a sword, not to mention our friend here," said Ketchum.

"Wonderful," Logan muttered.

———

"So much for clear and sunny," growled Logan as he stepped across a large mud puddle. In spite of the forecast saying otherwise, it had been raining since before sunup.

At the edge of the parking lot was a large sign with the words University of Oklahoma 35th Annual Medieval Faire. There were tents everywhere, ranging from small affairs to the huge army surplus GP3s. All of them were decorated with banners and devices of every conceivable kind to aid in creating the illusion of a genuine Medieval Faire. Of course, the several dozen wagons and trailers adorned with logos of everything from Mazios Pizza to Coors Beer did something to disrupt that illusion.

Coming around the wall of porta-potties, Logan found himself standing on the edge of a small crowd of fairgoers who were watching a pair of men in Musketeer outfits, swords drawn, shouting insults at each other. Under other circumstances he might have been calling for backup, but this was all part of the "show" that would be repeated several times over the course of the day.

A quick glance at the map supplied by the Faire's coordinating office indicated the performance area he was looking for was just ahead, beyond a stone bridge. Large tents had been pitched there, each one bearing a banner of a hawk flying through several rings. The area in front of them was marked off by rope and colored streamers, with several racks of unattended weapons and shields at either end.

Just to one side of the tent was a large sign, with a heraldic badge that featured several animals that Logan didn't recognize, and the words 'SWORD MAGIC performances on the hour.' A grey-haired man in a long black robe, open in the front to revel a Grateful Dead tee-shirt, stood near the entrance.

"Good morning," Logan said, holding out his credentials. "Would you be Cecil McCall?"

"I'm McCall." He said after eyeing the badge. "What can I do for you, Detective?"

"Just a few questions, sir." Logan offered a photo, the body in the ally, for McCall to see. "Do you recognize this man?"

"Afraid not. As pale as he is, would I be correct in assuming that he's dead?"

"Yep. Someone offed John Doe here last night, behind the Wal-Mart."

"John Doe?"

"When we don't have a name to go with a body, it's listed as John or Jane Doe, with a number indicating how many unidentified bodes we've had since the beginning of the year. So he became John Doe # 12. Cause of death appears to have been a sword."

"A sword? Is that why you're showing me this poor fellow's picture?" asked McCall.

"No, this," Logan held out a second photo, this one of the sword found at the scene. The design on the handle resembled the one on the banners hanging from the tents.

"Interesting. This could be one of my weapons; a few have turned up missing. I'll have one of my students do an inventory, but I would need to see the original to tell you for certain. Do you have it with you?" he asked.

"No, it's with rest of this fellow's personal effects," he said. "One of the local martial arts instructors who also teaches swordsmanship suggested that I talk to you. Seems, unlike the other performers at the fair, you folks work with real blades."

"Indeed we do," said McCall. "But my students do this only as a form of martial arts; their skills are not intended to, nor would I continence them, harming someone else.

Now, if we're done, I need to get some things ready. We perform on the hour."

"Even in the rain?"

"A true warrior never lets something as paltry as the weather stand in his way."

———

The rain had gotten heavy enough for Logan to seek shelter inside a concession tent dubbed The Cross-Eyed Tavern. Armed with a cup of coffee and a doughnut, both of which were highly over-priced, Logan sat down at one of the tables.

Even in the rain, people were moving around the fairgrounds, some walking confidently as if it were a sunny day, others dashing from tent to tent in an effort to minimize their contact with the rain.

"It's a good thing they aren't the performers. Running with a sword can be dangerous, especially in this weather."

Logan had seen no one else come into the tent after him, let alone sit down two chairs over, but there was a man there now. He seemed fairly ordinary, medium build, clean shaven, brown hair; the sort that a witness to a crime would describe and could be talking about any one of a hundred people.

"You're right about that," agreed Logan.

"I know they're professionals, like stunt men, but I can't help but wonder, if something goes wrong and somebody gets skewered with one of those swords, what would happen," said the stranger.

Logan shook his head, staring out into the rain.

"Let's hope we don't ever find out."

"Didn't I see you talking to that old geezer who runs the Sword Magic show?

Did he tell you what they have scripted for today?"

"No, but I suppose you could ask him." Logan turned to look back at the man, but there was no one sitting in the chair.

———

Logan stood in front of the cold storage unit at the Norman City Morgue, staring at the little card with plain block letters spelling out the name John Doe #12.

"Let's just see if you have some visitors tonight, my friend," he said softly.

Just after midnight the groaning of hinges came from the hallway in the direction of the men's room. A few seconds later he saw the door open, a familiar, and not unexpected, figure, dressed in the same robe and tee shirt from earlier, emerged.

McCall picked his way carefully down the hall, stopping at each door to see what was painted on it, until he came to the one with the words Cold Storage Vaults. Once inside, McCall began to look around on the desk near the door.

"No need to bother," said Logan, gun drawn as he turned the lights on and stepped where he could be seen. "What you're looking for is in unit number 12."

"Ah, Detective," said McCall. "How to nice to see you again."

"Now, didn't you tell me that you didn't know who he was, Mr. McCall?" asked Logan. "I assume you are here to claim the body of John Doe #12."

"Indeed," said McCall. "You were right. I did know him; I've known him since he was a child. His name is O'wan, one of my students."

"I'm sure we will be more comfortable talking about this down at the station," Logan told him.

A dart whizzed past Logan's ear and embedded itself in the wall behind him. Before he could do or say anything else, a fist slammed into his jaw, after that it was just dark.

———

When Logan woke up, McCall was gone and so was John Doe #12. It didn't take a rocket scientist, or Sherlock Holmes, to figure out where they both might be found. The Medieval Faire site was officially closed until 7 a.m., but that didn't mean it was empty. Some of the merchants slept on site, in their tents or in the RVs and vans that they traveled in. There was security, mostly private security guards, but several were off-duty policemen picking up some extra money. Running into them was not part of the game plan, so McCall picked his way carefully through the maze that was the faire site at night.

A dim light came from the center of one of McCall's tents. Peering through a side entrance, Logan could see McCall and another man, dressed in a leather bomber jacket, standing next to table where John Doe #12 had been laid out.

"Now, gentlemen," Logan said stepping inside, gun drawn. "We can do this easy or we can do this hard. It's going to be your choice, but we are definitely going to be dancing the next round together."

McCall turned toward Logan, an almost amused look on his face. "It's very nice to see you again, Detective," he said.

The other man took a step around the table toward Logan, but McCall raised a hand that stopped the other man in his tracks.

"Looks like you've got him trained well. Does he also bring you your pipe and slippers, along with the evening paper?"

"Please, Detective," said the older man. "I had hoped you would not lower yourself to such clichéd humor at Haylen's expense."

A dart embedded itself between the eyes of the man in the leather jacket; he began to raise his hand, as if trying to see what had hit him, but never completed the action, collapsing like a marionette whose strings had been dropped.

From a nearby rack McCall grabbed a sword, the blade moving slowly in gentle arcs as he turned, studying the darkness that enfolded the tent.

"Detective, this isn't your fight, any more than it was at the morgue. I think if you leave now, you have a chance. The man behind that dart is after me, not you. Tradition demands that he only carry one dart at a time, but he has plenty of other tricks up his sleeve."

"I go from having one murder to two. I think I want to have a word with whoever fired that dart. Plus a few with you, as well," said Logan.

A shadow moved across the back of the tent. Logan hoped it wasn't one of the Faire security guards coming to investigate. True, more firepower would be appreciated, but that also meant more targets, as well, along with quite a few more questions than there were answers right now.

A small figure dropped from the top of the tent, landing in a crouch. In spite of the size, this was no kid. Logan pulled the trigger of his gun twice; both times nothing happened. He looked around for a replacement weapon.

A staff with metal wrapped around both ends was the first thing that Logan saw. He grabbed it and swung hard toward the smaller man, who had pulled a sword from the rack and was bringing it down in a hard chopping arc. The jolt as the two weapons collided was hard enough to make Logan feel like a car had run into him.

Over the man's shoulder, Logan caught sight of McCall just as the older man slammed something hard against his attacker's back. That was enough to send the small man down, and this time he stayed down. In the dim light of the tent Logan couldn't tell if the man was alive or dead. It was no sword in McCall's hands, but a Louisville slugger baseball bat instead.

"Thanks," he said, between gasps. "But this doesn't change the fact that I think I'm still going to have to arrest you."

"Maybe you should take a look at our friend before you make any final decisions," said McCall.

Logan reached down, checked for a pulse, found none, and pulled back the hood that covered the attacker's face. The face was that of the man he had talked to briefly in the concession tent, then it was that of one of the officers from the murder scene. Over the next thirty seconds a half dozen other visages rolled across the man's face, some of them most definitely not human. It finally settled into one, with pale skin and a long cascade of white-blonde hair.

"I've removed a particular spell, and if you were to go look at O'wan, your John Doe #12, you would see the same racial characteristics as this fellow and myself. By the way, that spell is what kept your gun from working."

"Okay, I'm now officially weirded out."

"Please, Detective, the explanation is simple, if you are willing to believe it."

McCall walked over to a cooler and pulled out two bottles of beer. He held both out, letting Logan choose, then opened the remaining one and took a swallow. Logan followed suit, enjoying the feel of the cold liquid.

"So?" Logan gestured at the two bodies.

"First off, we are not human; I think you've figured that out. My students and I are refugees. O'wan, and the others are all that remains of the royal families of the Three Kingdoms. I rescued them. It has been my charge these past eight years to keep them hidden until the time was right for them to free their people. I knew that some of them would die, but I didn't expect it to be O'wan and Haylen, and certainly not before we returned home."

"I presume you're the resident magician and sword master. Should I call you,

Yoda or Gandalf?" asked Logan.

"Please. I'm a scientist, Detective, although I suppose much of our science would seem like magic to you." McCall pulled a candy bar from his pocket and took a bite out of it.

"But you're performing in the Medieval Faire?" asked Logan.

"Actually, in a number of them all year long. It helps us keep a roof over our heads, and it sharpens my students' skills. Hiding in plain sight, I suppose you could call it."

"Speaking of students, where are they?"

"My boys have developed a fondness for old movies. They've gone for pizza and to see a midnight movie at the campus student union." With his beer bottle in one hand, McCall began picking up the weapons from the floor.

"And bozo here?" Logan asked. "I should say the late Mr. Bozo. I hope you have something in that bag of tricks for disposing of bodies."

"I do," said McCall, "I hope he was just freelance and happened to stumble across us by chance. If he wasn't, then things may start to get dicey. So, have you made up your mind if you're going to arrest me? If you are, I need to leave a note for my students. I wouldn't want them to worry too much."

"Why do I have a feeling the jail wouldn't hold you for long." Logan mused. "I suppose I could be suffering from the effects of some new designer drug you slipped me, combined with a concussion, but I believe you, sorta kinda."

"Do you mind if I ask you something, Detective?" said McCall.

"Go ahead."

"It's going to be several years before we're ready to return to our world. I could use an extra hand with security, especially since I've been considering settling in one place. Norman seems like it might do," he said. "Think you'd be interested? Besides, you seem to have some skill with that quarterstaff. I might be able to teach you a trick or two with it, and a sword, as well."

Okay, he didn't completely buy this whole interdimensional ninja/assassin refugee thing. Remembering a couple of the faces that he had seen on the killer, he wasn't that sure just what McCall and his students might be. But one thing he did know, if he reported it, the chief would probably lock him up in a padded cell and through away the key.

Well, he wouldn't be the first cop to take a second job, Logan reminded himself.

"We can talk," he told McCall.

✦

SKIMMING STONES

L aying flat on my stomach with my face less than a foot from the river was not the way I had planned to spend Friday night. Especially when I knew that waiting at the Shadow Creek bar, there was a martini, possibly several, with my name on it.

Not that I had a whole lot of choice in the matter. I work for the City of Tulsa as an electrical maintenance engineer, so I end up doing a lot of work in places that I would prefer not to even think about, if I didn't have to; all in the name of keep various facilities around town running .

The hours weren't the greatest, but I was pulling down decent money and didn't have to spend my days in a cubicle. This girl wasn't complaining; I'd gotten enough of that from my ex-husband, Luke; he didn't like my hours, the fact that my pay check was bigger than his or much of anything in our relationship. When he finally took off, three days after our first anniversary, with that dye job blonde, Denise, I couldn't have been happier.

With budget short falls and layoffs my department was short-handed. Truth be told, we'd never had enough people, so making due was a way of life. That was why on a Friday night, I was in coveralls, laying on a stage floating on the Arkansas river, instead of wearing my new leather mini-skirt, boots and suede jacket and bar hopping with my best friend, Jani.

The floating stage is anchored in a small cove. They use it for outdoor theater productions, performances by musicians, and any formal city-type ceremony that the politicians want to conduct under the open Oklahoma sky.

The problem with the place is that it was designed by an idiot. At least once a month my department got a frantic call from the stage manager saying something was wrong and it needed to be fixed, yesterday. Since Tulsa Opera was supposed to do a benefit preview at two on Sunday afternoon, the powers-that-be thought it would be sort of nice if things worked.

143

I had come out with a four man crew around noon, then at six my boss called and told the others to go home. Less overtime, I suspect. "Look, Nancy," he had said. "You can handle it by yourself, shouldn't take you more than a half an hour or so."

Yeah, right! Three hours later I was closing the last access port and breathing a long sigh of relief when I heard something hitting the side of the stage. I trailed my flashlight along the water to find see what it was. There was something I thought it might be a mannequin, thrown away by frat boys at one of their drunken parties.

Okay, call me a Girl Scout, but I figured there was a chance I was wrong, so I dropped my flashlight and made a grab for whatever it was.

That took me several tries. The problem was, I couldn't get a good enough hold he dropped back into the water several times. In the process I heard the sound of coughing , that was proof enough that I wasn't trying to rescue a dummy or a corpse.

Once I did get him up on the stage I pushed his hair out of the way and discovered two important things, 'he' was a 'she, and *she* had my face!

———•———

Beyond a knot on the side of her head the size of a goose egg, some bruises and a cut on her cheek, my new-found twin didn't seem to have anything obviously wrong with her. City regulations, not to mention common sense, said I ought to call 911 or get her to the nearest hospital.

It was just that looking at that face, my face, just wierded me out so much, that I just could not see going by regulations right then as being the smartest thing in the world.

"Take it easy. You're okay. I got you out of the water," I told her.

"Where am I?" she said, her voice a cracked whisper.

"Tulsa," I said.

Don't ask me why, but right then I figured the best thing to do was get her away from there. The only place I could think of to take her was my house. I live in a suburb of Tulsa, somewhat isolated, which suited me just fine. I had been astonished when Luke had been willing to sign the place over to me as part of our divorce settlement. I took it, of course, after making sure he hadn't secretly mortgaged the place to the hilt.

Since her legs didn't seem to want to work for more than three or four steps at a time without going out from under her getting my guest inside was not easy. My cats, Paranoia and Schizo, were on the sofa but decided to take off for other places when they saw us come through the door.

Her clothes had dried some, but were still smelly and wet. I managed to get one boot off of her and was just untying the other when my guest said,

"If it's seduction you have in mind, I'm afraid that you're going to be rather disappointed. I'm not feeling up for anything just now."

"Don't worry about that. I've got better ways of picking up dates than fishing them out of the river. Besides, I don't think you're my type."

"If she's not, Nancy, am I?"

Standing in the living room door was Kent Sabiani. At six-one, his lanky frame and gray-streaked goatee gave him a vaguely satanic look, which went over great with some of my more religious neighbors.

He moved so quietly that sometimes you would just look up and there he was. Kent was an Emergency Medical Technician, so I had called him on my cell phone to come give my visitor a quick once over.

"Damn it, make some noise when you come in the door!"

"Hey, I did make noise; it's not my fault that you didn't hear me. So who's your friend?"

"Name's Sian," she said in a whisper.

I saw the look on Kent's face when he got a good look at Sian. He was cool, didn't say a word, just cocked an eyebrow at me and went to work.

I excused myself to the kitchen, where I found a couple of beers in the back of the fridge. Kent was just unwrapping a blood pressure cuff from Sian's arm when I came back. I handed him a beer.

"Thanks. Other than the obvious, bruises, scratches and contusions, Sian seems in pretty good shape," he said. "How far did you fall?

"Don't know, but it hurt like hell," she said.

"Must have felt like hitting concrete."

Sian nodded

"All right, that's enough," Kent said. "I would say a few hours sleep are in order. The interrogation can wait."

———

The next morning I came in the kitchen and found Kent rummaging around in the cabinets, a look of frustration on his face. "So. where did you put the frying pan *this* time?" he asked when he saw me.

"Just for using that tone, I'm not telling you." After all, it was my kitchen and *I knew* where it was. "Besides, why should I help you? You left your socks and shirt hanging on the dresser mirror, again."

"Be that way and you get to cook." He grinned.

That was a good argument. I'm a decent cook, but it's nice to have someone else do the work, and I stand in awe of what Kent can do in a kitchen. "Cabinet! Just to the right of the stove!" I said quickly.

Kent pulled the skillet out, fetched eggs, milk and a variety of other things from the refrigerator. I've never been able to figure out if he has specific recipes or just works with what's there. The results speak for themselves.

"Is there anything I can do to help?"

Sian walked into the kitchen wearing my heavy red bathrobe. A shower and some sleep seemed to have done her a world of good. The bruises were still prominent, but in the light of day looked like they would heal. She moved a bit stiffly, favoring her right leg, but, given the circumstances that was understandable.

"Just grab a stool," I said. "Kent is working his magic."

"A moment later he presented us each with a tall glass of orange juice. The odor of blueberry muffins began to fill the kitchen, followed a few minutes later by Kent setting a plate of them in front of Sian and me. He turned his attention back to the stove. I knew omelets would soon follow.

"Okay," I said. "So, feel like answering a few questions?"

"Ask away," Sian said, slicing a muffin and layering butter onto it. "This is very good. She was right when she called it magic."

"Thank you. So, what happened?." Kent said, without turning around.

"You wouldn't believe that I just got a little bit plastered and fell into the river?" I just arched an eyebrow at her and didn't say a thing. "Well, I didn't think so, especially if you've looked in the mirror anytime. The long and the short of it is, I'm you."

"Really?"

Sian nodded as she took a sip from her glass. "If you were able to run a DNA test on the two of us you'd see that we are genetically the same person. Only I'm not from this world."

"Unless you were cloned by aliens, or are a part of some sort of secret government conspiracy, that leaves only two possible explanations," said Kent. "Time travel or parallel world?"

Sian looked at him, shocked. "I'm impressed. You keeping him around on a long term basis?" she asked me.

I didn't answer. Instead I reached across the counter and grabbed Sian's left arm, pushing back the sleeve. Midway up the arm was a formation of veins, making the letter H, clearly visible beneath her skin. A jagged scar, about four inches in length, bisected it. I bared my arm to show an identical mark, but reversed. I'd definitely call this a bit more than circumstantial evidence.

"I *am* from a parallel world," she said. "Where history, as you know it, ran differently, because of different choices."

"So how did you end up in our corner of the time-space continuum?" asked Kent.

"To make a long story short, I'm a run-away princess." Kent had to struggle to keep from laughing, this was beginning to sound like something out of those fantasy novels he's so fond of reading.

"Let me see if I have this straight," I said. "You're me, from a parallel world, where you're a princess. But you decided to take it on the lam from your life as one of the royals and came here."

"Not at first. I left just over a year ago. I've probably been in seven or eight different worlds before this one."

Sian made a gesture in the air and a small globe of light appeared just above the palm of her hand. It hovered there for a moment and was gone.

"Kent isn't the only one who can do magic. It looks like magic, but there are sound principles of science behind it," she said. "Problem is that is about all I can do."

"A handy talent. So why *did* you leave home?" Kent asked.

Sian laid the remnants of her muffin down on a napkin. "They wanted to make me Queen."

"Queen?" I said. "I don't think you have any glass ceiling where you come from."

She cocked an eyebrow at me but went on. "My Daddy had decided it was time for him to have a co-ruler; someone who would do most of the work while he took it easy. I may be the eldest, but my brother is far more suited to the throne. When he wouldn't let me abdicate I faked my death and ran. Problem was he didn't he didn't believe it. He commissioned the Guild of Head Hunters to find me and bring me home. They've come close too many times."

"You figured to hide from them here in Tulsa?" Kent asked.

"Actually..no," she sighed. "I left a trail for the Head Hunters to follow, I had planned to lay a trap for them and then permanently lose them in the desert."

Permanently lose? To me that said kill them and dump the bodies.

"So, why are you in Tulsa?" asked Kent.

"Because of her," Sian pointed at me. "For reasons that I don't understand whenever I enter a new world, I tend to end up close to myself, if I'm still alive in that world. There have been a few where I was dead or had never been born."

"I bet that was a fun discovery," I said.

Kent picked up a muffin from the tin and began to gingerly peal the paper cup from around it.

"Sian, one thing that you haven't mentioned is just how you're able to go hopping from parallel world to parallel world. So what went wrong?" I asked.

"What makes you think anything went wrong?"

"A thirty foot drop into the river sort of suggests that things didn't work the way you planned them to work," I said.

Sian laughed. "Oh, they definitely didn't work the way I had planned them. Travel between the worlds is a combination of making your mind perceive things differently and then stepping through the gate. Ideally you need a set of rune stones to open that gate. I grabbed some of the best before I left home

"The only trouble is that I lost my rune stones. My fathers chief warlock taught me ways of duplicating the rune door with my mind, using a variety of herbs, native flora and pharmaceuticals. The problem is the last two worlds haven't have what I needed and I had to use substitutes. They didn't always work right."

"So you're saying, when you do this you're on drugs," Kent grinned. "Talk about your ultimate bad acid trip. So if you don't know where you are, does this mean that those Head Hunters of yours won't be able to find you?"

Sian stared at the counter for a long time. "I can only hope so."

"Well, I never had a sister, so you're about the closest I'm going to come to one," I said, putting my arm around her shoulder. "You're welcome to stay here for as long a visit as you want."

If she was going to stay around, Sian was going to need "a life", at least on paper. Kent just said to leave it to him. He knew a hacker who could do the job.

"Is this guy good?" I asked.

"Oh, yeah," he grinned. "The guy I have in mind is the one who teaches the CIA forgery department how to do things."

That done it was time to do something else, just as important. I looked at Sian's clothes, we'd left in the laundry room. They were not in good shape. She was going to need more than what I had found her in, and more than just borrowed things from my closet. Time to go shopping.

We hit the local mall and found everything Sian would need, not to mention some neat things for myself. Just after noon I decided it was time to introduce Sian to native dishes, i.e.: pizza. Meals in hand, we found a table near the stage at the center of the food court.

There were a bunch of guys there, dressed in combat fatigues, faces painted in camouflage paint all holding weird looking metal guns. The weapons looked like the sort of things my cousins Tim and Randy had played with when we were growing up, not practical looking but the sort of thing that thrills a twelve year old male.

When they began showing off some round balls and inserting them in the guns it dawned on me that these weren't real army types, but paint ball gamers.

I explained the concept to Sian and she just shook her head. "They do this for fun?"

I was about to turn my attention back to a slice of pizza when I looked toward the rest rooms. The air in front of them had begun to shimmer and fold in on itself. Then someone was standing there. He was big, six-four at least, wearing a dark floppy hat and a leather jacket.

"Slowly look over toward the rest rooms," I told Sian. "I think we have a visitor."

"I don't have to," Sian was staring at the shinny metal wall of the chinese fast food place. She could see a slightly blurry version of this fellow without a problem.

"A Head Hunter? Does he know you're here?" I said softy.

"Remember what I said about being drawn to this area because you were here. Look up on the stage." She pointed at a man standing at the back of the group of camo dressed performers. he was shaggier and maybe didn't weigh as much, but I could see the resemblance.

I was about to suggest that we ease our way out of there, when things began to go a bit haywire. One of the paint ball guys tripped over something, his own feet probably, gun in hand and almost feel. One thing he did do was accidentally squeeze off a shot that went straight out into the audience and hit the Head Hunter square on the chest. I can imagine where he would have hit if there had been time to aim.

The Head Hunter looked down, touched the fresh paint with one finger. "I just had that cleaned!" he said and headed for the stage.

Not being your shy retiring type, Sian grabbed one of the metal chairs that filled the food court. As the Head Hunter passed she brought it down hard across the man's back. That proved effective enough to put him on the floor, surprise is the best weapon. A quick grab under his shirt and she jerked something loose.

"Let's go!" she said.

We made it to the car and I hit the gas. How we got out of there without being stopped did it I still don't know.

"Damn, damn, damn," she muttered as I pointed the car toward the street.

"What was that you got from him?" I asked.

"These," she opened the small leather back and poured out a half dozen flat stones, each one of the carved with an intricate rune.

———

Sian spread the rune stones out on the my dinning room table. There were six, none bigger than a quarter. All were slick and cool to the touch.

"This isn't good. If one of them found their way here, that means the others know where he went. So if he doesn't report back, and he can't without these, then they will come looking for him." she said.

"Then why did you take them?" I asked. "I know, I know, it seemed the thing to do at the time. Can we just smash them and hope the others don't show up on our doorstep?" I got my answer with just the look in Sian's eyes.

Smashing those pebbles would be a very last resort.

"How long will it be before the other show up?" asked Kent.

"If I've read these alignments correctly," she nodded. "I should judge sometime late tonight, give or take a couple hours. They are going to try for an area along the river, probably somewhere north of where I arrived, something solid I would expect. They can't walk on water any more than I could."

"Good, then maybe its time for your to stop running," said Kent.

"I'm not going back!" protested Sian.

"You don't have to, if we work this right." The look on Kent's face suggested that he had something in mind. "It strikes me that there is a fairly simple answer to your problems, in my never-to-be-humble opinion."

"Oh, really?" asked Sian.

"Sure, we're just going to have to kill you."

———·——

Standing, at two a.m. on an abandoned bridge a mile north of the floating stage, with a strong northeasterly breeze blowing off the river, I was definitely not what you would describe as a happy camper. More like an irritated, cold and angry camper. I didn't think that Sian or Kent were any more comfortable right then than I was.

When Kent had breezed back in late that afternoon he was carrying half-a-dozen large boxes. "Have a look at these," he said. "I think you'll find them interesting."

Interesting was a good word. I was wearing the contents of several of them; a one piece black leather cat suit, covered in chains and metal studs, that was so tight I could barely breath. Sian had had to help me get into the thing and get everything zipped. Even the ankle length duster didn't do a thing to keep me warm, though it did provide a place to keep a loaded berreta and a fully charged Taser.

If Sian had read those stones correctly, this was where the Head Hunters were supposed to show up. That was a big if to my way of thinking. Of course we might get lucky, have them miss and end up drowning in the middle of the river. I wasn't counting on that.

Frankly, I was about ready to give up this idea and revert to Plan B, once we came up with Plan B, when something happened to the air about twenty feet off to my left. I motioned for Sian and Kent to stay hidden.

The air seemed to waver for a moment, fold in on itself and then there were two men standing in the center of the bridge. After our first Head Hunter I think I expected some sort of cross between a barbarian and a biker.

That wasn't what we got; more like a matching pair of lawyer boys, one was scarecrow-thin with a smile that seemed to take up three fourths of his face, the other was short, bald and looked like one of my cats could take him two falls out of three.

"I think this may be the place we're looking for. It feels right," the tall one said.

"I hope so, its about time our luck changed," his companion said.

That was my cue. I pushed the duster back and strode forward. "All right, you two scumballs. This time you are completely out of luck. You're mine!" Hey, even if I was cold and scared out of my wits, I think I presented a fairly fierce picture right then.

Seeing me, they just stood staring for several seconds. That was enough time for Kent to come over the side of the bridge, where he had been perched, and clobber one of them with a blackjack. I enjoyed very much using the Taser on the other. Once they were down, I made sure they were still breathing, then we hogged tied them; feet and hands together behind their backs, with nooses around their necks.

"I guess this is places for Act Two," I said as Kent waved capsules of smelling salts under their noses.

They jerked awake and it didn't take them too long to figure out that they were in trouble. The smaller one looked around and started to speak, but thought better of it. The other one just stared at me, his face impassive and waiting.

"Good evening, boys. So, do the two of you have names of any sort?"

"Aye, m'lady," the taller one said, pronouncing each word carefully. "I'm Carson Sal'se and he's Vernon Myth'rn. If we have offended you, or broken any local laws we do most humbly apologize."

"Well, isn't that just too, too cute. You've made a serious mistake, showing up on my lands, just when I'm in a very, very bad mood!" I said.

I began to pace back and forth. In the distance I could see the lights of the 21st street traffic bridge, flanked by the expressway bridge fifty yards beyond that. I couldn't help but grin at the idea of how the passing drivers might react to this scene. Of course explaining this whole scene to any police officers who showed up might be more than a bit difficult.

"The treasury is a little low right now and the price of two prime slaves like you two would certainly help fatten it up. I understand that there is a shortage of workers in the okra fields to the south. They'll be here shortly, for my little package over there. You fellows wouldn't happen to be with her, now would you?"

It wasn't easy for either of the Head Hunters to see where I had pointed, but they tried. One of Kent's other boxes had contained a filmy affair of white silk and transparent gossamer fabric.

Wrapped around Sian it looked as exotic, in its own way, as what I had on. It made what I had on look warm and comfortable. Kent dragged her forward to stand closer to the rest of us. Sian was blindfolded and her hands bound behind her.

"It's her! I told you we would find her!" said Myth'rn. He tried to get to his feet, but got no more than a couple of inches when the rope around his neck choked him off.

"You dared to violate my territory for that?"

"Yes, m'lady. She is to become a queen in her own right."

I began to laugh. "I doubt that she will be good for anything like that, not now anyway. This wench showed up here three days ago, tried to take me in a fight and lost. Instead of killing her I had her dosed with a drug that I use a good deal in my business. The stuff helps new slaves adjust to life in the bawdy houses I operate. That is if I don't decide just to get ride of her, like I'm thinking of getting rid of you two." I knew one thing, I had to keep them more than a bit uncertain of just what was going on, before they started asking too man questions, like how we happened to be there just where they were going to show up.

The look on the faces of the two Head Hunters was something akin to grief and shock, with a healthy dose of fear thrown in for good measure.

"This wasn't how you had wanted things to work out?" I asked.

"No, m'lady. Our guild accepted the commission to return her to the throne. Its obvious now, we have failed," he said. "When we return we will be in disgrace."

"If I allow you to return. Maybe I should just feed you to the fishes. Can either of you swim?"

"Swim? N…no, m'lady."

"You two are such pains. But then so is she, and I'm not in the mood." I pulled out the Taser and jammed it aginst Sian's neck. The effect was quick and certian, she jerked like a marionette whose strings had been dropped, then crumpled to the ground. She lay there, eyes open and empty, her tongue hanging limply from her mouth.

"We'll just compost what's left of her," I said.

I let my words digest with them for several moments as their eyes darted between me and Sian's still form. Then I reached over and pulled their shirts open, just as Sian had told me to expect, there were two identical leather bags hanging around their necks. I yanked them free.

"I was going to kill you, and dump you over the bridge, but the river's too polluted as is," I said. "I have a better idea."

I gestured for Kent. He grabbed the shoulders of the smaller man and I grabbed his feet. We rolled him on top of the other one, face to face. I shoved one rune stone each between their lips.

"Don't swallow fellows," I laughed. "You've got one chance, scum. I 'd advise you to take it."

They understood what I was talking about, leaned forward and touched the stones together. The air shivered, folded in on itself and the two Head Hunters were gone.

"That's one way to make an exit," Kent said.

Sian moaned and began to blink her eyes. Kent scrambled to her side, checking her vitals. "Did it work?" she managed to ask.

"You betcha, sis," I said. "I have a feeling they're going to be required to think very fast to explain what happened. In fact I'm fairly sure they won't be able to admit a thing about what really happened. As far as your father is concerned you are gone and will not be returning anytime soon."

"That's good, I just wish it didn't have to be this way. I love Daddy, but he can be hard headed," she said. "Oh, but that thing you hit me with, sister mine, hurt like you wouldn't believe. Look, before we go much further, would somebody mind untying me. And I would appreciate a coat of some kind. It's cold out here."

Kent took a knife and cut the ropes around Sian's wrists, helping her stand up in the process. "We need to have a long talk, Kent, about your taste in women's clothes." she said. I didn't have to look over there to know he was putting on his totally innocent "I don't know what you're talking about face just then.

I had to say it had been an interesting weekend. I reached in my pocket and touched the rune stones. It occured to me that smooth and flat as they were they would be perfect for skimming. I wondered how far I could throw them.

"No, maybe another time," I said to the wind.

"I don't know about you two, but I could do with some hot coffee," said Kent.

"What's coffee?" asked Sian.

✦

MONEY'S WORTH

I had my hand on the dagger before I was fully awake. Sleeping with a knife under your pillow isn't the most comfortable thing to do, though you can get used to it. I'd rather be uncomfortable then wake to a sword at my throat.

When I had leased the villa last month the caretaker had apologized profusely about the number of things that needed fixing; after all, the place had been empty for nearly two years.

One of the problems he had mentioned was the hinges on the master bedroom door; they squeaked and needed replacing. He had sworn by any number of local gods that he would have it fixed quickly.

It hadn't been. Right then I didn't have a problem with those squeaky hinges. They had been enough to awaken me.

There were two intruders, small hunkered forms clinging far too closely together as they came across the floor. When they sprang I threw my blanket over them as I rolled over the other side of the bed.

"So what enemies have tried to ambush me?" I demanded, my voice as melodramatic as possible, since I already knew the identities of these intruders. I threw the blanket aside and fought hard to suppress a grin at the scene in front of me, a jumble of legs, arms and tangled hair, mixed in with gasps and giggling. "Is it some demon or perhaps an advance scout for the Kelmigie Horde? Whatever foul creature it is I will crush it under my heel and serve the remnants to the dogs! "

"No!" The bundle of arms and legs separated into two forms and scrambled madly toward the far side of the bed.

Kellian was eight; his sister Jayce was two years younger, but nearly as tall. Their red hair came from my side of the family. Their chaotic nature was a legacy from both their father and myself.

155

"It's us, Mother," Kellian yelled!

"Really it is," his sister added.

"I don't know! Those could be very good disguises. You could de dwarfs from the deep mines. I'd best beat you severely, just in case."

Jayce turned to her brother. "I told you this was a bad idea, that Mommy would be mad and punish us."|

I wasn't mad; I was actually quite pleased with the two of them. They had been at each other's throats for the last several days, over some incident that they had both forgotten by now. That they had made peace and decided to attack *me* was a good sign.

"Mother, we were just playing! We thought it would be fun to play Kyber assassins!" Kellian proclaimed.

Kyber assassins?! It didn't surprise me that they had heard of the Kyber Guild.

There were half a hundred tall tales about the Guild, told by children and adults to frighten each other, most all of them far, far from the truth.

Nothing in my possession had the Guild name on it; only a seal, hidden away in a compartment in one of my trunks even bore the emblem.

"All right! I believe you aren't dwarves wearing a disguise spell to make me think you are my children. I will let you off, this time, young Kybers." I picked up a piece of fruit from the table next to my bed, and broke it into several smaller sections. "But only if you help me eat this. Do you agree to my terms?"

"Yes!"

———•———

Six weeks ago I had announced that I was taking an extended holiday, officially to escape the seasonal heat in the capitol, as were many others who could afford to move to the mountains or the sea for a few months. Unofficially, I just I needed some time away from not just the Kyber Guild but the various businesses I ran as a part of my "everyday" identity.

I had chosen Yallon's Bay because it was several days' travel from the capitol, far enough away for some privacy but close enough not to be completely out of touch.

Of course, this was not the first time I had come to Yallon's Bay; that had been decade and a half before with my beloved Micah.

Here he was remembered as one of the five thousand men lost in the Battle of Summer Falls. I had no intention of disillusioning anyone about that tale; besides, who would want to hear that he had died in an attempt to assassinate General Zyon, one of our officers who had defected to the other side. I preferred to let our "friends" think of Micah as a dead war hero and myself as a rich, respectable widow.

The down side of Yallon's Bay was a number of "social" obligations that I would cheerfully have ignored; however, attending them was part of my public persona.

"Lady Danya, it is most gratifying to see you again," Lord Junius had said as I arrived at his home for what had been billed as a small gathering. Conservatively, I estimated that, excluding servants, there were well over fifty other guests: human, dwarves, and elves, along with a smattering of other races.

"Danya, are you alright?"

I turned to look at Cyma Tamu, her thin face furrowed as if she was uncertain of what she wanted to hear me answer. She was an inquisitive sort, but Cyma did have the good sense to know there were some questions that were best left unasked.

I realized that I had been staring out at the bay, studying the ships. There were three new ones that had arrived on the morning tide. They were small, compared to the large merchant men more common near the capitol. But Yallon's Bay was off the major trade routes and too shallow to take the really large vessels.

"Oh, it's nothing, Cyma," I said. "It was just seeing the bay right now, something about the way the light is falling on it reminded me of the first time that Micah and I came here."

I let a long sigh write a look of nostalgia on my face. Let Cyma take whatever interpretations of it that came to her mind; she was very good at that. Truth be told, Micah and I had first come here seeking a hideout. A mission for the Guild had gone wrong and we needed to be someplace where no one knew us.

That had been a good time. For a moment I let myself miss Micah more than I had in a long time.

"Now, Danya, you must accept the fact that Micah is gone. Remember always, he died a hero of the Empire; that is something that you and the children can be proud of. While I didn't know him, I have the feeling that he wouldn't want you to lose yourself mourning for him forever. You are still young and very beautiful."

I smiled. "Beautiful, hardly; but thank you, Cyma."

"You are definitely beautiful, don't deny it," she laughed. "In case you haven't noticed, someone can't take his eyes off you."

"Indeed?" I asked, searching my memory for any recent arrivals that I was not aware of.

"Oh yes." Cyma gestured toward a tall man, dressed in silken finery, at the far end of the room. Even at this distance I could see the marks of Elvin blood in him - silver streaked hair, long fingers and a narrow face.

"Interesting" I said

"He's been asking about you," Cyma said, a slight purr in her words.

"Does he not have the courage to come and face me himself?"

"Who knows what will happen. This gathering has at least several more hours of life in it. Then there is the rest of the night." The suggestive purr was back in Cyma's voice.

"Indeed." I admit I was a bit intrigued. I looked back to where he was standing but the man was nowhere in sight.

An hour later I found myself back at the balcony, having made a half transit of the room, speaking with a number of my neighbors, letting them see the "me" that I wanted known around the town. It would be a bit longer before I could withdraw and return home without committing a social faux pas.

I caught sight of the stranger only twice, always at a distance. It seemed an odd little dance the two of us were doing.

The sun had begun to disappear over the horizon, letting dusk streak itself across the waters of the bay as the three-quarter moon appeared in the sky. The full moon would come in a day or so.

"Is the wind from the south, Lady Sable?" It was my admirer stepping up beside me. His words were pitched low, intended for me alone.

"Pardon me, m'lord?"

"Is the winds from the south, Lady Sable?"

I was a little taken aback. No one should have known my Guild name, let alone *that* phrase, in Yallon's Bay.

"Ask about the weather and it will change in a blink."

Sign, countersign.

"How do you know me?" I demanded.

"The Widow told me," he said. "After the proper payments, of course. I hope I get my money's worth."

I wanted to turn and walk away. This man knew far too much about me for my liking.

"Very well, but this is not the place to talk. There are too many ears attached to wagging tongues," I said.

It wasn't that I really wanted to hear what he had to say, or, frankly, gave a damn. I just didn't want anyone else hearing it.

Besides, I was not happy at his being here at all. Of course, knowing The Widow, enough money would make her forget my decree. She also knew, of course, that I would say no; that is an option all of us have. I'd been very specific about my wishes; but the Guild would have the money, the introduction fee was non-refundable.

"Fear not, I've laid a minor glamour around us. All anyone will hear will be whispers that no one can quite make out and none will approach, thinking it a near romantic tryst," He reached up and took my hand. He didn't lean forward and kiss it, just did a slight bow.

"You are prepared."

"I try"

"I need you to kill someone, and it must be soon."

No big surprise there. "First, there are some niceties to be observed, m'lord," I told him. "The courtesy of your name would be a good start, though I suspect I could find it out easily from any one of a dozen people around us."

"My name is not necessary. The only name you need is that of she who I want you to kill."

"On the contrary, it is very necessary. You have sought me out, at some great expense if I know The Widow. Obviously you know who and what I am."

"A killer," he said with a certainty in his voice. "As are all the Kyber Guild."

"Understand this," I said. "I know of five ways to kill you, where you stand, without even breaking a sweat or staining my clothing with blood. Three of them would look like you had just died a natural death. So shall we start again?"

I could see him thinking, wondering just how far to take my challenge to him, wondering perhaps just how far I would go right now.

"Very well. I am Rathbin of the House of De Costa." I vaguely knew the family name, one of the lesser Elvin houses, too much human blood for the High Houses to give them more than the briefest acknowledgement, too much elf blood to "fit in" as more than a token among the higher born human clans.

"See, that didn't hurt at all," I said.

De Costa scanned the garden just below us. He gestured toward the far end where I could see a woman, dressed in a fur edged cape.

"That is her, your target. Her name is Layra. She is my sister."

On more than one occasion I had heard my children threaten to kill each other, but the next moment they would be laughing and playing together. De Costa was taking sibling rivalry a good ways further along the track than normal.

"I must decline your offer."

De Costa's face went paler than it had been, then ran red with anger. 'What! You can't! She must die by your hand!"

"Not by my hand. Do it yourself if you are that adamant. I decline. I'm on holiday; there is no argument that will persuade me otherwise"

He grabbed me, his face a grim mask of hate, long finger tightening around my arm. "It must be you!"

With my free hand I slapped him hard and then drove my knee into his groin. That was more than enough to get him to let go of me. I stepped away and saw him draw back, my unexpected attack being quite effective.

In spite of the glamour that de Costa had cast, that little exchange caught more than a few people's attention.

Cyma came running up. "Are you all right?"

"Lord de Costa just needs to learn that when I say no, I mean no."

I left Cyma doing what she did so well, draw the wrong conclusion.

Over the next two days I saw de Costa a half dozen times, always silently staring with the same grim face. I didn't give a rat's ass if he wanted his sister dead, I just couldn't figure out why he insisted that I had to be the one to do it.

That was why, two hours after sunset, on the third night since the party, I was sitting, concealed in the branches of a tree just outside of his house.

I had plumbed certain local sources to find out what I could about the man. It turned out not to be much. He had come from the south, but no one knew exactly where, arriving in Yallon's Bay a month before, having purchased the house through an agent earlier in the year. That proved he had money, but I knew that since even a chat with The Widow can cost an arm and a leg, not to mention your firstborn.

What bothered me was that there was even less to discover about his sister than about de Costa, save that she lived only a mile from her brother. There was endless speculation, but no hard facts.

I had taken to my bed early in the afternoon, complaining of a sour stomach, leaving instructions that I was not to be disturbed. If anyone looked into my bedroom they would see a figure enshrouded in heavy blankets.

De Costa had spent most of the evening in the house's library, studying a number of documents and books that looked very old. Just before midnight he finally blew out the last candle and left the room. I remained on my perch for a slow count of a thousand before dropping onto the balcony outside his window.

Once inside I lit a small candle and put it into the metal holder I had brought; the shutters could be opened one at a time to direct the light where I wanted and to keep it to a minimum

I sat down and began to study what he had left behind. The books were old and had the smell of ages on them. One of them left the palm of my hand tingling after I touched it. I could make out only a single word embossed on the cover, *Aubic*.

There were also loose papers, written in a clear concise hand, spread over the desk top; most were business dealings, nothing personal.

"I think you might find something interesting in the lower right hand drawer, Lady Sable." A section of the bookcase on the far side of the room had swung open. De Costa stood there, a much too satisfied look on his face.

Damn it! I would have read the riot act to any first year apprentice who didn't check for hidden doors when they invaded a room.

"Good evening, Lord de Costa. I get the feeling that you were expecting me. I presume that you've got a spell on the chair to keep me from getting up."

"Actually, no," he said leaning against the bookcase frame. "But before you decide to bolt or to use any number of those skills that I know you possess, I think you really should look at what is in the drawer."

I rose up slightly, just to test his words and could feel no restraints, sorcerous or otherwise. It would only be the matter of a few seconds to get me out of the window.

Opening the drawer, I found a wooden casket. The wood was smooth, almost silky, to the touch. The hinge and latches were almost impossible to find; whoever had made it had been a master craftsman. I doubted that there would be any sort of contact poison. That seemed to be a far cry from what de Costa had in mind.

Inside was a silver blade laying on a red silk piece of cloth. Two glyphs were emblazed on the blade; I recognized one of them as a Dakarian Moon, the other I did not know but even the sight of it sent a shiver down my spine.

"A Moon Dagger?"

Moon Daggers were few and far between; no more than a dozen were even rumored to exist. They were said to have been forged from sky metal by a Dwarven smith nearly a hundred years ago for an order of sorcerers that had been destroyed in the Three Sabers War.

I personally knew where six of them were; safely buried under several tons of rock in the ruins of the Fulgrham temple. If this happened to be one of those, then there was a lot more to de Costa than I thought.

"I searched for more than a decade after I first learned of them," he said. "Then one day I saw it lying on a fishmonger's table. He accepted a rather large payment and never knew what he had."

"Some people have all the luck."

"I want you to use it this very night."

"On you perhaps?"

"I'm sure that would please you to no end. Before you try, I would suggest that you look at what else is inside that casket." He moved over to a bookcase and picked up a small statuette, running one hand across its surface.

I lifted the cloth and found a pair of small hand mirrors. De Costa nodded, indicting that this was what I was looking for. Hefting one of them I stared deep into it and felt my heart drop out from me.

Instead of my own reflection I saw my daughter. She was asleep. In the other one I saw my son. Both children were seemingly undisturbed. A small dark spot hovered over each, gradually shifting form into that of a dagger, identical to the one lying in front of me.

"Those are echoes of the Moon Dagger. I assure you that neither of those fine young people will come to any harm, they will simply sleep the night away," said de Costa. "Provided you do as I have requested. The spell that I am weaving will require the heart blood of the house of de Costa. You have two hours to plunge that blade into my sister's heart. If you don't, those blades in the mirror will plunge into your children's hearts."

"You slimy bastard." It took all my concentration to control myself. Losing my temper would not save my children. "I should use this on you."

"I wouldn't. I crafted the spell so that should anything happens to me, then the knives do their work," he said casually. "As for my sister, with her defenses, I can't enter her sanctum, nor she mine, without an invitation. Trust me; neither of us is going to be issuing the other one of those. Now, be on your way, the moon is full. I need her blood spilled with the dagger while the moon is full."

He picked up the two mirrors and looked into their surfaces, smiling.

———

Given the minimal amount of time involved, there was no way to plan a quiet way into the house of de Costa's sister, so I opted for something simple and straightforward-- I went in the front door.

It wasn't barred and there was no sign of any guards. Given the siblings' magical interests, that didn't surprise me, any more than the distinct feeling that I was being watched from the moment I crossed the threshold.

If I believed de Costa, then his sister would be asleep in the master bedroom, toward the rear of the house. He seemed to think that I should be able to waltz right in, carve her like a goose and wander away at my leisure. I, on the other hand, had my doubts about that plan.

"Why don't we have a drink and talk about it?"

I had barely stepped into her bedroom when Layra de Costa spoke. Like her brother, she seemed able to turn up when no one expected her.

It took a moment for me to locate her, sitting in a large throne-like chair just to the right of the bed.

"I'm not going to insult you by assuming that you don't know why I'm here." I said.

"Lady Sable, you're quite direct. I like that." That she knew my Guild name made wonder just how many people had paid The Widow for information about me.

I suppose I expected Layra de Costa to make some sort of magical gesture and conjure up a globe of light or some such thing like that. Instead, I heard the very distinctive sound of flint being struck, followed by sparks and a shard of wood glowing as its tip burst into flame.

She held it out to the wicks of several candles nearby; the light was enough for me to see her face. Layra de Costa wore green, so dark it was almost black. Her silver streaked hair spilled loosely over her shoulders. I could see the resemblance to her brother.

"Half-brother, actually; our father, shall we say, got around a bit and had a taste for human women. In our cases, two different human women," she said.

"Interesting, you can read minds." That would be all I'd need in someone I had come to kill.

"Not actually; it just seemed a logical thing that you might wonder," she said.

Simple and straightforward, I liked that. I reminded myself that no matter how much I might like her; there was the matter of those two ghostly daggers hanging over my children.

"Did he at least provide you with a reason that he wants me dead?" Layra said, pouring two glasses of wine and passing one to me.

I waited until she had taken a sip before lifting my own, not that I drank from it, but there are ways of appearing to.

"Nothing specific, something about tapping the power of your late father, though he did give me some damn good motivation to follow through on his wishes." I held my hand on the pommel of the Moon Dagger, its metal now ice cold to the touch, letting her see the weapon.

"Did you see a very old book, with the word Aubic on the cover?"

I nodded and mentioned the fact that touching it had left my hand tingling.

"Our father's grimorie; then it is obvious that my dear brother has broken the seal and found the spells that were the source of our late father's power. From what our parent said, it *would* require the blood of our family to do such a casting," she said.

"Wouldn't your father have had to have a Moon Dagger to do it in the first place?"

Layra reached down to the side of her chair and brought out a blade identical to the one I held.

"He had one." She said.

"It figures," I muttered, then I let fly with the Moon Dagger.

I probably should have been a lot more discreet, given the large bag I was carrying, when I went back to de Costa's villa. I wasn't in the mood for subtlety; I just wanted to make sure my children were not within reach of his slimy fingers one minute more than they had to be.

De Costa was behind his desk when I entered. "Welcome, Lady Sable, welcome," he said. "I trust all went well and as I requested."

"It did, and I have brought you proof of my deed." I laid the bag down on the floor, near the bookcase with the sliding panel. Very carefully I untied the ropes at the top and pulled it open. In the dim light Layra's face was pale as her head rolled lifeless to one side.

"Unnecessary; her blood on the Moon Dagger would have been sufficient. If you felt you had to bring proof I would have been happy with just her head," he said. "Oh, sweet sister, I've never been more pleased to see you." For a moment it was as if the two of them were alone in the room.

De Costa came around the desk and toward the body. I stepped in between him and his goal.

"Hold it right there. You get her, and I frankly don't care what you do with her," I said. "But only when you fulfill your end of the bargain by taking those ghost daggers from my children's throats!"

I watched his jaw tighten as he stared at me, unblinking. I already knew that he wasn't used to people telling him what to do, and didn't like it when it happened, but I didn't care. I was prepared to do some serious damage to him if that was what was necessary to keep the children safe.

"Very well, Lady Sable," he said at last, his voice as casual as if talking about the time of day rather than children's lives. "You did as I asked and my word is my bond."

De Costa went back to the desk and picked up the casket that the Moon dagger had been in. I could see the two mirrors from where I stood and I felt a tug at my heart seeing the vague forms in them that were my son and daughter.

Holding the mirrors in one hand, he smashed them down against the corner of the desk. Shards of glass flew everywhere. For a moment I felt like I could see the forms of the blades over the pieces of glass, then they dissipated.

I wanted that to be the end of it. But what you want and what happens are often two different things.

"As promised, both of your little darlings are safe," he announced.

"One thing," I said.

"Our bargain is completed. Your Guild will have its fee, and you have your children. What more is there to say?"

"There *is* more," I continued, ignoring his attitude. "Why me when there are any numbers of street thugs, mercenaries, even other Kybers you could have hired? Why did you insist on me?"

De Costa laughed: it was a sickening cackle. "The night I acquired the Moon Dagger I had a vision: my sister, dead, the hand that had wielded the blade was yours. You were a key pivot point to achieving my destiny," he said. "Does that satisfy your curiosity?"

I nodded and stepped to one side. I've dealt with any number of magic users over the years. The necromancers like him left me repulsed. Kneeling beside her, the man moved the cloth further away from her head, and then gently ran his fingers along her hair.

"Not that you weren't planning to do this to me, Layra. You shall bring our father's power to his rightful heir, me."

De Costa grabbed the bag and began to rip it down the center, revealing Layra's blood stained blouse right over her heart. I caught myself wondering if the man knew where that was; he certainly didn't seem to have one.

Even with his back to me I could tell when he realized that something was wrong.

"The Dagger, where is it?" He screeched in a voice that was almost feminine. "I will need it to finish this night's work."

"Oh, is this what you want?" I asked innocently, holding the blade up.

"I think not, brother," said Layra. Her eyes were open, a look of pure hatred on her face. Since she couldn't enter the house without an invitation, I gave her one. It wasn't that I didn't trust de Costa fully to keep his side of the bargain, but it pays to have a backup plan.

Layra brought out the other Moon Dagger. Her aim was good; as close as she was to her brother, it would have been hard to miss. The blade drove easily through cloth, flesh and bone and into de Costa's heart.

I could tell when the shock passed and pain swallowed Rathbin de Costa. Blood began to run around the edges of the blade, spewing out after a few moments to strike Layra, the furniture and even me. He trembled and then collapsed backwards.

Layra sister struggled out of the bag and to her feet. She stared at her brother for a time and then began to chant. I couldn't understand the words; there are more dialects of elfish than there are grains of sand in the desert.

Any possibility that it might be a mourning chant passed quickly. I could feel the magic stirring in the air around me. I realized she was doing exactly what her brother had planned. I had the feeling that this was not a good thing. Apparently, she had known more than she had let on.

Vague images formed in the air above the body, most of them things that I did not want to even put a name to. But when I saw Killian and Jayce there, I knew what I had to do.

I stepped up behind Layra, threw my arm around her neck and brought the Moon Dagger around. This time it did not strike into the chair to one side of her, as it had earlier, but drove directly up under her rib cage and into her heart.

"I could ha…"

That was all she got out before the light faded from her eyes. I let go of her and she fell down into the arms of her brother.

"I guess you got your money's worth." I told the dead sorcerer.

✦

WHEN TO STEP AWAY

"**I**t's about time you decided to show up for work," said K-Bar, My young associate grinned at me as I stepped over the pile of bricks that bracketed the rather large hole in the wall of what had been a very high end jewelry emporium. When I say high end, I mean *High End*—no sign on the door, just a small brass plate with the words By Appointment Only engraved on it, and you didn't get an appointment unless your credit score was somewhere in low-earth orbit.

"That's a smart way to say hello to the guy who signs your paycheck every week, whether you've earned it or not," I said. "Didn't they teach you that in business school?"

"If I remember correctly, that was a 7:30 in the *ayem* class. I think I slept through it, both times, boss, " laughed K-Bar. At six two, with perfectly combed hair and in his scarlet and black uniform, he was the perfect image of what a hero was supposed to look like. The problem was sometimes he sometimes acted like he was about fourteen years old.

"Why am I not surprised?"

The shattered remains of display cases, mirrors and Louie 17th chairs littered what had been the stores main display floor. The whole scene reminded me of that place down in the Village a couple of years ago where Thunder-Rider had had been thrown through a wall by "something" that he had referred to as The Chihuahua.

I had once tried to see the file on TR s opponent, but it turned out to have been classified very, very Black. I got told not to ask any more questions, ever; not only was it above my pay grade, but it was hinted that seeing it might be beyond my life expectancy, as well. The only reason I even know the perp's name was due to the fact that, a year later, TR got blotto at his little brother's bachelor party and told me.

"Looks like somebody knew how to party," said K-Bar, looking around at the chaos and shaking his head.

"You think so?" I said. K-Bar didn't have a retort, he may sometimes act like an idiot teenager, but he had the smarts, at times, to know when not to say anything.

A pale skinned, medium-sized man picked his way around one of the shattered display case and came up to me. His dark suit, which looked expensive, was covered in dust, a shoulder seam had ripped and a thin trickle of blood ran from a cut on his forehead had run the length of his face to stain the material.

"Just who are you?" he demanded.

"Boss, this is Don Edwards. He's the Managing Director of this place," said K-Bar.

Managing Director, fancy way of saying general manager, which meant that he had to report to somebody who was probably too rarefied to even darken the doors of the shop.

I thumbed a business card from the Ether and passed it over to him. "Shadowfall, Inc. We work with the city and state on cleaning up sites like this," I said.

He stared at the card for a minute, and then looked at me, his head twisting slightly.

"Don't I know you?" he asked, which didn't surprise me, since the card had my real name, not my code name, on it.

"No, sir," I told him. " To the best of my knowledge I don't think we've ever met. I doubt that I would have shopped here or at your other three stores." He stared for a moment, surprised that I knew about the other stores. There is one thing, among many, that I can say about Mayfly, our resident computer geek and communications specialist: she never fails to supply me with relevant information. I make it a policy to not ask her where a lot of it comes from.

I could almost mark the moment when Edwards recognized me; it's happened before.

"Wait a minute. Aren't you The Stygian?" he asked.

"I've been called that, among other things. Okay, here's how this is going to go down. I'll make a quick preliminary survey. Then my people will be here in the next few hours to process the area and remove anything "untoward". Once they have signed off on the site you can get your insurance people and contractors to work." I told him, hoping that I wouldn't get stuck with listening to the long "I need you to do something now". All it does is let the people vent and slow us down getting things done that need to be done.

"Okay," he said. Right then his Blackberry began to buzz and what little color remained in Edwards face drained away. The store owners were probably on the other end of that call.

"Give me the situation, Seymour," I said, turning to K-Bar.

"Boss, please don't use that name, at least not while there are civilians within hearing distance" he muttered "Or, preferably, ever."

I had worked with Seymour Aloysius Barker IV for just over two years. He as a good kid, but he had issues, not the least of them was his name, which frankly I didn't blame him one bit for disliking.

"The situation, Seymour," I repeated.

K-Bar pulled his PDA out and began to call up the incident reports. Knowing him, he had probably committed most of information to memory already, but he liked to show off his technical expertise. "The perps were first reported at 0930 just north of Hammett Park. There were a dozen robots. Varying reports place them at anywhere from eight to twenty feet tall. There were also a couple of guys in powered exoskeletons who seemed to be running the whole show, mixed in with them. They fanned out in a fairly military style and started hitting stores. Two of the robots hit this place forty five minutes after they opened up. It was a nicely done operation; they were in and out in three minutes," he said.

"Who was first at this location?"

K-bar moved several screens around on his PDA. "Looks like it was The Myth, and a couple of Force Five. They took out one of the robots, I think our guys did more damage to this place than the perps did." He gestured toward the corner of the showroom, where part of a robot lay, its head and left arm the only remaining visibly complete parts of the machine.

I'd rather have to sort through damage to property than have casualties among the civilians. Picking up pieces of human beings is definitely not fun. That little fact was something that people, and politicians, finally accepted; otherwise Congress wouldn't have passed the Kane-Shuster Meta Human Shield laws.

K-Bar passed me his PDA. I scanned over the sensor logs. Every one of Shadowfall's cars is equipped with a state-of-the-art sensor setup. Whenever we do a clean up, standard operating procedure is to have a full spectrum sensor sweep going from the minute any team arrives on scene. When you are dealing with the sort of cutting edge, possibly alien, possibly extra dimensional, technology that some of these guys have, you try to be ready.

"Okay, time for me to go to work." I said.

I ran my hand over several of the bricks along the edge of the hole in the wall. They were still warm. Since the attack was more than an hour ago, that said a lot about what kind of weapons the machines were using. Of course, the shape of some of the wall supports suggested that they had been twisted both coming in and going out which said a lot about the power of the machines and the attitude of the men behind it. I didn't envy the metas who were tangling with the main force of robots.

"Well, it's not my job to worry about it," I muttered. That was for people like Force Five and the others. I had willingly stepped away from the front lines, and even if I could I didn't think I would go back. The life expectancy of most so called super heroes isn't that good; we tend to really screw up the insurance actuarial tables. If you are going to live to see your family grow up, or to even have a family, you have to know when to step away from the spotlight.

That's why I'd done, after a run in with the Undermen had messed up my leg. Together with a couple of other retired crime fighter types and some younger heroes who needed training I'd started Shadowfall, Inc., we follow in the wake of hero/villain fights and clean things up, making sure everything is safe for the civilians. I didn't realize just how busy we were going to be; in the last couple of years we've expanded threefold. Thanks to super villains, would be dictators and megalomaniacal 1 mad scientists I haven't been bored and my bank account has been quite healthy because of it. After all, someone has to get paid for cleaning up the mess the others leave behind.

I knelt down next to a pile of bricks and laid my hand on some of them. I could feel the micro fractures that radiated out from broken edges. I shifted my vision into the Upper and Lower spectrums to survey the wall supports and the crossbeams in the roof.

There wasn't a single one that had not been strained, some almost to the breaking points. The worst were the two that ran through the central part of the ceiling; it felt like if someone even sneezed, they would come apart.

I took a deep breath and shut myself off from everything except the beams. It took some doing, but I reinforced the weakest sections of the metal. They would hold until Lamplighter and The Cape showed up to process the scene and clear it for the repairmen.

Standing up, I felt a sharp emptiness in my stomach. Manipulating things on a sub-atomic level takes a lot of energy. Since the only thing I had had to eat this morning was a granola bar and a handful of dry cereal, I didn't have a lot of reserves to draw on.

I shoved my hands into my pockets and once again was very glad I had long ago given up wearing a "costume". When you're wearing tights there really is no reasonable place to put your hands, except for resting them on your hips or crossing them over your chest. Both of those poses make it look like there is some ass about to be kicked.

Trust me, it is way much cooler to plunge your hands into the pockets of an Armani suit, push back your jacket and look like you are about to say something profound than to have to stand there and try to figure out what to do with your hands. Not to mention a properly tailored suit, like the one I had on, can hide a leg brace a lot easier than skin tight spandex. I get reminded of that every morning when I get ready for work.

My own phone began to buzz to indicate an incoming text message. The screen had the words "Mr. Steed, you're needed."

"K-Bar, stay here; this is the third site on this run. We should have teams on the first two locations by now, so it may be awhile before our people get here. Make sure that the civilians don't contaminate the scene," I said.

"I'm on it, boss."

<hr>

Once I was behind the wheel of my SUV I slid my PDA into the com unit. After I punched in my ID code I held my thumb over the scanner. Supposedly this was to make sure it was actually me, the idea being that someone might be able to hack the code or even get my DNA, but the chances were slim they would be able to do both.

Mayfly's face was on the navigation screen and the PDA at the same time. I made a mental note to see if we could rig this thing to do only one picture; two just didn't seem right.

"This is Stygian," I said.

Mayfly grinned at me and waved, it seemed silly and unprofessional, but from her the gesture was perfectly normal. She looked in her early twenties, in spite of the retro 60's granny glasses and hippie clothes that she insisted on wearing, but I knew she wasn't. There are some bonuses to being able to read pre-employment security clearance reports, like getting to know a whole lot about your potential employees.

Mayfly's solid blue eyes didn't seem quite human, but her eyes weren't the reason I hired her; it was her ability to literally get inside of any electronic equipment and make it do handstands, wash the car and take the cat out for a walk

"Hey boss, are you having fun yet?"

"I'll be having fun when we get this thing wrapped up," I said.

"Sounds like someone has a hot date," laughed Mayfly. "I presume it's with Cassi."

"None of your business, not get back to work."

I had a weekend planned with Cassandra Van Pelt at her place in the Hamptons. I really didn't want to have to explain to her why I might be late, again. Most of the time she seemed to understand about my erratic work schedule; you never know when some super villain type is going to try to conquer the world or rip off an ATM. Cassi didn't have a whole lot of room to complain, since she's an actress and they have their own erratic schedules.

"Hey, kiddo, can you patch me through to Site Two. Is something going on that I should have been told about?"

"Not that anyone has mentioned to me," said Mayfly. I saw her turn to a bank of machinery to one side of her work station. "Okay, I am getting some major interference and nothing on our main com channels is coming through from Site Two."

I had a bad feeling in my gut right then. I have every confidence in my people, but even the most powerful Meta-human's can be taken by surprise.

"Keep trying. I want to know what's going on and I want to have known five minutes ago. Also, keep my channels open. If I yell for help I want it there fast."

"You got it."

Top Hat and The Crimson King were the ones handling Site Two. So if something were going on it might mean a very large damage potential.

By the time I got there I was relieved to see that things looked normal, or as close to normal as anything can look after giant robots have blasted through an area. Top Hat and some local LEO's were standing on the far side of the street, just beyond an overturned car.

The Crimson King came out from beneath the overhang of a newspaper stand that seemingly had not been touched by the river of chaos that had washed around it.

"Hey, Stygian. What's going on?" he asked.

"You tell me. I got your text message and got over here as fast as I could. That was an interesting way of getting my attention." I said

"I thought you might appreciate it. I got the idea when I saw that autographed picture of Mrs. Peel in the dominatrix outfit at your place," he grinned.

"How did you get into my condo?"

"We can talk about that later, have a look at this." He gestured over toward Top Hat. A few feet in front of her were the remains of an arm of one of the robots. This one had been brought down without any superhuman help. Apparently, a civilian had dived out of his car when the robots attacked and the car had slammed into it, wiping both the machine and the vehicle out in a hell of an explosion.

The interesting thing was that the remains of the rest of the robot were at least four hundred yards away from where arm was. To throw this thing that far would have to have been one hell of a blast. The preliminary report said that the driver had been headed for a gas station, so that meant that more than likely there hadn't been all that much go-juice in the car's tank.

I cocked my head one way, then another, before I noticed the light reflecting off the air above the arm. There was a force screen around the thing; the hum of a porta field generator sitting a few feet from Top Hat, confirmed it. I looked over at Top Hat and she smiled; even in the baggy company coveralls you could definitely see her nicely endowed figure. She'd been with the company for only a few months, but I figured to use her in some of our advertising.

"You catch it first?" I asked. Top Hat can create a force field up to a hundred yards away. The closer she is to the target, the stronger it is, and she can hold it as long as she has the target in line of sight.

"Yep," she said with just a trace of her south Arkansas accent coming out. "Before we knew it, the arm had come active and had its hand around the bumper of a police cruiser. Then it made a grab for that blonde reporter from The Daily Sentinel ."

"You should have heard her scream before I got it off of her," said The Crimson King.

"No one was hurt?" We have immunity to lawsuits thanks to The Kane-Shuster Act; even so, I keep a good supply of liability insurance, not to mention some top notch lawyers on speed dial, the next number down from the best takeout pizza place in the city.

"Just some spilled coffee was all." Top Hat smiled sheepishly. "Hell, the civilians even brought lunch out for us afterwards. I think they thought it was part of the show."

I suspect that being caught off guard had upset Top Hat. She is barely eighteen and her powers only manifested six month ago and is still insecure and trying to find her confidence. It takes time. I should talk; it was more than three years before I was convinced that I wasn't going to rip buildings apart with my powers. It took an aquatic invasion and an earthquake to shoo most of my fears back into the anxiety closet in my mind.

"I called Disposal. They should be here in a bit with an adamantium container that ought to hold that thing. The Porta unit is good for another hour and a half," said Crimson King. "Personally, I suspect it has some sort of regeneration circuitry and it was looking for material to rebuild itself."

"That makes sense," I muttered. "Have Mayfly expedite Disposal, prior ity one."

"We're on it, so don't worry about it. You got enough grey hair as it is."

"Thanks for reminding me." I said. "So was there any kind of warning?"

King motioned me over to a car where he had his laptop set up. Two keystrokes brought up the general sensor logs.

"Everything looked normal right up until the time that piece of junk started trying to cop feels of any and everything it could find," he said.

I flipped through several screens and could see nothing so I ran through all the readings twice more. Then I back to one screen and stared at it for nearly a minute. The readings didn't look odd, at first. Then I realized what I was looking at and things had just gone from bad to worse.

"Oh shit," I said.

I can just imagine the look on Crimson King's and Top Hat's faces when I lit out for the SUV at a dead run. Fast exits come with the cape, even though I wasn't wearing one and had never liked the damn things to begin with. It gives the bad guy something to grab onto, not to mention that they have a tendency to get whipped around over your face at very inconvenient and usually dangerous moments.

I hit the starter and the com unit at the same time. Mayfly's face came on both screens. Mayfly was looking at something off screen and I heard her mutter things about her equipment and the way it was reacting that would have made the most hard core rock and roller blush.

"Can it!" I said. "Get a hold of K-Bar! Now!"

I maneuvered the SUV between two buses and just barely missed hitting a United Pharmaceuticals semi that was stopped at the police barricade. The bald-headed driver flipped me off as I went past.

"Sorry boss, something has scrambled communications out the yin yang! It's going to take me at least another half hour to clear things up," she said, the screens behind her dancing with color and static.

"Keep trying," I said. "If you get through, tell him we may have an imminent threat situation with the remains."

It felt like it took a half hour for me to make it back to the jewelry store; point of fact, I think it couldn't have been more than ten minutes at the outside.

The thing was, when I got there, as it had been with Site Two, there was nothing happening other than what should have been going on . The coroner's vehicles had swarmed over the place to pick up the ones who hadn't been lucky this morning. I hoped that I was wrong, but one of the sensor screens that that Crimson King had shown me was identical to what I had seen on K-Bar's PDA.

I came of the SUV and was a dozen steps from it when I heard someone yelling from the direction of the jewelry store. I had really hoped I had been wrong, but this proved I wasn't.

A moment later, a figure in a police uniform came flying through the hole in the jewelry store's wall. He crashed into the ground and lay there like a limp rag doll.

I made it to the door in time to see K-Bar himself go crashing into one of the few intact display cases on the back wall. I punched a three digit code into my comm unit. Hopefully, that would bring help as soon as possible.

This was not what they paid Shadowfall, Inc for. Even so, there are times that you do what you have to do and this looked like one of them.

The source of the problem was a cyborg. Part of it had been what was left of the robot that I had seen earlier. Attached to the robotic torso was a human arm that was flailing about, and legs that the remnants of dark trousers, now stained with blood and gore, covered. The thing's face was part machine, the rest belong to Edwards, the store manager. Evidently Crimson King's guess about the regeneration circuitry in the thing had been dead on and Edwards had supplied it with the raw material the machine needed.

"It's about time you decided to come and work for a living," yelled K-Bar. He picked up a two by four and let fly with it. The improvised javelin struck the robot, splintering into a rain of wood.

"Is that what I over-pay you to do?" I said. "Get creative!"

"You want creative? I can do creative!" said K-Bar.

In the far corner of the store was a plastic container that bore my company's cape and star logo. K-Bar dived for it, rolling to one side when the robot made a grab for him. I let fly with several large chunks of concrete. That bought K-Bar enough time to get into the container. He pulled out a handful of sensor spikes and, in almost the same movement, sent them flying toward our foe. Every one of them missed, striking the wall and rubble behind the cyborg.

"Hey boss, got a light?" yelled K-Bar.

I reached out with my mind and found the power sources in the spikes. It was the matter of just a few moments' effort to push them far beyond the limits of what they were supposed to do. The results were exactly what I wanted. All of those rather expensive pieces of equipment blew up at the same time sending a shower of bricks an rubble over the newly created cyborg.

I hadn't expected the explosion to do much more than delay it for a moment or two, and that it did. I turned my attention to the girder that I had examined earlier and reversed the repairs that I had done, ripping out additional parts of it as well. That was enough to send several tons of steel, along with assorted amounts of brick and mortar, crashing down on top of it. I hoped I would live through that.

"Now, that's entertainment," said K-Bar.

———•———

"Why did you do it, boss?" asked K-Bar.

I typed three more words and hit save before I looked toward the office door. K-Bar was there, not in his scarlet and black work uniform, but in a faded concert sweat shirt and ripped jeans with holes in several places.

"Do what? The only thing I've been doing is going over the after-action reports, and, by the way, I still don't have yours yet. You know what I'm talking about, the paperwork that lets me afford to keep you on salary, Seymour," I said.

K-Bar dropped into the chair to one side of my desk and just stared at me. In the couple of years that I have known him, K-Bar, had never been one to not say what he was thinking.

"We need to talk?"

"What's the matter? Some young lady's boyfriend and or husband show up at the wrong time and you need an advance on your salary to get out of town?" I asked.

"It's about that whole thing at the jewelry store. You never even told the press that it was you who brought the roof down and stopped the robot. All I did was put the sensors where you could blow them up," he said. "It was you who should have gotten the coverage, not me. You're the veteran hero, I'm just a newbie."

I shrugged. "Hey, they want a handsome young hero to show off to the viewing public, not some grizzled old meta-human."

"True, but I saw you being interviewed by that reporter from Channel 42. You present a good image for the company, maybe you'll pull in some extra business for us," is said.

"Isn't that what the villains are doing?" he asked

"Besides you were loving every minute of it, my friend, not to mention she was a knockout. Did you get her number?"

"Married with two kids," he sighed.

"That's not what I asked you, Seymour. Did you get her number?" I repeated.

K-Bar reached into the pocket of his jeans and pulled out a business card. I recognized the station logo and could see a phone number and e-mail address written across the back.

"I really hate being predictable," he said, "but I wasn't the one that they should have been interviewing."

"Oh, shut up and get out of here," I said. "I've got paperwork to fill out. We're going to need the money. Cassi just called and told me where, to make up for missing our date last night; I'm taking her to dinner and let's just say that it *is* expensive."

After K-Bar left, muttering to himself about how he would never understand what went on in my head, and how I deserved the credit and not him, I couldn't help but smile. In the time that Seymour Aloysius Barker IV had worked for me I had seen him mature into someone who was willing to let someone else take the spotlight, as log as the job got done. That was an important step for someone who people would call a hero.

I picked up my cell and punched in Force Five's direct private number. Exactly three rings later a familiar voice echoed in my ear.

"This is The Major. That you, Stygian?"

"Of course it's me, Michael" I said. "Who else has this number? Look, you mentioned last month that one of your people, Aquaton, wanted to retire. I think I may have a possible replacement for him, code name K-Bar."

"Tell me more."

✦

BACKSTAGE: AN AFTERWORD

Whenever I've seen something happening on stage or on a movie screen, I've always enjoyed knowing what was happening backstage what went into creating the story I was watching.

As a kid sitting in theaters watching movies like The Exorcist, and while other people were getting scared, I was trying to figure out what the film makers had to do to get a particular effect. I've never had a problem knowing how magicians make their stage illusions work; to me that just adds to the enjoyment of it. My wife has been involved in live theatre since before we meet. Soon after she came into my life I discovered what a blast it is to be standing in the wings and seeing what is going on back stage.

One of my personal favorite things about short story collections is to know what caused the writer to tell his particular tale, and why. In many cases, as with most of the stories in this collection, but not all of them, it was because an editor asked me to submit a story.

I know that some people are reading this Afterward before they've read the stories, which I openly admit is usually my habit, while others will wait until they've read them before reading it. Whichever, you are welcome to my worlds. If you will follow me now, we'll go backstage and see a little bit about how the magic works.

WHERE THE SHADOWS BEGAN

One of my favorite writers Philip Jose Farmer created what has become known as the Wold-Newton universe ie: connecting many different literary characters into the same extended family with his fictional biographies of Doc Savage and Tarzan. Blackcoat Press has continued Farmer's tradition with their series *Tales of The Shadowmen*. Through a set of circumstances that could only happen in the 21st century I got invited to submit a story to them. The conditions of the story were that it had to involve already existing literary characters. I have always had a fondness for Lovecraft and especially his seminal story "The Call of Cthulhu" so I combined his Inspector Largesse and had him chasing down a very dangerous theatre company. Oh and for good measure I managed to get the Old Gentleman of Providence into the story as well. I honestly think it is one of my best and scariest.

LATE NIGHT DOUBLE FEATURE

They say write what you know, Well, I grew up around movie theaters, drive-ins and walk-ins both. So to do a story set in a theater wasn't a surprise. The problem for me was the story just didn't want to work. At first I did several different versions, using different voices and narrators. What actually was a surprise for me was when I realized just who my first person narrator had to be. Let's just say I have been a Humphrey Bogart fan since my father sat me down in front of the TV and said we were going to watch this movie about a detective called *The Maltese Falcon*.

LINES IN THE SAND

Sometimes you think that a story is fairly simple and you will be able to tell it quickly, other times it takes forever. This is one of the latter kind of stories. Some years ago a good friend was editing an anthology of fantasy stories about Marylyn Monroe. Around that time I saw a beach photo shoot of Monroe where she and the water and the sand just seemed to fit so perfectly together. I still didn't have a plot so I started writing about someone walking along the beach. At first I didn't know who the narrator was. Only gradually did I realize it was Marylyn and that she was about to encounter a younger version of herself. Once I knew that, I read a bit on Monroe's life and found mention of a seaside date she had, shortly before she signed her first acting contract. The interesting thing was, it mentioned that while her date parked the car she had walked on the beach for a few minutes. I didn't finish the story in time to sell to the anthology, though the editor told me, when she heard me read it, that she would have taken it for the book. Eventually it did find a home and I'm still pleased with it.

SERPENT'S TOOTH

Collaborations that work are wonderful things, producing a story that neither writer could have done on their own. A few years ago I got asked to write a story for an anthology that was about different takes on classic fairy tales. It happened Sue had started a retelling of Cinderella a few years earlier, in the form of a letter by the stepmother to her mother. The problem was, she couldn't figure out how to finish it. I took the story and finished it. She revised it and the result was something that neither of us could have done on our own. One fun bonus on this was finding two checks from the editor waiting on the table one day when I got home from work. Sue thought they were both addressed to me; they weren't. I got to hold one up and say 'This one is yours." I really wish I had a picture of her expression.

THE ADVENTURE OF THE OTHER DETECTIVE
I have been a Sherlock Holmes fan for a very long time. I can remember watching the Basil Rathbone moves on TV with my Dad when I was very small. When I discovered that other people were doing stories about the world's first consulting detective, I thought it would be cool if I could do one. That battered tin dispatch box seems to have been bigger on the inside than it was on the outside. One day I sat down and started writing one, with no idea just where the story was going. Very quickly (but not surprisingly, given my turn of mind) I found that Watson ended up some place I didn't expect. Oh, in the original version of the train station scene at the end, I had Watson notice a man in a bathrobe talking to another man in a floppy hat and a long scarf, standing in front of a strange blue box. My wife suggested that I should leave that part out. In retrospect I realize that she was, as she is in so many things, exactly right.

LOCATION SHOOT
There is an old tradition in the science fiction and fantasy field of writing a story around an already existing cover painting or drawing going back to the pulp magazines of the 1930s. A few years ago I saw the cover of a humorous fantasy anthology that caught my attention. It featured a girl in a chainmail bikini doing a photo shoot with an elfin photographer. That image lingered in my head for a long time. I kept trying to figure out how that might come about, then a couple of lines of dialogue about a movie stunt woman came to me. This, along with watching a news story about movie companies that went on location to save money, caused the light bulb to go off over my head. The result was "Location Shoot". I've been tempted to take this movie company to other location shoots, but haven't found the right one; not to mention that I would love to do something more about one of the secondary characters. After all, who wouldn't enjoy more of the adventures of Bambi the Barbarian?

WIND AND SHADOW
Some years ago the writers' group I belong to had a member who would write an entire short story while he was at lunch. They were actually pretty good stories. One day I decided to try doing that myself. That morning, on the way to work, I had driven past a cemetery and happened to notice a man

standing by the gate, sort of lost in thought. By the time I pulled into work I had the basic plot and yes, I did manage to write the first draft in, long hand, in just under an hour.

AND THE WIND SANG

When the good folks at Tekno Books asked me for a story for their *Knight Fantastic* anthology, I decided to do something more about Lancelot, but this time I decided to go back in time to only a few years after the fall of Camelot. I had originally intended to tell the story of how he became a vampire (Guinevere put the bite on him) but when I started working on it, I quickly realized that wasn't the right story.

OATHS

This story had its origins in the fact that my good friend P.N. Elrod (author of the extremely good Vampire Files series, which, if you haven't read, I urge you to go forth and find them) was putting together her first anthology. It was called *Time of the Vampires* and the premise was simple: historical stories that involved vampires. She called me at the last minute and asked if there was any chance I go do a story for it, but she needed it in a week. I said yes and started wracking my brains. I usually get an image in my mind and build a story from there. In this case it was a knight on horseback who was soaking wet and feeling miserable. That came to me as I was driving to a local pizza place to meet my wife for dinner. By the time I pulled into the parking lot I knew the knight was Lancelot du Lac, formally of Camelot, and he was the vampire. I managed to make my deadline, in spite of working a full time day job, dealing with a cranky computer printer, air conditioning that had gone out in July and packing to go to Dragoncon in Atlanta.

CENTRAL PARK

Sometimes you never know who you will walk around a corner and meet. Sue and I were at the World Science Fiction convention one year and I happened to bump into one of the editors from Tekno Books. We chatted for awhile and he complimented me on "Oaths" and the character of Lancelot. I said I wanted to do more about him. It happened that Tekno was putting together an anthology about Merlin and asked if I wanted to submit a story about Lance. I said sure and that I would make it a modern day story. On the spot I came up with the title—"Central Park."

FINAL SCORE

In the ancient days of the early nineties, there was a computer network called GENIE, where a large number of sf/fantasy/horror writers congregated. Twice a week a bunch of us would get together for live chats. During one of those chats one guy mentioned that he was editing a series of reprint vampire anthologies, with one story set in each state of the Union. I privately contacted him and asked if he had a story for Oklahoma, which he didn't, and if he were interested in original stories, which he was. So Final Score was born, since I had for a number of years made an annual trip to the Medieval Fair in Norman, both as a visitor and as a part of the Society for Creative Anachronism. I had wanted to do another contemporary story with Lancelot and this proved the perfect venue. I have three more stories planned with him: the story of how he becomes a vampire, one set in 1893 and one in 1932. After that, who knows.

JOHN DOE # 12

One thing I've learned about writing is to not be precious about my words or plots. If something doesn't help the story, then get rid of it. When I wrote the Lancelot story "Final Score" I had at one point intended to have a policeman involved in the story who was investigating another case. That story line just didn't seem to work so it had to go. One day several years later I found the original manuscript of the story and realized how I could make the cop story work on its own. However, the background, i.e.: the medieval fair in Norman, seemed just too perfect. So the events of this story are happening at the same time as "Final Score". Who knows, maybe at some point I'll do the sequel "Second Job" where the cop and Lancelot will finally meet.

SKIMMING STONES

One evening, around sunset, I was crossing the Arkansas River on the new highway and saw the old bridge, a hundred feet or so away. That bridge had once been part of Route 66 and had seen a lot of history, but for safety reasons was now closed off. I know no one was there, but for a moment it looked like there was a figure standing near the rail, wearing a cape. That image hung on the edge of my mind for several weeks and periodically I would try to figure out who it might have been. Then one weekend we went to Oktoberfest on the west bank of the Arkansas River and I saw a workman hanging over the side of the floating stage doing repairs. That's when things started coming together for me and fairly quickly I found myself with a fantasy/sf story, set here in Tulsa. All the locations are real, including our home and the cats that make an appearance in one scene.

MONEY'S WORTH

When editors solicit a story for a themed anthology, they usually give some examples of what they are looking for. One day I opened an e-mail asking me if I could write a story for an anthology about assassins. One of the examples was an assassin goes on vacation, and that intrigued me. Several people, including the editor of the book, have said how sudden and unexpected the violence in the story is. Well, that's the way it happens in real life, sudden and unexpected. I have plans to eventually revisit this venue and find out more about the Kyber Guild and its rather lethal members.

WHEN TO STEP AWAY

Okay, I admit to being a comic book fan from way, way back. I loved them when I was a kid and still do. The writers' group I belong to has a contest at the annual Christmas party where the members write a short fragment of a story to a specific theme. It's read out loud without anyone's name being attached, then the members have to guess who wrote it. The theme one year was giant robots, so I decided to do one about a retired super hero who runs a company that comes in after the other heroes have battled the villains, in this case giant robots, and cleans up things. The fun thing was, no one at the meeting guessed it was my fragment. Actually, I liked the four pages that I wrote enough to go on and finish the story. Prior to this collection, it has only appeared in a small chapbook in the UK.

So look, up in the sky, it's a bird, it's a plane it's…

✦

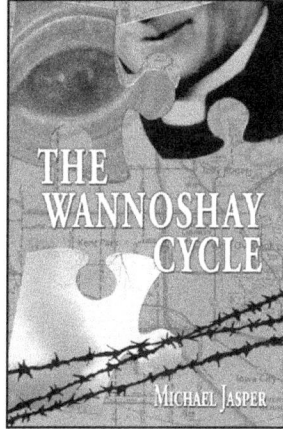

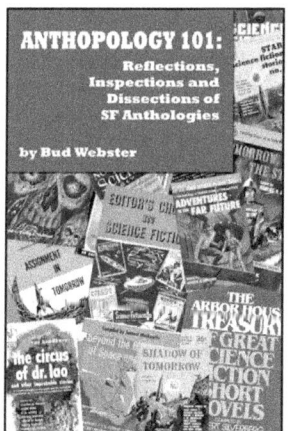